So Long, Chester Wheeler

Also by Catherine Ryan Hyde

So Long, Chester Wheeler

A Novel

Catherine Ryan Hyde

LAKE UNION
PUBLISHING

Text copyright © 2022 by Catherine Ryan Hyde, Trustee, or Successor Trustee, of the Catherine Ryan Hyde Revocable Trust created under that certain declaration dated September 27, 1999

Published by Lake Union Publishing, Seattle

www.apub.com

Amazon, the Amazon logo, and Lake Union Publishing are trademarks of Amazon.com, Inc., or its affiliates.

ISBN-13: 9781662505775 (hardcover)
ISBN-10: 1662505779 (hardcover)

ISBN-13: 9781542021593 (paperback)
ISBN-10: 1542021596 (paperback)

Cover design by Shasti O'Leary Soudant

Printed in the United States of America

First edition

So Long, Chester Wheeler

Chapter One:

The Bad-Neighbor Lottery

The first thing I need to say, and the most important thing you can know, is that for most of the time I was forced to know him I despised Chester Wheeler. And I mean with every fiber of my being. I'm always tempted to say *hate*, but I feel that's a line I never want to cross. Nobody wants to harbor hate or feel hateful, and it might even be fair to say that the reason I hated people like Chester is because they made it so easy to hate. Like there I was, trying to live a peaceful life and harbor no ill will for anyone, and then Chester came along and found that little seedling of hate and just pulled it up and out of me until it was laid bare in the light, like the most dominant characteristic of my life. And then people like him, they get to say, "See? You're every bit as hateful as I am," while pointing to what they inspired. And he did say that to me on at least one occasion. But I'm getting off to a bad start, running away on a tangent.

I can pinpoint exactly the moment I came to despise Chester. In fairness, he hit me with his attitude on what I can honestly say was the worst day of my life. I don't suppose he knew that when he opened his big mouth, but I don't think that makes his rudeness any easier to forgive.

And I should mention that it wasn't just me. Everybody hated Chester Wheeler. Even his grown children. But there I go with the *H*-word again, and I've been trying to avoid it.

I'll start more or less at the beginning. Maybe a little before what someone else might see as the beginning. Because it's impossible to know how deeply Chester hurt and offended me without knowing the details of how he chose the worst moment in the history of my life.

I had a very good job that was just about to get better. Or so I thought.

I was working at a software company as a developer, and I had been promised a raise that would bring me into six-figure territory for the first time in my life. It may not sound all that earth-shattering to someone else, but for a twenty-four-year-old guy, it looked like a lot of money.

I had just picked up the first paycheck that would reflect my new raise.

I decimated the envelope tearing it open, and my eyes landed on the figure. And it hadn't changed. It was exactly what I'd been getting every two weeks since my first six months at the company.

Then a flash of pink, still inside the envelope, caught my eye.

If somebody had asked me prior to that moment, I would have ventured a guess that pink slips are not actually, literally pink. I would have been wrong.

I just stood there in the hallway for a time with my face burning, thinking nothing. I don't know if I was purposely trying not to think, or if I was trying and failing.

What might have been several minutes later I marched down the hall to Edward's office. I think I had it in my head somewhere that this was all a horrible misunderstanding. A case of mistaken identity, maybe. If anyone at the company was unhappy with my work, I think I would have known it.

I knocked on Edward's door.

I heard a mumbling from the other side—sounding a bit unbalanced and frightened—that suggested I was not to open the door.

"Sorry, no, not now, I'm sorry, I can't . . ."

I opened the door.

He looked up at me as though I might be the person who would end his life, and this might be the moment I did so.

"Lewis," he said.

I opened my mouth, but nothing happened. No words came out. But I was standing in his open office doorway with the paycheck and the pink slip crumpled in my hand. It's not like he didn't know why I'd come.

"It wasn't my decision," he said. "And it wasn't anything about you or your work. And you're not the only one. We needed to downsize or else. Or we'd go under. I had to lay off four employees. But I'll write you a hell of a recommendation, old boy."

That sounded like a strange thing to call a young person, but it's not as if that part was important.

"Worst time in the history of everything to find another opening."

"I know," he said. "I'm sorry."

And by the tone of his voice and the look on his face, I knew he truly was. And I knew it was not a misunderstanding. Not a case of mistaken identity. And there was no point getting angry with Edward, because clearly his hands had been tied.

I walked back out into the hallway and more or less collapsed. Not like fainting, exactly. I'm not sure what it *was* like, exactly, because I didn't exactly feel myself doing it. I just remember I ended up on my butt on the linoleum floor with my back up against the wall, my head in my hands.

It may seem like an extreme reaction, but there were a few factors I might mention.

First of all, as I'd said to Edward, the job market was horrendous. Unless I wanted to get a job flipping burgers for one-fifth the money.

Even then, I'd be duking it out with a bunch of other degree-holding developers for the honor of flipping said burgers.

Second, I was in a promising but fairly new relationship with a man I hoped to be with for the rest of my life, but had so far only been with for ten months. I had been the big earner between the two of us, and now I had to go home and tell him we'd be living on his salary until I could find something new. Which—see dilemma number one—might take time.

It might also help to know that when I was four years old, my father lost his job. He and my mother immediately started fighting, and he left the family for parts unknown. I haven't seen him since.

I'm sure that bit of youthful trauma factored in.

Tim and I also had a dream of leaving the dull gray sky and dirty snow of Buffalo and living near the ocean in California. We'd been saving up to make it a reality. As I sat there in the hallway with my head in my hands, I watched it fly away. In my imagination it had actual wings, that dream, which it flapped in a sort of dreamy slow motion. I think I might have waved goodbye in my head, behind my closed eyes.

When I dropped my hands and opened my eyes again, Carol Linley was standing over me.

"You too?" she said.

"Yeah," I said. "Me too."

"You going to be okay?"

"I don't think I am," I said, "no. But with any luck I'll turn out to be wrong. I've been wrong before."

"At least you don't have to move back in with your mother."

"We'll see."

Truthfully, I knew that was out of the question, as my relationship with my mother had always been . . . strained. To put it the most polite way possible. But it sounded like a good line.

Her face took on a wry, twisted smile, and she moved off down the hall.

"Take care of yourself, Lewis," she said over her shoulder.

"Thanks," I said. "You too."

Then I got up and fetched my briefcase and walked out to my car, which I liked very much but which wasn't yet paid for, and which I knew might be the next casualty. Trying not to like it any more than necessary, I drove home.

———

When I pulled up in front of our two-story brick rental house, Tim was loading packing cartons into the rear of his older hatchback car.

I stepped out and stood in the street, more or less in front of him, and too much into the traffic lane. A tricked-out sports car blared its horn, then swerved around me, which I figured it could have done in the first place. You know. Without all the histrionics.

I was seized with a sense of very recent déjà vu. Standing there watching him load his car felt so similar to standing in the hallway at work staring at the pink slip. Knowing and not knowing, understanding and not understanding. All at the same time.

"What are you doing?" I asked.

I hadn't meant to ask it out loud. Because that, of course, would be inviting him to tell me.

"Moving to California," he said, avoiding my eyes.

"By yourself?"

"Yeah."

"Any special reason?"

He looked right into my face, and I immediately wished he hadn't.

It's weird how you think you know somebody, but then suddenly you don't. How you think you know what a person thinks and how they feel, but then it turns out you only knew what they chose for you to know. How there are two whole people in there, and one is a perfect stranger.

"You don't really need me to explain that," Tim said, "do you? Really?"

I'm deeply ashamed to report this next part.

I'd had no idea he'd been unhappy. I couldn't even have ventured a guess as to what he thought the problems had been. I couldn't even choose a general area of our relationship in which to begin shooting in the dark.

"I guess not," I said.

I'm not even sure why I said it. Because I didn't want him to know I was too thick to have seen the truth? Because if I asked, he might tell me? Because I was already exhausted from the day and couldn't take any more? More shots in the dark.

"I have a few more things to pack," he said. "Could you help me carry some boxes?"

"No," I said, without giving it a moment's thought.

I knew I had no choice but to stand there helplessly as he left me. My only choice was whether or not to contribute to the effort. Helping him move out would have felt like abandoning my own army and joining the enemy side.

I sat on the curb while he finished, and he drove away without saying goodbye. Without a hug. Without giving me an address to forward his mail to, or a promise to call when he got settled in safely.

I guess he was mad because I wouldn't help him carry his boxes.

I sat listening to his car's old, rattly muffler fade away down the street. The sun had dipped to a long slant, and it was almost dusk. I had two thoughts, one right after the other. The first: I don't have to break it to him that I lost my job and we'll be living on his salary. The second: I have nothing to live on.

I got up, dusted off the seat of my good work pants. Turned around.

My next-door neighbor, Chester Wheeler, was sitting out on his front porch in his wheelchair. His Dominican health-care worker was standing behind him, her back up against his front door, smoking a cigarette.

I ignored Chester as best I could and walked up the pathway to my front door.

"Well, well," Chester said. "Things are looking up."

I stopped cold. I should have let it go by. I knew, as I didn't, that I should have.

"How do you figure?" I asked.

"I used to live next door to a whole bowl of fruits. Now at least we're down to one piece."

Our friend Anna had lived with us as a roommate until about a month previous. I figured she constituted the rest of the "whole bowl." Anna was straight, but, then again, this was Chester Wheeler. Not what you might call a reliable narrator.

He had the world's least believable comb-over, and a red, jowly face. He wasn't ancient. Maybe seventy. But his health was clearly on the rocks. I didn't know the details, or want to know. Or care.

"You're a hateful old man, Chester," I said. "No wonder nobody can stand you. No wonder you can't keep a health-care worker. No wonder your kids never come to visit. You're insufferable."

I must've struck a nerve, because on that note he painstakingly turned his chair around and wheeled back into the house. Agostina had to jump out of his way.

She stood on the porch for another moment, grinding out the cigarette on the sole of her hot-pink athletic shoe. She was a woman in her forties with her long hair piled up on her head in intricate designs.

"How can you stand him?" I asked her from my front porch.

"I can't," she called back.

"But you still take care of him."

"Not after seven o'clock tonight I don't. I'm quitting. This is my last day."

"Does he know yet?"

"Not yet. Unless his ears are better than I thought and he heard me just now. It's going to come as bad news to him, because the agency has no one left to send. He drove every last one of us away. I was the only holdout because I needed the money. But it's not worth it, Lewis. They can't pay me enough to make it worth it. I'd rather starve."

"When do you tell him the bad news?" I asked, fairly squirming in my delicious schadenfreude bath.

"Maybe never," she said. "I might just . . . not tell him at all. I don't want to hear what happens when he stops holding back for fear of losing me. I think I'll just go. When I never show up again, I expect he'll figure it out."

"Good," I said. "He deserves all of it and worse."

She tucked the half-smoked cigarette back into the pack and narrowed her eyes at me.

"Where'd Tim go?"

"California."

"Without you?"

"Right."

"You didn't let on."

"I didn't know."

"Oh. Sorry. You gonna be okay?"

"I don't think I am, no. But with any luck I'll turn out to be wrong. I've been wrong before."

"Be well, Lewis," she said.

"You too, Agostina."

It felt like a genuine connection, made just at the moment I knew we would never see each other again.

True to her word, and my assessment, I never saw her after that.

—

"The drinks are on me," Anna said.

And I said, "They'd pretty much have to be."

It was the following evening, and we were in a bar downtown. It was a gay bar. I hadn't selected it. Anna had selected it. I'm pretty sure I mentioned that Anna is not gay. I wanted to ask about her choice of places, but there were so many other questions slamming around in my head.

We were standing at the bar, waiting to get the bartender's attention.

"You did get a paycheck," she said. "Right? Tell me you got a paycheck."

"Yeah, of course I did. I got my final paycheck. The problem is . . . it's my final paycheck."

"Right," she said. "I get that. But you have that savings."

"I don't have any savings."

"You had all that money. That you and Tim were saving for California."

"Yeah. Well. It's somewhat fulfilling its destiny. It's on its way to California. With Tim."

"He took it all?"

"Every last penny."

Since calling the bank, I had been angry about this, and I mean a full-on hamster wheel of anxiety and resentment. I expected more of the same as I opened my mouth to answer her questions. To my surprise, I had slipped past it and into depression. Who knew?

"Can he do that?"

"He already did, so I'm going with yes."

"But, I mean . . . legally. Can he do that?"

"It was a joint account. It was in both of our names."

The bartender finally fit us into his busy schedule. Anna ordered us a pitcher of beer and then we sat down in a booth to wait. It wasn't hard to find a booth. It was only 6:30 in the evening.

Her hair was long and straight, a sort of amber color, and I honestly think she'd forgotten to comb it before leaving the house to meet me. She might have been napping when I called.

"So," I said, preparing to wade deeply into enemy territory, "you never told me your thoughts on Tim's parting words."

"The part about how he was sure you'd know why?"

"That's the part in question, yeah. Does that make sense to you?"

"Yes and no," she said.

The pitcher arrived, and she poured for me first. She was that kind of friend.

"So you knew he was unhappy?" I asked when the waiter guy left.

"Yes and no," she said again.

"What does that *mean*?" I asked, trying to hide my irritation. Probably failing.

"Isn't it self-explanatory? It's a yes. Followed by a no."

"Let me rephrase. Can you please elaborate on the 'yes' part?"

She took a long swallow of her beer. She was avoiding my eyes, which was undoubtedly a bad sign. I waited. Not patiently.

"He seemed . . . I don't know. Tense. Or aggravated. Or . . . I'm not sure what the word is I'm searching for. He seemed a little distant, but I figured that was just Tim."

And I hadn't even noticed any of it. It made my head spin. Almost literally. What world did I live in? What relationship had I been having for the past ten months? Obviously not the same one as Tim.

I spent a minute falling fully into my own sense of deficiency. Somehow, in some way, I was not enough. Hence the missing partner. The fact that I didn't know what way, and he figured I should, only added fuel to the fire.

I decided to take the conversation in an entirely different direction. The current one was too unsettling.

"I have to tell you this really offensive thing the neighbor said to me."

"You mean Chester Wheeler?"

"That's the guy."

"Don't tell me, then."

"I just need to get it off my chest."

"That never works," she said. "People think complaining about a bad thing will make them feel better. But it just stokes it. It keeps it alive. It's like feeding it. This is why I never liked the expression *pet peeve*. Why keep a peeve as a pet? Why give it a dish of water and a nice spot to lie down in the corner? It's just choosing to be peeved. Look, I more or less know what Wheeler said. Something idiotic. Because he's an idiot. We already knew that. It's utterly unsurprising. It's not exactly breaking news. Don't give the guy so much space in your head. You want to be keeping better things in there, right?"

I only sipped my beer for a time, feeling a little stunned. It was unlike Anna to give me such a sharp dressing-down. Or, anyway, that's what it felt like.

I never answered.

"Look, I get it," she added. "I'm not without empathy. He upset you, and the upset needs time to move through you. It usually takes me about three days to let a thing like that move all the way through my system and move on. But while you're waiting, try not to feed it."

"Okay," I said. But it didn't feel okay. I still felt a little stung.

"Moving on," she said. "Obviously the timing utterly sucks."

She didn't elaborate. She didn't need to. She had moved out less than a month before to give my relationship with Tim more space, and a more private feel. And now I had no one to share the rent.

"I don't suppose you could—"

But she didn't even let me finish.

"I signed the lease on the new place," she said.

"You didn't tell me that."

"Why would I tell you that?"

"I thought we told each other everything."

"I told you I was *going to* sign it. I didn't think touching the pen to the paper would be big news."

"I guess I need a new roommate."

"Or two."

"Right. Or two."

"If I were you, I'd get right on that," she said.

I sipped my beer in silence for a moment, looking around the place. The sky was still barely light outside. Two middle-aged guys had put a slow ballad on the jukebox and were dancing. It burned in my gut, because I had honestly thought Tim and I would last long enough to do that. To be that.

Why was I such a fool?

"Why did you pick a gay bar?" I asked Anna.

"Because you're single."

I snorted something that was meant to be laughter, but it made me sound like a donkey. Albeit a quiet one. Probably because I found no humor in the observation at all. In fact, I think it only dawned on me in that moment. I think it hit me when she said it. Tim was gone. I was not a person in a relationship. I was single.

"I've been single for, like, hours," I said, trying to wrestle the moment into submission with my ability to appear casual.

"I'm not suggesting you should meet somebody right now and live happily ever after. I'm only saying that it might be time for you to accept being single. You know. Make the transition."

"I hate transitions more than anything," I said.

"Oh, honey," she said. "I know you. Don't I know how much that's true."

Chapter Two:

Oh

It was several days later, but I don't remember how many.

The knock on the door came at 8:35 a.m. I had been up until all hours worrying about such matters as money and my future, and so was sleeping soundly.

I got up, put on my old faded corduroy robe over nothing, and grumbled my way to the front door. When I opened it, the light was absolutely brutal in my eyes. I had to shield them with one corduroy-clad arm.

The guy standing on my stoop was wearing a sleeveless T-shirt and tight jeans, despite being a bit too old for the look. I made him to be in his late fifties.

"I'm Rick," he said.

"The guy who called about the roommate situation?"

"Right."

"The one who said he'd come at nine thirty."

"I'm a little early."

I said nothing. I was still half-asleep, and I mistakenly thought if I gave him enough time, he would see his transgression as clearly as I did.

"You know," he added.

"What do I know?"

"Well. Just that . . . I didn't want to be late."

"Or early," I said, trying for a voice only damp with sarcasm. Not actually dripping.

Just then we heard the dreaded voice of Chester, calling over from his front porch.

"Filling up the fruit bowl, I see."

Rick turned around to look. I looked past Rick. Apparently Chester had found a new caretaker after all, because there was an oddly short fortysomething woman with a bobbed haircut, and she was sweeping the porch behind him and his wheelchair.

"And nuts," Chester added. "A fruit and nut bowl. Because if you're a fruit, it goes without saying you're a nut."

We all just stood there in awkward silence for a time, because it's hard to know what to say in response to such an embarrassingly childish attempt at mean-spirited humor.

Finally Rick turned back to me.

"Why did he say that?" he asked.

"Because he's an idiot."

"Are you gay?"

"Yeah. Does that make a difference?"

"Not really. I mean . . . maybe just because you didn't tell me."

"Tell you when? In my ad? We haven't even had a conversation yet."

"Right," he said. "Right." Then, inexplicably, he said "Right" a third time. "Well, it's not really that so much. But I don't want to move in someplace with nasty neighbors. Who needs it, am I right?" he added, extending his love affair with the word "right."

He turned on the heel of one gray snakeskin cowboy boot and walked to the curb and his car, which was a vintage fire-engine-red Chevy. It was a convertible with the top down on a chilly morning, and it had one of those bizarre chain steering wheels.

I looked back at Chester's porch, ready to read him the riot act about chasing my prospective roommate away. Granted, that one had been an unusually poor prospect. Still, it was the principle of the thing.

He had apparently gone back into the house. Only the elfin forty-something woman was still outside. She looked up at me with something like an apology in her eyes.

"You the new health-care worker?" I called over.

Of course I had it on good authority that Chester had burned through every single health-care worker at that agency, but I figured there were other agencies.

"I'm his daughter," she said. "We're having trouble getting somebody new."

"My condolences," I called back.

"On having trouble getting somebody? Or on being his daughter?"

"Sorry," I said. "Never mind. Forget I said it, please. He brings out the worst in me, but I don't need to take it out on you."

"It's not like I've never met him," she said. "It's not like I haven't heard it before."

She came over to my side of the porch and leaned on the railing, where we were only about twelve feet apart.

"You know somebody who needs a job?" she asked.

"Yeah, me. But not if you mean . . . No, never mind. It doesn't matter. I have no experience in home health care anyway."

"No experience required. At one time we thought it would be nice, but we're way beyond that now. We just need somebody to do his errands and make sure he takes his meds and call 9-1-1 if he's in trouble. At this point any sentient human being will do. And having someone who lives right next door would be a big plus. We can't afford a live-in, but this would be nearly as good."

I took a deep breath and tried to remember to be kind.

"Look," I began. "You're probably a perfectly nice person, and I expect you've been through enough without me being rude to you.

15

But, honestly, I only lost my job a few days ago, and I'm not nearly that desperate yet. I'd rather flip burgers. I'd rather sleep on a friend's couch. Hell, I'd rather sleep under a bridge. I'm sorry. Life is too short for Chester Wheeler."

"Okay, got it," she said. "Let me know if you change your mind."

"I won't change my mind," I said.

Then I went inside and put myself back to bed.

———

It was the following Friday when I came home from my two lackluster job interviews and walked in on something that looked suspiciously like a surprise party. In my own house.

It wasn't *literally* a surprise party. Well. It was literally a surprise. But it wasn't the sort of thing where everybody hid and then jumped out and yelled "Surprise!" at the same time, at a coronary-inducing volume.

Still, I walked in, and there were a dozen people in my house.

I knew them. But . . . still.

They were all standing around, ignoring perfectly good places to sit, holding cocktails and talking in low voices. It vaguely reminded me of the wake after a funeral.

All eyes lifted toward me as I walked in the door. A few people looked mildly surprised to see me, as though they'd forgotten who lived in my house.

Anna was the only one with an outsize reaction. She raised her arms, then flipped them over with palms up, as though about to raise the roof. Then, her face twisted wryly, and in a fairly deadpan voice, she said, "Surprise."

"I certainly am," I said.

"Then my work here is done."

"You still have your key to this place," I said, "don't you? You never gave it back to me."

"You never asked for it back."

"Remind me to ask for it back," I said.

Anna only rolled her eyes.

"It's not my birthday," I added.

"I know it. It's not a birthday party. It's a rent party."

"Oh," I said. "A rent party. I'm not a hundred percent sure what that is, but it sounds like something I could use right about now."

I walked around for a time saying hello to people. Barry and Ted. Carol Linley, formerly from work. Some guy I'd never met. They had lots of condolences. Their foreheads furrowed when they told me how sorry they were. About everything.

Anna caught up with me again and handed me a margarita.

"Thank you," I said.

"How did the job interviews go?"

"Not well."

"I'm not sure I believe that," she said. "You do a great interview."

"I'm sure I was fine. What was bad about them was that they both had one single job opening and more than a hundred applicants."

"Oh," she said.

Knowing her as I did, I expected her to find something buoying to say. When she never did, the gravity of my situation settled hard on my poor, exhausted head.

She took me by the sleeve of my good job-interview sport coat and towed me over to the dining room table. There were helium balloons tied to my silver candlesticks, waving on long pink ribbons. They made an odd sound as they bumped together just below my ceiling, responding to the air currents we stirred up as we approached.

In the middle of the table was a silver bowl. There were checks in it. Personal checks, in several patterns and styles.

"Just to prepare you," Anna said, "it's not a lot. Everybody is strapped. But we did what we could, and anyway, it's something."

I sifted around with my fingers. Most of the checks were for twenty-five dollars and fifty dollars.

"Oh," I said. "Here's one for two hundred dollars from Chris Marsecki. That's particularly nice, especially since I've never met a Chris Marsecki."

"He's that new guy I've been seeing. I hope you don't mind my bringing him."

"*Mind?* My short-term future appears to rely on it."

I picked them all up and shuffled through them, doing the math in my head.

"I know," Anna said. "Believe me, I know. It's only about half a month's rent."

"Well, I'm not going to complain. It puts me half a month closer to making rent than I was before. Besides, it's the thought that matters, and . . . something something. No, seriously, though. I mean it. People are helping as much as they can. I appreciate it."

Paul Segal raised his glass to me on his way back from the kitchen. "Sorry it can't be more, Lewis," he said, and kept walking.

"Don't feel bad," I called after him. "You're doing better than I am."

When I looked back at Anna, I caught her in a deeply pitying expression. She wiped it away as quickly as she could, but it stung.

"You'll find something," she said.

"I did get one job offer."

"Really? That's great!"

"But—"

"No buts, Lewis. Don't 'but' it. It's a job. Maybe in the short run you can't afford to be too picky."

"You'll change your tune when I tell you what it is."

"If it's honest work, though . . ."

"Yeah, it's honest work. Caretaking for Chester Wheeler."

I watched as her face changed. She looked much the way I imagined she would if I had taken the top off a very ripe trash bin positioned directly under her nose.

"Oh," she said.

"Yeah. Oh."

"*That* desperate you're not."

"Not yet anyway."

"Don't you need some kind of training for that?"

"They're pretty much looking for any warm body at this point."

"Hopefully not yours," she said.

"No. Hopefully not mine."

"Because that would be really . . ."

"You don't have to finish that sentence," I said, despite the fact that she had pretty much trailed off and abandoned it anyway. "It's not as though I haven't been imagining it."

We stood still a moment, purposely not meeting each other's eyes.

"Well," I said when the silence got awkward. "It's my party. I should go mingle."

———

The following morning the phone blasted me out of sleep. Possibly for that reason, or possibly because I was still mostly dreaming, it took me a minute to realize it was the phone.

When I understood I could deal with it without getting up and getting dressed, I reached over and picked up the receiver. By then it was on about the fifth ring.

"Hello?" I said. I'm pretty sure it sounded bad. No, I take that back. I'm completely sure.

"You were sleeping?" a deep, scratchy male voice said.

"Who is this?"

"It's almost nine in the morning."

"Again . . . ," I said. I was trying to sound patient. I was also trying to wake up fully. ". . . who is this?"

"It's Chester Wheeler. Your next-door neighbor."

The news that his voice, his words, had found a way inside the walls of my home was an electric shock to my gut. On the plus side, it brought me fully awake.

"How did you get this number?" I asked, probably after a bit of pesky stammering.

"It's listed, nimrod."

"How do you even know my last name?"

"Because it's . . . *on your mailbox*? Jeez."

"Let me try this another way," I said. "What the hell do you want, Chester?"

"I heard my daughter offered you the job."

"Yeah. She did."

"Don't take the job."

"I have no intention of taking the job."

"Well, just don't," Chester said.

"I just said I had no intention of it."

"I'm telling you not to."

"Holy crap, Chester," I said, amazed at how quickly he had dragged me down to his elementary school level of discourse. "You are the most irritating man in the world."

"Good," he said. "Then don't take the job."

I held the phone away from my ear for a moment. I tried to count to ten but only made it to four.

"I'm hanging up now," I said. "I'm going back to sleep. Don't ever call here again."

He said something in reply—or anyway, he tried. I could hear him talking extra fast to get the last word in, but I hung up before the last word could be delivered.

It took me almost an hour to get back to sleep because I was so irritated. But I eventually did, which felt like a small victory.

A very small victory.

———

Probably no more than fifteen minutes after that pathetically tiny victory, a knock blasted me out of sleep. I know. It's all very redundant. Now imagine how it felt living inside all that repetition.

I got up and stumbled to the door, shrugging into my robe as I went along. I was thinking, *If it's Wheeler, I'll kill him. How could any jury convict me?*

I opened the door so suddenly that the woman on the other side of it flinched—shrank away from me as if I had raised a baseball bat over her head in anger.

I blinked pitifully into the light.

It was Wheeler's daughter.

"Sorry," I said. "It's been a bad morning. Well. A bad week. Or more. Well. I don't honestly know how long it's been. It's just been bad."

"It's after ten," she said. "I didn't think I'd wake you."

"Long story." Actually it was a short one, but also one that would involve her own flesh and blood and a lot of curse words. "What can I do for you?"

"I just wondered if you've thought about that offer."

I opened my mouth to say something harsh, and in a harsh tone on top of that, but her vulnerability caught me and set me back on my heels. Her hair, bobbed just below her ears, made her look like an elf or a pixie, but I might have mentioned that before. She was wearing an expression that reminded me of a puppy looking up at a rolled newspaper.

"There's really nothing to think about," I said, purposely not harshly. "It's a hard pass."

21

"Before you completely dismiss it, though . . ."

"I've already completely dismissed it."

She went on talking as though she hadn't heard me. ". . . I wrote up a figure. It's somewhat open to negotiation, but only to a point. My daughter is about to give birth in a few days and I *really* need to get back home to her. So I've already gone up a little from what I was originally thinking."

She pulled a piece of folded paper out of her pocket and extended it in my direction. I purposely ignored it and held her eyes, which she seemed to find unsettling.

"He has no other grown children to come take over for you?"

"I have two brothers. But . . ."

"They won't come," I said.

It was not a question. I knew.

"No," she said.

We stood in silence for a moment. She was looking down at her feet and so was I. She was wearing these huge, wild bedroom slippers that looked like they were made of imitation poodle fur.

"Look," she said, when it was clear I wasn't about to say more. "I know my father is not the easiest man in the world . . ."

She braved a glance up into my face.

"We both know what your father is," I said.

She quickly looked down at the crazy slippers again.

"At least take a look."

She held the paper out in my direction, and this time I took it from her. And unfolded it. And read the number. And I was immediately disappointed. I'd wanted it to be a low figure, to further justify my decision. It was not a low figure. Not at all. It was surprisingly generous. Not what I thought I'd be making as a developer after my raise, but close to what I'd been making before it.

Underneath that magic figure she had written her cell phone number.

I felt my resolve waver. I needed the money. Soon. Badly. A simple "yes" would solve everything.

Then I remembered Wheeler's rude phone call earlier that morning. It snapped my resolve firmly back into position.

"He called me on the phone and told me not to take the job," I said.

We stood a minute, and I watched her face fall.

"With all due respect," she said, "it's really not his decision. Not anymore."

I shifted uncomfortably on my feet. My bare soles felt uncomfortable on the chilly concrete of my front stoop. It was uncomfortable to be wearing only a robe while talking to a clothed person. Every aspect of my life chafed in that moment. I was living in a sandpaper reality.

"Here's what I don't get," I said. "You told me it was pretty much any sentient human being at this point. So why do you need *me*? I realize he's alienated every professional in this town, but he couldn't possibly have alienated every single job seeker in Buffalo. Somebody else out there will be desperate enough to take this on."

"But we can't afford to pay someone to live in," she said. "You're right next door."

"Right. Come to think of it, I guess you mentioned that. But—"

"You could work ten hours doing what he needs and then go home, but if there was an emergency, you could get over as fast as if you were living in the spare bedroom. We could put in an intercom, or get him one of those alert things you hang around his neck that's set to dial a certain number."

"An intercom," I said. "So that way he could tell me what he thinks of me in my own home at any hour of the day or night. As appealing as that sounds, I'm still going to pass. My sanity is still worth something to me."

"I could go a little higher than the figure I just gave you. Please think it over for a day or two. That's all I'm asking."

I sighed. Which was too bad. It meant I was conceding at least that one small point to her.

"All right," I said. "I'll think about it. But I wouldn't get your hopes up. I doubt my answer is going to change."

She waved expansively, and, without further words, retreated from my front porch.

I went back inside and did not even attempt to get back to sleep.

Chapter Three:

What's Wrong with That Man?

The following morning I sat at the breakfast table and drank two coffees with that fancy, sweet toffee-flavored creamer. All the while, as I drank them, I stared at that paper with the numbers on it.

I could feel myself going back and forth in my brain as to whether I should even think more about it. Whether I even wanted to ask more questions.

When I had rinsed my mug in the sink, I decided questions couldn't hurt me. Chester Wheeler could, but asking about him was safe enough.

I had planned to get dressed and walk over, but then I decided I wanted to minimize my chances of seeing or hearing from the man in any way. Which, really, when you think about it, should have been my answer right there.

I carried my phone to the window and stood there, pulling back the curtain slightly and staring at the dreaded Wheeler household. Then I dialed the number I'd been given.

She picked up on the first ring, which was a bit startling.

"Mr. Madigan?" She sounded breathless, as if she'd been waiting for a call about a missing loved one while the sheriff dragged the river for bodies.

"Calling me Lewis is fine," I said. "I'm sorry. I never got your name."

"It's Ellie. Don't worry about that. I'm just so happy you called. You must have thought more about it."

"Don't be too happy," I said. "Don't read too much into it. I just wanted to ask a question."

"I'm just happy you even have a question. Go right ahead."

"What's wrong with him, anyway?"

A little blunt, granted. But it needed to be asked.

She sighed out a bit of irritation that I hadn't expected.

"Now how can I answer a question like that? Who can ever answer a question like that one about anybody? He just . . . is what he is. He's what he's been as long as I've known him. Everybody is—"

I interrupted as gently as possible.

"Wait. Please. You misunderstood the question. Maybe I wasn't clear. I meant what's wrong with him physically? What's happening with his health that he's in a wheelchair and needs nearly full-time care?"

"Oh. I'm sorry. I thought you knew. Cancer."

"Of . . . ?"

"I'm not sure I understand the question," she said.

I was startled to see her face appear in the window next door. She had come to the window on the side facing my house and pulled back the curtain. Suddenly we were looking right at each other, albeit from some distance. It felt like we were bookends, or some kind of mirror image of each other. I had not been expecting that feeling.

She waved with mostly just her fingers, and I awkwardly returned the gesture.

"I guess what I meant to say," I began, "is that cancer tends to choose a part of the body. So I was just asking . . . you know . . . cancer of the what?"

"Pretty much 'of the everything' at this point. It started out in his lungs but it's all over now."

It seemed like an interesting double entendre, though likely unintentional.

"And the prognosis?"

"Oh, it's not good."

"How long do the doctors think?"

"Three months, if he's really lucky."

"I see," I said.

Which was a deeper statement than it might have sounded on the surface. Suddenly I did see the situation, clearly and very differently.

On the plus side, this would be a very short gig, if I took it. I could try to line up a better job over the next three months, and I wouldn't have to worry about the rent or bills in the meantime.

On the minus side, I felt I had no right to despise Chester Wheeler anymore, because what kind of monster harbors hate for a dying man? I immediately felt vulnerable and naked with those feelings stripped away, and would have done nearly anything to pull them home again.

"Well," I said, ending what I think was a weirdly long silence. "Give me another day to think about it."

Even at the considerable distance, I could see her countenance change. She stood up straighter, and seemed to bounce on her toes a little.

"Of course! Yes, of course I will. I'm just so happy to hear you're even considering it. Thank you, Lewis! Call anytime, day or night, when you decide."

I mumbled some polite closing words and ended the call.

She disappeared from her window immediately.

I stood at mine for a long time, staring at the house next door. I was thinking, *What the hell did I just do?*

—

In the evening I sat across the table from Anna in a perfectly stereo-typical Italian restaurant. Red checkered tablecloth, potted candle in the center of the table. Trellis laden with grape leaves stenciled onto the wall.

I was eating spaghetti because I felt guilty that the meal was on her. The meals had been on her since I'd lost my job, and, though she was doing better than I was, she was hardly made of money. I didn't want to stress her delicate system. Now and then I would glance across the table at her veal piccata in a vaguely drooly, unfortunately covetous manner.

"So here's the thing," I said.

I wound spaghetti around my fork and took another huge mouth-ful. Which is—let's face it—weird behavior when you've just said to someone "So here's the thing."

Unfortunately, Anna knew me all too well.

"Got it," she said. "Really not looking forward to admitting this next thing to me, whatever it is."

I swallowed hard, but the mouthful was not fully chewed, and it caused discomfort going down.

"I got some new information about that job looking after Wheeler."

"And you're actually thinking of taking it," she said.

She didn't say it as though she was passing judgment. Really, if I had to characterize it, she sounded . . . almost . . . impressed.

"Only because I'm getting desperate."

"What information could possibly have changed your thinking?"

"He only has three months to live. Unless he has even less."

She ate in silence for a full minute or two, nodding every few sec-onds. Leaving me just waiting to hear what she would say. With my stomach twisting into knots.

"And you could use the three months to line up something better," she said at last.

"That's what I was thinking, yeah."

"I guess you could put up with anything for three months."

"Maybe. Or maybe he'll reduce me to a quivering pile of anxiety and insecurities."

"And maybe this could be your chance not to let him. Maybe it won't be such a bad thing. Oh, don't get me wrong. It'll be terrible. It'll be your worst nightmare. But how many of us get to stand face to face with our worst nightmare and just . . . bushwhack our way through it?"

I digested those comments for a moment, trying to think how to phrase a request for more details.

I needn't have bothered.

"This might be a really interesting challenge for you," she said. "Because this is . . . and this won't come as news to you . . . your Achilles' heel. You can't stand to be disrespected and criticized, or insulted in any way. Oh, don't get me wrong. I'm not suggesting anybody *likes* it. But it seems to me that you don't really have that solid core of confidence that lets you shake it off and not take it personally. I hope you don't mind my saying so."

"I guess I don't," I said, though I pretty much did. "You think it's possible to *grow* such a thing?"

"I think this is your chance to find out."

"I'll have to think about it."

She dropped her fork onto her plate. It made a lot of noise. Other diners jumped and turned to stare.

"Holy crap, Lewis," she said. A little too loudly, considering that people were already staring. "All you've done is think about it since it first came up. What you have to do now is *decide*."

I sat in silence for a few beats, nursing the sting. The other diners grew bored with staring and got on with their lives.

"I'm sorry," she said, more quietly. "I didn't mean to yell. But you have a way of pushing decisions down the road. It's like you're waiting to be sure how it'll pan out before you decide. But that never works. We can't ever know that going in. I think you just need to choose a path and see where it takes you."

I opened my mouth to say, "Okay, I'll think about it." I swear I almost said it.

Then I closed my mouth again and said nothing at all.

We ate in relative silence for the rest of the meal.

———

When I got home, Ellie was sitting on my front porch steps. I had left the outside lights on for myself, and my headlights shone on her as I pulled into the driveway, so I was able to see her clearly. She looked frazzled. Harried. All the words one might use to describe an overworked housewife in a black-and-white 1950s television commercial. She looked like that exhausted mother with the strand of hair hanging down over her eyes, who you just knew would blow it upward and out of the way in an exaggerated and slightly cross-eyed gesture.

I didn't bother putting my car in the garage. I just stepped out.

I looked down at her and she looked up at me, and I had this mental image of looking for a life preserver to throw to her.

"You look . . . ," I began. But it was a hard sentence to finish while still being polite.

"My daughter is going into labor," she said.

"Oh. I thought that was still a few days off."

"Didn't we all."

"I guess it only matters what the baby thinks."

"I guess."

"How long will it take to get back to her? Can you drive?"

"Oh, no. I have to take a plane. And I couldn't get a flight out until midmorning tomorrow. I still have no idea what to do about my dad. I was thinking, if you could just cover me for a handful of days. Just so I can be there with her. When the baby comes home from the hospital, and she's a little more settled in, I'll come back and look for somebody permanent." She stuck on that final word. It felt as though we both did.

"Long range, I guess I should say. Or at least a little more long range. I would double what I already offered you if you could cover him for a week. Any chance you could help me out?"

"Sure," I said.

You know the old saying "You could have knocked me over with a feather"? You could have. But her, not me. Okay, maybe a little bit me, too.

Trouble was, I liked her. I liked her almost as much as I didn't like her father.

She was still stumbling for words, so I added, "You don't have to double anything. Just what you wrote down on the paper was fair."

She leaped to her feet surprisingly fast, and without warning.

Next thing I knew she had me in her grasp. Her arms around my waist felt strong for such a small person. It was almost hard to draw a full breath. The top of her head barely came up to my shoulder.

"I don't know what to say. Just . . . thank you. You won't be sorry."

Then we backed apart, and caught each other's gaze—and both burst out laughing at exactly the same time. It was an odd moment for mirth, but what can I tell you? Life is odd.

"Oh, I think we both know I'll be sorry," I said.

"Okay, true. But . . . I promise I'll pay you. What else can I say?"

"That's all I really ask. What time do you leave for the airport?"

"About seven thirty. Any chance you can come by about seven? I know you're not an early riser, but I need to show you everything. Well. I can't show you everything. I'll show you as much as I can. You'll have to call me on my cell phone a lot at first. He'll tell you things, and you need to check them with me. He'll tell you, 'Ellie lets me do this.' But probably I don't."

"So he lies," I said, and then wished I had phrased it more diplomatically.

"He likes things his own way." She paused there in my driveway, staring down. As though she had lost something important in the half

31

dark. Then she looked up, and I saw shame on her face. "Yes," she said. "He lies."

"Okay," I said. "Thank you for the candor. I'll see you at seven o'clock sharp."

I watched her walk away in the dark for a moment.

Then I called out to her. "First grandchild?"

She stopped and turned, and in my porch light I could see her beaming.

"Why, yes!"

"Congratulations."

"Thank you," she said. "You're very kind."

Then she walked back to Chester's house, leaving me with a feeling that I had made someone very happy, even if I had made myself very unhappy in the process.

Chapter Four:

I Want a Drink

Chester Wheeler's house was . . . how to say this kindly . . . frozen in time. That's probably the highest compliment I could pay the place. It looked like a dim den used by someone who had given up on life decades ago. The more I followed Ellie around, glancing at everything in my peripheral vision, the more I came to accept that this was probably exactly the case.

The couch was this overstuffed royal blue affair with tufts of stuffing poking out near the seams at the edges of the cushions. It looked like something you'd see dragged out to the curb to sit beside the garbage cans on trash day. You might go over to take a look, because after all it was free, but when you got closer, you'd just keep walking. The carpet was 1970s shag. Yes, shag. No, I'm not kidding. I can't say for a fact that it had been installed in the 1970s, but judging by its condition it was not out of the question.

There were no pictures on the walls. I had never seen a home with no pictures on the walls. Not only were there no framed memento photographs of family, there was not even generic art, like a cheesy oil painting of a wave crashing on a big rock or a Labrador retriever holding a duck in its mouth.

It did have a fair number of potted plants, but they were droopy, sickly looking things.

It gave the eerie impression that the person who lived there didn't love anyone or anything.

Speaking of the person who lived there, Chester was nowhere to be seen.

"He can't really wheel himself from place to place much in his wheelchair," Ellie said, and it brought me back into the moment. It reminded me that I was following her around, ostensibly learning. "He just doesn't really have the arm strength or the cardio for it these days. So you'll have to wheel him places."

We had just moved into the kitchen, a drab room with ancient white appliances that were clearly decades older than yours truly. We stopped in front of a counter that was home to a sea of brown prescription medicine bottles. And I do mean a sea.

"I saw him wheel himself into the house," I said.

She looked mildly perplexed.

"How long ago was that?"

"Oh, I don't know. Let me think. It was the day I lost my job. So more than two weeks now."

"He must've been highly motivated," she said. "Needless to say, the situation worsens by the day. Now. Getting back to the meds. You have to keep track of his meds. He can't, and probably wouldn't if he could. Other than calling 9-1-1 in an emergency and putting him back in his wheelchair when he falls out, that's probably the most important thing."

She indicated the medications with a sweep of her hand, a signal that we would continue talking about them. I didn't let her get far.

"Wait. He falls out of his wheelchair?"

"Oh, yes. Regularly. He tries to do things he knows he shouldn't do, like move himself onto the toilet."

My head literally swam. It made the room twist in an uncomfortable way, and sickened my stomach for one uneasy wave.

I was going to have to help Chester with his toilet routines. I should have thought of that. Why hadn't I thought of that?

Meanwhile she was back to talking about medication.

"I've made a written list, and it's right here by the pill bottles. You have to check it against what you've given him, and it can be a little complicated and confusing, especially at first. But it's important to get it right. You hand him the pills and a glass of apple juice. He doesn't like to take pills with water. He doesn't like water, period. He wants apple juice. And you stand right there until he's swallowed every last one. If you walk away and leave him on the honor system, he'll ditch them in the potted plants."

I looked around, and the obvious question came into my head.

"Where *is* Chester?"

"He closed himself into the bedroom."

"He didn't lock himself in, did he?"

"No, we took the locks off the doors so he can't."

"So he knows I'm the new hire."

"Oh, yes. He knows."

"He couldn't have been too happy about that. He can't stand me."

"No offense, Lewis, but don't think you're so special. My father can't stand anybody. He barely tolerates *me*. Now, over on the fridge here I've put all the phone numbers. You know. The doctors and all."

I followed her over there to look. There were a lot of doctors.

"What about hospice?" I asked. "Won't they come out now and then so he won't be alone if I have to go somewhere?"

"Oh, you can go out if it's only an hour or so. Just make sure he has your cell phone number. There'll come a time when we'll need hospice even to go to the store, but it's not quite here yet." Having reminded herself about time, she glanced at the huge round elementary-school-style clock on the kitchen wall, and frowned. "I have to go. I have to get to the airport. But I wrote it all out for you. You can read it and then call me with questions."

"You need a ride to the airport?"

"No, I have a rental car. But thanks."

She hurried off toward one of the bedrooms, presumably to get her bags. I was left with a dizzying sense of panic and dread. I had wanted to drive her to the airport as a way of getting out of that horrible place. Now I would have to stay in the den of darkness.

"Wait," I said, and she stopped. "What about treatments?"

"Cancer treatments?"

"Right. Doesn't somebody have to take him in for chemo and radiation and . . ."

"No. He's refusing all further treatment."

"Oh. Really? That seems . . ."

"It wouldn't have bought him very much time anyway."

Upon saying that, she disappeared into the guest bedroom.

I waited for her for several minutes. When she didn't come back after a time, I wandered over to the only closed bedroom door. I stood in front of it, breathing purposefully, for what felt like a long time.

Then I rapped softly. Very softly.

Chester's gravelly voice came back at me immediately. It was not soft.

"Leave me alone, Ellie."

"It's not Ellie," I said through the door. "It's me. Lewis. Can I open the door?"

"Absolutely not."

"Now how can I take care of you if I don't open the door?"

"I don't care. I don't need you here. Just go away and leave me on my own. I'll call you if I'm dying."

"I'm going to open the door now, Chester."

"No. Do not open that door."

I opened the door.

The room was dusty and depressingly dim. Everything had such a dank feel, and the air was so heavy that it was almost too thick to breathe. It felt weirdly like being underwater.

He was sitting in his wheelchair by the window, as though looking out. But he couldn't possibly have been looking out, because the shades were drawn. That seemed odd. Then again, it was Chester Wheeler. Did I expect anything non-odd?

He looked at me and I looked at him. And for a moment, that's all we did. Just looked at each other.

"You know that's not the way it's going to be," I said. "I have to do things like come into your room."

I could see his jaw working as he ground his molars together.

"I told you not to take the job," he said, his voice a sandpaper growl.

"Do *you* do what other people tell you to do?" I asked.

It was the right question. Because he had no answer for it. No way to argue the point.

I heard Ellie's voice behind me, so I stepped back and closed the door.

"I hope you don't mind," she was saying. "I took the liberty of making an appointment for this afternoon for a man to come out and install the intercom. It'll be on all the time, so you can hear if he falls or goes into coughing spasms or whatever. You can fix it so he can't hear everything you say and do, but you'll have to have the guy show you how to work it so you still have your privacy. You'll need to let him in over here and also over at your house."

"Sure," I said. "Fine."

But of course it wasn't fine. It was a live, real-time feed of Chester Wheeler, twenty-four hours a day, in my home. It wasn't remotely fine.

On the other hand, it was what I had agreed to tolerate.

She stood in front of the door with a suitcase on either side of her, their wheels buried in all that ridiculous shag carpeting. She offered me a nervous, unbalanced smile.

"Let me help you with your bags," I said.

"No. It's fine. I've got them. Just promise me . . ."

But then she seemed unwilling or unable to finish.

"What?" I finally asked. "Go ahead and say it."

"He's going to give you a hard time. He'll try to drive you away. But I need you to stay for at least the time you committed to stay. Otherwise I'll have no other options."

"Don't worry about it," I said. "I promise. I'll be miserable. We both will. But I'll stay till you can get back."

She sighed out a breath that sounded as though it might have been held for hours, if not days.

Then she ran over, gave me a brisk hug, and towed her suitcases out the door, leaving me alone with the most horrible man on the planet. At least, in my own fairly limited experience. Still, I expected I could have knocked around in a few more places for a few more decades without anybody evicting Chester Wheeler from the top spot of honor.

—

I rummaged through the prescription medication bottles for a few minutes, lining them up and comparing them with Ellie's written instructions.

She was right. It was confusing.

Just as I was getting it all sorted out in my head, I realized I didn't have the answer to the most obvious, most important question of all: Had he already had his pills that morning?

I pulled my phone out of my pocket and called Ellie's number.

When she answered, it was clear from the background noise that she was still driving.

"Lewis," she said. "Can I call you back when I get to the airport?"

"Yeah. Sure. But it's a really quick question. I just want to know if he's had his morning meds."

"He has. Sorry. I should have told you."

"No problem. Thanks. No need to call back. That's all I wanted to know."

I hung up the phone and immediately heard Chester call out to me from his bedroom.

"I want a drink!" he shouted.

I walked to his bedroom doorway.

"I'll get you a glass of apple juice," I said.

His face contorted into a mask of contempt.

"No, a *drink*," he spat. "A real drink. A man's drink. Typical pansy—you don't even know what a real man drinks. There's whiskey in the cupboard."

I took a deep breath and let the insult move through me. Or anyway, I tried. It stuck here and there going through. But I tried to focus right past it.

"I'm not sure if you're allowed to drink whiskey," I said.

"Ellie lets me drink whiskey."

"Ellie told me you would swear up and down that she lets you do all kinds of things that she would never let you do."

"I'm not a child!" he shouted. "People don't *let* me do things. I should get to be in charge of my own life."

"Just following orders."

"Sure," he said. "Got it. Exactly what Adolf Eichmann said."

I pulled in a few more deep breaths. Really made an effort to steady myself. In that moment I decided, without really thinking much about it, that the best way to fight back against Chester Wheeler was to stay steady. The more he tried to knock me off balance, the more I would stay steady.

"Tell you what," I said. "I just talked to Ellie. She's still driving. Let's give her a few minutes to get to the airport and get checked in. I'm going to go around and open the drapes. Let a little light into this place. And I'll open a couple of the windows to give the house a good airing out. And then I'll call her and see if she thinks you can have a whiskey. And if she says yes, great. Happy hour is here."

I didn't point out that it was still very much morning, because I wasn't sure how to make him care about such a thing, and I wasn't even convinced it was right to try. When you're living out your last couple of months on earth, does it honestly matter what time it is when you pour?

"Leave the curtains right where they are," he said.

"Nope. Sorry. We're going for light and air."

"I hate light and air."

"I'm sure you do. But I don't. And if you'll stop complaining about it, I'll call Ellie and see about getting you that drink. If you insist on grousing about your need to sit in a dark place with no air, then I'll just assume she doesn't allow whiskey and go from there."

He gave me a look I can only describe as loathing.

"This is going to be hell," he said. "Isn't it?"

"I'm pretty much figuring we're already there."

I stepped out of the doorway and began to walk around the house, letting light in. I opened one of the front windows. The air that flowed in felt decidedly cool, but that was not necessarily a bad thing. Traffic noise also flowed into the living room, but it felt like a welcome reminder that people were alive and attending to their day out there in the world.

I opened a kitchen window for cross ventilation.

Then I walked back to Chester's room and wheeled him out into the light.

"It's freezing out here," he said as I parked his chair near the couch.

"I'll get you a blanket."

"I don't want a blanket."

40

"You just said you were cold."

"I don't want to sit here with a blanket on my lap or around my shoulders like a frail old man."

But you are *a frail old man,* I thought. I kept the observation to myself.

"I'll get you a jacket, then."

"Fine."

I looked in his bedroom closet, but found only shirts. I opened doors in the halls that I thought might have been closets, but they contained shelves of threadbare linens and old worn towels, or in one case an ironing board.

"It would help if you told me where a jacket might be located," I called in.

"This whole thing was your idea," he called back.

I finally found the coat closet off the living room, and laid my hands on a royal blue down jacket. What was it with Chester and royal blue?

He clearly wasn't going to lean forward or offer to put his arms through the sleeves, so I draped it over his shoulders, wheelchair back and all.

As I did, he looked up at me. Just for a split second I thought I saw deeply into his unhappiness, a place I was not normally allowed to go. When he saw me looking, he quickly closed that window into his interior again.

"When did you last shave, Chester?"

His cheeks and chin were covered with longish, spotty stubble, mostly gray.

"I don't know," he said. "Who cares?"

"I think you might feel better if I shaved you."

"I don't want you shaving me. I don't want you touching me. Besides, I can shave myself. My arms aren't broken, you know."

Then why didn't you? I thought. Again, I kept it to myself.

41

"Fine," I said.

I wheeled him into the tiny, cramped bathroom. There was barely room for both of us in there at the same time.

I looked at my reflection in the mirror, standing behind his wheelchair, and it knocked me entirely off balance. When you catch a glimpse of your reflection unexpectedly, it's like seeing yourself from the outside.

I didn't know who I was looking at anymore.

I knew who I so recently had been. I had been a software developer. A good earner. A boyfriend. I'd been that person saving to move to California. But who was I now? I had no idea. Other than the fact that I was just . . . absolutely . . . lost.

"What?" Chester said. "Stop looking at yourself in the mirror. You're not that pretty a girl."

I pulled my attention back to the task at hand, and buried that personal crisis as deeply as possible.

I took two towels down off their racks. Put one on his lap and one around his neck. Then I looked around in the cabinet over the sink and found shaving cream and an old-fashioned safety razor.

"What am I supposed to do for water?" he said. "I can't reach the sink."

I squeezed out of there and walked to the kitchen. Opened a few cabinets and took down the biggest bowl I could find. I filled it half-full of water in the kitchen sink and then handed it to him through the open bathroom doorway.

He reached out to take it, but as soon as I let go I could tell it was too heavy for him. I grabbed at it again and helped him settle it onto his lap.

"I can do it," he said.

"Fine. Knock yourself out."

Somewhat nervously, I left him alone with the task.

I retreated to the cool living room, where I dialed Ellie a second time.

"Sorry to do this to you again," I said. "Are you still driving?"

"No, I'm wheeling my bags over from the rental car desk."

"Do you let him have a drink of whiskey?"

"*One*," she said, her voice quite firm. "He can have *one* drink. He's already a fall risk, and if he has much more than that it can open up a world of problems."

"Got it," I said. "Thanks."

"So . . . ," she began, ". . . is it . . . going okay so far?"

"I guess. I opened the curtains and I'm airing the house out a bit."

"And he didn't pitch a fit about that?"

"I told him if he'd stop complaining, I'd ask you about that drink."

A brief silence, which I instinctively took as a bad sign.

"I think you're better at this than you realize," she said. "I think you're going to do just fine."

"One more question. Can *I* have a drink? I could use one right about now."

"If *he* can have one, *you* can have one," she said. "By the end of the day it might be all that's keeping you sane."

———

I made the glasses of whiskey stiff and tall, and wheeled him back into the living room. He looked more human and more comfortable now that he was clean shaven.

I parked his wheelchair next to the couch and handed him one of the glasses. I sat down on the ridiculous couch with the other.

"Now doesn't that feel better?" I asked him, taking a long sip.

"Doesn't what feel better?"

"A good shave."

"What do I care if I'm shaved or not?"

I decided that my attempts at talking to him were not going to make things better for anybody. Then I wondered why I hadn't known that all along.

He slammed down his whiskey in just a few long gulps. He belched, and held out the glass to me. I took it from him.

"I have to take a pee," he said.

My heart fell.

"I'm not sure how we—"

"I don't want you anywhere near me. I don't want you looking or touching. I can do it. Just bring me the bedpan and go away. But when I have to take a dump, you'll need to help me onto the can, and I'm not looking forward to that, believe me."

"Neither am I," I said. "Believe me."

———

The intercom installer guy showed up around one o'clock.

Chester had closed himself into his bedroom as the result of an altercation we'd had regarding apple juice. You wouldn't think two people could really get into it in any serious way over apple juice, but Chester and I had managed.

The short version goes a little something like this: Chester said I watered down his apple juice with water from the tap so it hardly tasted like anything at all. I said he was delusional. Spoiler alert: I knew who was right. I was. I was there when the apple juice was poured. I poured it right out of the bottle. Nothing was added. Case closed.

The installer guy had short-cropped hair and a blue work shirt with the name "Dean" embroidered over the pocket. He looked me up and down, apparently to see why I wasn't Ellie. Then he asked straight out why I wasn't. Not in so many words, but that was the gist of it.

I sighed and invited him in.

"She had to go home," I said. "Her daughter is in labor. The bedroom is this way. You have to install one in Chester's room. Then another in my house, next door."

He followed me down the hall and I rapped on Chester's closed door.

"I told you to go away and leave me alone!" he bellowed.

Dean jumped back a step.

"Gladly," I said. "But this guy who installs intercoms needs to come in and do . . . you know. What he does."

I opened the door.

Chester was sitting by the window, and he had managed to get the curtains closed again.

"I don't want an intercom," he said.

"It's not really up for debate. Ellie's orders."

"I'll tear it right back out of the wall."

I looked at Dean and he returned a questioning gaze.

"Put it up nice and high," I said.

"I don't want that damn thing. I don't want people snooping and spying on every word I say."

"That makes no sense," I told him.

"It makes perfect sense to want your privacy."

"But during the day I'll hear what you say anyway. This is for the night, when you're here all alone. Unless you call for help or fall out of your wheelchair, there won't be anything to hear. Why would you say any words at all if you're home alone?"

Oddly, Chester never answered the question.

When Dean grew tired of waiting, he said, "I'll put it up nice and high."

I left them to work it out between themselves.

———

When he had finished his job in Chester's room in spite of its occupant—and I use the word "spite" quite literally—I led Dean over to my house.

"Boy, he's a piece of work, huh?" Dean said.

"Yeah, he's one of a kind."

"Your father?"

"Nope."

"Grandfather?"

"No blood relation. It's just a paid gig. I just told his daughter I'd look after him for a week or so."

He stopped dead in my driveway.

"A week?"

"That's right."

"And after that?"

"Don't know. Don't care. They're on their own. Why?"

His face took on a quizzical expression. Then he shrugged and resumed walking.

"Just seems like a lot of money to spend for a week. You know. Getting an intercom installed."

"Well, it's her money," I said, and opened my front door for him. "It's her decision."

"Sure, sure. It just sounds like she's hoping you'll stay on the job longer."

I never answered. Not only did I not know the answer, I had no idea why the question hadn't occurred to me on my own, without the savvy counsel of Dean the intercom installer.

———

At 6:00 in the afternoon I told Chester I was leaving. He was already in bed, and he had been properly fed.

"You're supposed to stay till seven," he said.

"Well, I'm not going to. I've had enough."

"I'll tell Ellie. She'll dock your pay."

"She'll give me a medal for having stuck it out *this* long."

"It's a nine-to-seven gig," he said.

"I've been here since seven in the morning."

That shut him up, which was a small miracle all in itself.

———

I lay awake until nearly midnight, listening to Chester toss and turn. He also snored like a buzz saw once he really went under, punctuated by sputters and gasps.

I stared at the ceiling, wondering how I could possibly make it through the week.

Then something odd happened.

Chester began talking. Not to me. Not giving me a bad time, as though he knew I was listening. He began talking in a soft voice, as if to someone in the room.

I couldn't make out every word, but I heard a few sentences in their entirety.

"No, honey, don't get up. I'll get him, Sue. I'll take care of it."

Then something unintelligible.

Then, "He probably wants a glass of water. You go back to sleep."

Then incoherent mumbling, followed by "I'll show him inside the closet and under the bed. We'll shine a flashlight in so he'll know not to be scared."

Then, suddenly, almost perfect silence. He must have rolled onto his side, because the buzz saw was gone, replaced by just the lightest trace of sleeping breath.

In time I must have drifted off to sleep myself.

Chapter Five:

Nocturnal Redemptions

When I opened my eyes, the world was light.

I reached over to my phone, which was charging on the nightstand, and hit Ellie's number.

She picked up on the third ring.

"Everything okay?" she asked immediately.

"Yeah. Sure. Just a question."

"Okay. Whew. Good. Baby's here. A little girl. Seven pounds, ten ounces. I got here just in time."

"Nice," I said, and pretty much meant it. Even though I wasn't much of a baby person. *She* was, and that was all that mattered. "Congratulations."

"Thank you. What's the question?"

"Is your dad . . . ever . . . does he have . . . delusions?"

"What kind of delusions?"

"Like the kind that would have him talking to someone who wasn't there."

"Oh, my. Not up until now, no. You mean right there in broad daylight with his eyes wide open he was talking to someone who wasn't there?"

"No, it was at night. I heard him on the intercom."

"Oh, that's just him talking in his sleep. He talks a blue streak in his sleep. I meant to tell you."

"Interesting," I said.

"I'm not sure what's so interesting about it. Half the time I can't make out a word he's saying."

"Maybe because you never had an intercom between your rooms. That thing could pick up a page turning. What's so interesting about it is that in his sleep he seems . . . okay."

"I don't follow. Okay how?"

"Like . . . an okay person. Like a nice enough person."

For a moment I heard no response.

Then she said, "Well, you never know about people. Maybe one is buried in there somewhere. If you can find it, you're doing better than I am."

Then she had to go, to help her daughter with the breastfeeding.

———

When I got over to Chester's, he was in a deeply foul mood, even for Chester.

I couldn't help wondering if it was constipation. The result of holding it in to avoid that moment we both dreaded.

"You want coffee?" I asked him.

"Of course I want coffee," he said. "I'm not a savage."

I didn't question why he associated coffee with civilization. I took the conversation in an entirely different direction.

"You have a great-grandchild," I said.

"And?"

"Just thought you'd want to know."

"I've already got five," he said. "What's one more?"

He didn't ask if it was a boy or a girl, or how much it weighed. He didn't even ask if it was healthy. All he asked was if I would hurry up and make the damned coffee.

———

After breakfast he said the dreaded words—the sentence we both knew was coming sooner or later, though I'm sure we had both wished hard for later.

"You gotta help me onto the can."

"Okay," I said.

Then I just sat there with my face tingling, saying nothing.

We were still at the breakfast table, and he was looking down at his lap to avoid my eyes. At least, I assumed that was why.

"I guess we should get started," I said.

I found myself wanting to put the whole uncomfortable mess behind us.

"I want you to wear a blindfold," he said.

I was feeling pretty unfiltered, so I said the first thing that jumped into my mind.

"That's the stupidest thing I've ever heard in my life."

"It's not stupid. I don't want you looking at me."

"I'm not going to be looking at you."

"Oh, you're gonna be looking."

"I'm not attracted to every man on the planet, Chester. I'm twenty-four. You're, like, seventy. Do you honestly think I'm interested in you?"

"I'm only sixty-nine," he said, still looking at his lap.

"That final question still stands."

"You're a man. Marginally, anyway."

"I'm going to let that go by because we have important matters at hand. Here's a question. Did you make Agostina and the others wear a blindfold?"

"No, of course not. Agostina was a woman. Women don't have that lust thing going on. But if you're a man, you look. If I was taking care of a woman, even one who was that much older than me . . ."

"She'd have to be like a hundred and fifteen," I said in the pause.

"Anyway, the point is . . . I wouldn't be after her. But I'd look. How can you not look?"

"That's disgusting," I said. "Oh my God, Chester. You just hit a new low even for you."

I pushed away from the table. I was acting like I was going to get up and stomp away. But I didn't, because there was this . . . situation. This problem that needed solving.

Chester seemed unmoved by my disgust.

"It's just how men are," he said.

"This man isn't like that."

"Maybe if you really *were* a man, you'd understand." He allowed a pause for me to take the bait. When I didn't bite, he added, "But I'm supposed to believe a fairy has less lust than a straight guy? I'm having trouble believing that."

"I'm sure you have trouble believing all kinds of things that are true," I said. "And I'm sure you believe all kinds of things that are obviously fiction." I stood. Sighed deeply. "But come on. We need to get this over with."

I walked around behind him and grabbed the handles of his wheelchair. Started to pull him backward into the bathroom.

"Where did we land on the blindfold?" he asked, sounding a little off kilter.

"We landed on 'That's the stupidest thing I've ever heard in my life.' But if it makes you feel better, I'll look up at the ceiling and close my eyes."

"You better *keep* 'em closed," he said as I wheeled him in.

"Oh, Chester. If only you knew how much I *don't* want to see."

51

When we had managed to squeeze into the bathroom, I gave him my arm and we tried to pull him up out of the chair. It was harder than it had been helping him into bed the night before, maybe because in that case we were just swinging him over to a soft, safe place he could drop. This time I had to get him onto his feet and fairly steady. That was the first moment I realized, all the way down into my gut, how deeply weak and helpless he was.

When we had him pretty well balanced on his feet, still holding my arm, I carefully turned him around so his back was facing the toilet.

"Okay, this is the bad part," he said. "You have to hold me up while I get my pants down."

"Hold you up how?"

"You have to put your arms around me, under my armpits."

"While looking up at the ceiling with my eyes closed."

"Exactly."

There was no way not to think of it as a bear hug. I wrapped Chester Wheeler in a bear hug. While looking up at the ceiling. With my eyes closed.

I could feel him fumbling with his zipper down below my grasp. It was probably the most deeply awkward and uncomfortable moment of my life to that date.

Finally I heard the soft sound of his pants falling down around his knees.

"Now lower me down," he said.

"Don't you need to take down your underwear?"

"No."

"Why not?"

"Because I'm not wearing any."

I sighed deeply.

"Because of course you're not," I said.

I instinctively looked down as a way of beginning the task.

"Don't look!" he shouted.

"Sorry. Force of habit. I'm used to looking at what I'm doing."

"Well, don't."

I leaned forward, still in our bear hug, and let his great weight settle. Chester was a heavy man, and there was a moment when every muscle in my body trembled with the strain. But a moment later I heard him sigh as he settled his bulk onto the toilet seat.

"Okay, now go away," he said, his voice hard.

"Can you wipe yourself?"

It was a horrible question, because of the horrible possibility that the answer might be no. Which would have been horrible.

"Of course I can wipe myself. Just how weak do you think I am? Damn, Lewis. I'm not dead yet. Now get out of here."

With great relief, I did as I had been told.

———

I stayed over and we set up to watch *Monday Night Football,* in return for me coming in late the next day. Okay, *I* set up. Chester sat there in his wheelchair chanting something about the Buffalo Bills, which seemed odd because they were not one of the teams playing.

I brought him a beer—one beer—during the kickoff, and then retreated to the kitchen to make microwave popcorn.

When I got back out, he was pounding his thighs in excitement.

"What did I miss?" I asked, handing him the bowl of popcorn.

"What do you care? You don't watch football."

"How do you know I don't watch football?"

"Oh, come on, Lewis."

My stepfather had been a big football person. While I was growing up he'd sat glued to every game, shouting at the screen and drinking beer. I'd watched with him, and learned the game, as a way of trying to bond with the guy. It ultimately fell short of the goal. But I had no intention of sharing any emotional details of my past with Chester Wheeler.

I sat down on the couch about ten feet from his wheelchair.

"Who do we like?" I asked.

He briefly looked away from the game to narrow his eyes at me.

"*I* like Dallas. You can like whoever you want."

Before I could even respond, he became suddenly agitated over the conclusion of a pass play, and began throwing handfuls of popcorn in the general direction of the TV screen.

"Throw a flag!" he shouted in that gravelly voice of his. "That wasn't pass defense, that was a mugging!"

He followed his pronouncement with another handful of thrown popcorn.

I watched it bounce and roll on the shag carpet for a moment. Then I reached over and grabbed the remote and muted the game.

"Hey!" he shouted. "What're you doing? Turn that back up!"

"In a minute," I said.

"No, now! I'm watching this."

"And if you want to keep watching it, you'd better listen to what I have to say. Because I'm not turning the sound back up until I've said it."

"What? Hurry up."

"You don't get to throw popcorn on the rug."

"Can if I want. It's my house."

"But I'm the one who has to clean it up."

"So clean it up. It's what you're getting paid to do."

I could see his eyes nervously following the action on the screen. Then the game coverage broke for a beer commercial, and I watched his face relax some.

"No," I said.

"You can't say no. It's your job."

"Oh, I can say no. I can and I will. Just watch me. Here's the thing, Chester. Do yourself a favor and absorb this next part. If you were a nice guy who could employ any help he wanted without driving them away, you'd have more power. But you're not, and you don't. I'm pretty much Last Chance City in your life, my friend. You honestly think Ellie is going to fire me? To be replaced by whom?"

"*Whom?*" he repeated, mocking me.

"Yeah, 'whom.' It's called English grammar. You should try it some-time. Now listen up, Chester. Here's the way it's going to be. I will clean up the floor of anything that ends up there accidentally. If you purposely throw food on the floor, I'll leave it there. I'll leave it there until it molds, and ants and cockroaches and mice show up to eat it. Or, if you prefer, I'll pick it up this one time, after you make me a solemn promise that you'll never do that again. If you make the promise and break it, next time it stays there and becomes part and parcel of your shag carpeting. Possibly not the worst thing to ever happen to it, I might add. And, by the way, the reason there was no flag thrown for pass interference on that play is because the ball was uncatchable anyway."

I stopped talking, but Chester didn't start. He just sat there in silence. I think I had caught him speechless. A real occasion, consider-ing the source.

I thought, *Mark this day on your calendar.*

The game came back on, and I turned up the sound.

Just at that moment my cell phone rang, and the caller ID told me it was Ellie. I got up and took it in the kitchen.

"Everything going okay?" she asked.

"Yeah, pretty much. I'm being tough with him, and he keeps acting like he's in charge and can get me in trouble. But I know you'll support me on whatever keeps him in line."

"A hundred percent," she said. I could hear a hesitation in her voice. A slight nervousness. "I was just thinking . . ."

Here it comes, I thought, though I actually had no idea what was coming. Just that something was.

". . . it would just be so nice if I didn't have to fly back there. If you could stay."

"I'm sure it would be," I said, trying not to laugh in any derisive way. "For *you*."

"But I had that intercom installed and all."

I mentally bowed to the cognitive powers of Dean the Installer Guy.

"That felt slightly passive-aggressive," I said.

"Sorry. Will you at least think about it?"

"I'm pretty sure that's how you got me into this mess in the first place."

"Can't hurt to think about it."

"Fine," I said. "I'll postpone saying no till the next time you call. Hey. Mind if I ask you a question? I'm just curious as to why he's so immobile. I had to lift him onto the toilet this morning, and, wow. I mean, I understand he's weak, but I sort of picture someone weak from cancer as needing you to steady them by the arm while they move very slowly from place to place. This seems . . ."

"It's in his spine," she said.

"The cancer?"

"Yes. Among other places. His spine is all shot through with tumors."

"Oh."

Then I didn't know what else to say. Something bland like "That's too bad" only felt generic and lame.

"I'll call again in a couple of days," she said. "See what you decide."

Then she quickly ended the call before I could tell her, again, that I already knew what the decision would be.

I slipped my phone back into my pocket and rejoined Chester in the living room.

As I settled on the couch, he spoke. His voice sounded different than I was used to hearing it. Almost . . . humble. Or at very least, slightly chastened.

"I won't throw any more popcorn. So . . . if you'll pick up what's already there . . ."

"Sure," I said. "Now that we've established that it's the last food that'll go into that carpet on purpose, I'll take care of it."

I got down on my hands and knees in all that horrible shag and weeded it out one kernel at a time.

In one sense it put me in a degraded position. Almost like prostrating myself. But in another, more significant way it was a triumphant moment, because I had won that round, and we both knew it.

———

That night I was so tired I fell asleep straightaway, in spite of Chester's tossing and turning, gasping and wheezing.

Then, at what the clock would later inform me was after 1:00, he woke me with a single shouted word.

"No!"

It wasn't the kind of "no" you would shout to forestall disaster. It wasn't like a person in a horror movie screaming to the monster, "No!" as in "No, please don't kill me!" It sounded more like the decidedly vehement answer to a yes-or-no question I hadn't been privy to overhearing.

I sat up and turned on the light, then stared at the intercom for a few beats. But it, and Chester, seemed to have nothing more to say.

I turned off the light and tried to get back to the task of sleeping.

Just as I was pulling the covers over my shoulder, just as I was rolling over to try to get back to my sleeping position, I heard one clear sentence from him. It was, in fact, eerily clear, and spoken in a gravely quiet voice.

"I found the letters he wrote you."

I lay awake for an hour or two, but sleeping Chester had no more words to toss out into my once quiet and private living space.

Chapter Six:

Who Are You,
and What Have You Done with Chester?

I arrived at his house at the agreed-upon time. Stuck my head through his bedroom door.

He was wide awake, lying on his back and staring at the ceiling. He shifted his eyes down to my face.

Much to my surprise, he smiled.

I can't honestly say it was a happy or genuine-looking thing. More like something he pasted on, leaving a little strain showing through here and there behind it. Still, we're talking about Chester Wheeler, and it was a smile.

"Oh, Lewis," he said. "Hi. Good morning."

I only leaned there in the doorway for a moment, speechless, letting it all sink in. I could feel my forehead wrinkling with the strain of figuring it all out.

"Sorry," I said. "Wrong house. I was looking for a Chester Wheeler. You know him?"

"Very funny. Jeez, Lewis. I can't win with you. You want me to be nice, but then when I try to be nice, you give me a bad time."

"I don't mind your being nice. I just want to know why. I mean, you never were before, and this is out of the blue, and I'm just curious about the why of the thing. And you can't say, 'Because I'm a nice guy,' because you're not, and even you admit it."

"I never said I wasn't nice."

"Oh, sorry. My mistake. I must've confused you with everybody else on the planet."

———

I cooked bacon for breakfast. His breakfast, not mine. Not bacon and eggs. Not bacon and toast. Just bacon.

Ellie had made it clear when I'd spoken to her that morning that he could eat any damn thing he wanted. Anything that made him happy. His long-range health didn't enter into the picture, because he didn't have a long range.

Then she'd asked me again to think about staying on, but she'd quickly hung up before I could tell her I already *had* thought about it and the answer was still no.

"Did Ellie say when she's coming back?" he asked me with his mouth full of half-chewed bacon.

"Five or six days if I insist. But she's really hoping I'll stay on and she won't have to come back at all."

"You should do that," he said.

I narrowed my eyes at him suspiciously. "Which part of 'that' should I do?"

"You should stay."

I dropped my palm hard onto the table and it made him jump.

"Okay, Chester," I said. "What's going on?"

"Nothing. I'm just trying to be nice."

"No ulterior motive at all."

"Well . . . ," he said. Then nothing further.

He sipped at his coffee, his eyes scanning the ceiling almost nervously.

"Come on, Chester," I said. "It's coming out sooner or later. Go ahead and spit it out now."

"I guess I was just hoping you'd do me a favor."

"I *knew* it," I shouted, with more slapping of the table. "I *knew* there was a reason you were being nice to me. Why me? Why didn't you ask Agostina? She was here for months. I've only been here for a couple of days."

"Agostina didn't drive."

"Oh, I see. You need to go somewhere. Well. That doesn't sound so bad. Where do you want me to drive you?"

"Arizona," he said.

I honestly thought he was kidding. It sounded like Chester's brand of basic sophomoric humor. I laughed, and got up to pour myself a second cup of coffee. I figured in a minute he'd tell me where he really wanted to go. Niagara Falls, or the home of an old friend on the other side of town. Williamsville, maybe, or Cheektowaga.

"So does that mean no?" he asked after a time.

I sat back down with my coffee, sipped, and watched him start on the last slice of bacon.

"I'm still waiting to hear where you want to go."

"What, are you deaf?" he asked, skating right back into regular Chester territory. "Am I talking to myself? I just told you. Arizona."

"That wasn't a joke?"

"No. Why would I joke about a thing like that?"

"You want me to drive you to Arizona."

"Seriously, Lewis, are you having hearing problems?"

"Nobody drives from Buffalo to Arizona."

"I'd bet money somebody's done it."

"It's probably over two thousand miles."

"So? People drive over two thousand miles."

"This person doesn't. If I were going to take you to Arizona, which I'm not about to do, we'd go by plane."

"We can't go by plane," he said, very matter-of-factly. As if the comment were self-explanatory.

"Why can't we?"

"Because . . ." He seemed to stall for a beat. ". . . you can't fly when you have lung cancer."

"Oh. Well, I'm not driving to Arizona."

"Should've known," he said. "Should've known better than to expect anything good out of *you*."

He had finished with his breakfast by this time, so I moved the day along.

"We should take care of your shower."

"Whatever," he said. He seemed to be imitating a petulant teenager. Saying the fewest, least helpful words possible.

"I'll go get it set up."

I hadn't yet helped Chester take a shower in the forty-eight hours or so he'd been in my care, but I had instructions on how to do it. Ellie had left a waterproof lawn chair in the shower stall. I was to wheel him into the bathroom and loosely cover him with a giant bath sheet. He could wiggle out of his clothes underneath it. Then I had to help him up, keeping the towel still mostly wrapped around him, and move him into the shower chair. I was to turn on the water but then turn it off at the little switch on the head of the shower hose. I would hand the hose to Chester, who could move the towel and turn on the water after I had gone.

I wheeled him into the bathroom, set up the water properly, and left him for a moment while I fetched an extra-large towel from the hall closet.

"I just think it sucks," he called down the hall to me.

"You just think what sucks?"

"I'm a dying man."

I arrived back in the doorway with the towel and stood looking down at him. He looked up into my eyes with an expression I can only describe as hateful.

"Of course it sucks that you're dying," I said. "And I'm sorry."

"That wasn't what I meant."

"Oh. What did you mean?"

While I was waiting for him to tell me, I draped the big towel over the front of him.

"I'll wait out in the hall," I said.

"Thank you. I just think I should get a last wish. It sucks that I don't even get a last wish."

I stepped out into the hall before answering.

"I guess . . . I agree."

"You do?"

"Yeah, I guess. I mean . . . a last wish sounds fair enough. Unless it's being driven to Arizona. By me."

"You're going to feel bad about it after I'm gone."

"Probably not," I said. "I was barely on board with calling 9-1-1 or putting you back in your wheelchair if you fell out."

But, even as I said it, I knew he might be right. One day in the future I might be lying awake thinking I'd had a chance to fulfill the last wish of a dying man. Even if the dying man in question *was* Chester Wheeler. Would I regret that?

"You undressed yet?" I added, wanting to get this over with.

All of this.

"Not even close. I've barely got my shirt off. It takes me a while."

"Fine," I said. "I'll wait."

I leaned on the wall with my arms crossed in front of me, vaguely aware that it was a defensive pose. I was protecting my soft underbelly.

"What's in Arizona?" I asked after a time.

"My ex-wife."

"Ah. Looking for closure, eh?"

"Something like that."

"The phone is good."

"I couldn't see her face that way."

"We could do a Skype or a Zoom thing."

"No we couldn't. She wouldn't agree to do it. If I surprised her, she'd hang up on me."

"Then what makes you think she'd agree to an in-person visit?"

He didn't answer. But, in his silence, the answer came through.

"Oh," I said, drawing the word out long. "I get it now. A *surprise* visit. You want me to drive you to Arizona to *ambush* your ex-wife."

"I'm ready," he said, but I didn't think he was talking about an ambush.

I stepped into the bathroom again. Chester was mostly covered with the huge yellow towel, but his bare shoulders and lower legs were exposed. They were a strange milky white, as though his skin was too thin. It was weirdly translucent, his skin. I could see veins right through it, like looking at soft, blurry details through a fogged-over window.

"Okay, I'm going to lift you up," I said.

He wrapped both his arms around one of mine, and I hoisted. As I did, I had to use my other arm to keep the towel as far around him as reasonably possible.

I steered him backward into the shower stall and he flopped too hard into the chair, the skin of one massive white buttock exposed.

I averted my gaze and handed him the shower hose and a bar of soap.

"Now go away," he said.

Just on my way out the bathroom door I asked a question I hadn't felt coming.

"Is her name Sue? Your ex?"

"Yeah. How did you know that?"

I rarely lie, but in this case I did.

"Ellie mentioned it."

I didn't think he wanted to hear that I was piecing together a puzzle of secrets he'd been exposing in his sleep.

I left him and walked into the living room, where I called Ellie yet again.

"Everything okay?" she asked. Immediately. Breathlessly.

"He wants me to drive him to Arizona."

She didn't sound the least bit surprised.

"Oh, that," she said.

"I guess he wants some closure with his ex."

"I'm sure that makes one of them."

"I'm not going to do it."

"I understand. I didn't expect you to. I never meant that you should do that much. Just the basics is all I ask."

"So, listen. I didn't know people with lung cancer couldn't fly."

"Neither did I," she said. "But you should probably know that my father has a deathly fear of flying."

"Oh. So that might have been a lie."

"Might've been. I don't know. Did you tell him no?"

"About driving him, you mean?"

"Right."

"Of course I did."

"Then what's the problem?"

That caught me off guard. I stammered a little, trying to express the answer and figure out what the answer was, all at the same time.

"I guess," I said when I'd straightened out my tongue, "maybe I feel guilty. I said no and now I feel guilty. I mean . . . it's the last wish of a dying man. You know?"

"I wouldn't feel too bad about it," Ellie said. "You're already doing more for him than anybody else is willing to do."

Just then I heard the water shut off in the bathroom.

"Wow, he takes short showers," I said.

"If you can get him to take one at all."

"I should go," I said, forgetting that he would want to dry off in privacy.

Only after we ended the call did I realize I'd had the chance to tell her she'd need to fly home—that I wasn't staying on—and I'd gotten distracted and let it go by.

I sat on the arm of the horrible sofa and pulled up the internet browser on my phone. I typed in "Can someone with lung cancer fly?"

I clicked on the first article.

The answer was a qualified—but only slightly qualified—yes.

———

It's not my intention to mislead anyone with this part of the story, but I'm at a loss regarding how best to report this next happening.

When I woke up the next morning, I went over to the house next door and found Chester Wheeler dead in his bed.

Except that never really happened at all.

In reality I went home that night, fell asleep, and the part I just described was a vivid dream. But what a dream! It was so perfectly realistic, so detailed. While the whole thing was playing out I was positive it was real, and happening just as it appeared to be happening. Usually dreams have an element of dreamlike weirdness to them, even though you might not see that until you wake up and look back on the details of it. This dream followed the down-to-earth reality of waking life to a tee.

The sights and sounds of it are still seared into my brain. Even now I can close my eyes and see the slightly open-mouthed death mask of Chester's unshaven face as rigor mortis claimed what was left of him. I could smell the staleness of the air in his room. Feel the shock of the discovery in my belly.

I had all the thoughts and feelings anyone would have in that situation. My brain rushed in a swirl of failed directions.

I have to call Ellie. No—well, yes—but first I have to call . . . who? 9-1-1? But it's not an emergency, because we're not trying to prevent a man's death. It's already happened. Maybe just call the police and report it and ask them to send . . . ? No, maybe you don't even call them when somebody dies of natural causes. Maybe just call the funeral home to come pick up the body. Did Ellie leave me the name of the funeral home? I'll have to start plowing through what she left me.

Or maybe I should call her before anything else.

And then, the plainest, most affecting thought of all.

Why didn't I just take him to Arizona?

Granted, I said the dream was perfectly realistic, but that's not a hundred percent true. In real life I hadn't exactly denied him the chance to go on his road trip, because no time had elapsed. If he really had died that night, death would have denied him the chance. I would only have denied him a yes answer, which at least would have been some indication that I gave a damn about his need for closure in some important relationship from his past. And that was bad enough.

But back to the feelings of the thing.

I stood there over his bed, staring down at his forever-frozen, open-eyed face, thinking, *What would it have hurt you to take him?*

I mean, sure, nobody spent time with Chester Wheeler on purpose, and if they could avoid it. But I had agreed to be here anyway. One way or another I was going to spend those next few days with him. Was the open road somehow worse than the dank, faintly odorous world he had created behind closed doors?

Suddenly the trip sounded like an improvement.

And, for the love of all that's holy, it was his dying wish.

And I'll never get a do-over.

Except I was utterly wrong, because just then I woke up. There I was, sitting up in my bed in the dark, in the opening moments of the do-over.

I sat for a time, afraid to go over to Chester's, because maybe the dream was prophetic. Maybe I'd go over there . . .

I purposely didn't finish the thought.

I couldn't hear him snoring through the intercom, so I rose and dressed quickly. It was only five thirty in the morning, but I made my way next door in the dark and let myself into Chester's house with my key.

I stuck my head through his bedroom door and listened, but heard nothing. Not even the rhythmic sound of his breathing. I turned on the light in the hall to try to see him, but his bed was still in darkness. So I took a big, deep breath and turned on the overhead light in his room.

He immediately sputtered up into his normally combative consciousness.

"Holy crap, Lewis!" he shouted. "I was sleeping. What are you doing here so early? What time is it?"

"Sorry," I said. "Just checking in on you."

I opened my mouth to ask him some details about this proposed trip. What would we drive? My car? Did he have a car? Could his be trusted on such a long journey? Where would we stay along the way? Who was paying for all this?

Then I closed my mouth and said nothing along those lines.

"Turn off the light and leave me alone. I wanna go back to sleep."

"Sure. I'll make some coffee for when you're up."

I slipped into the kitchen in the mostly-dark and made coffee.

Then I sat at the table drinking a cup and thinking.

I wasn't feeling ready to tip my hand about the thing, because doing so would have been like jumping into the deep end of a pool. Once you jump, that's it. You've jumped. You can't unjump, because there's no such thing as unjumping.

But even in that no-man's-land of options and actions, I think it's fair to say that I already knew which way this part of the story was going to fall.

Chapter Seven:

Scrape Them

I woke again and lay on my back, staring at the ceiling for a time, thinking. Then I grabbed my phone off the bedside table and called Ellie.

"Hey," I said.

"Hey," she said back.

We had grown surprisingly comfortable with each other.

"So, look," I began. Then I stalled, and did not immediately tell her what it was we'd be looking at. "I'm not saying I'm actually going to do it. I'm not committing to any of this. So don't hold me to it. I'm just asking. Let's say, just for the sake of conversation, that I did agree to drive him to Arizona. What would we be driving? I hate to put that kind of miles on my car. Does he have a dependable car?"

"Oh," she said, obviously surprised. "I didn't realize you were even thinking about that. It's kind of you to even consider it."

"I can't really justify why a road trip would be any worse than just sitting in that musty house with him, doing nothing."

"I guess that's true," she said. "I would imagine you'd be taking his Winnebago."

"Chester has a Winnebago? Where?"

"He stores it somewhere, but I don't know exactly where. He'd have to tell you that."

"Is it roadworthy?"

"I think so. I know he took meticulous care of it. Better than he took of his family, believe me. But I think it's at least twelve years old."

"I guess we could have a mechanic look it over and offer an opinion. Who would be paying for all that gas?"

"I'd cover your expenses."

"Interesting. I guess I'll have to think about that."

"It's kind of you," she said.

"But I don't know for a fact that I'll do it."

"It's kind of you to even consider doing it."

"Well," I said. "It *is* a man's dying wish. I'm not really sure how you say no to a man's dying wish."

"Think it over and let me know what you decide."

I agreed that I would, then clicked off the call.

I rose, dressed, and walked over to Chester's house, even though it was earlier than I needed to be there. I knew if I did, I could leave work early that evening, which already sounded appealing.

I stuck my head into his bedroom.

He was lying on his back in bed, his hands clasped behind his head, staring at the ceiling. He had a look on his face . . . I'm not sure how to describe it. Almost like someone who didn't hate everybody and everything on the planet.

He turned to look at me, and he smiled. And not a smile pasted on over stress and hatred, like the last one. An actual, genuine smile.

"I underestimated you, Lewis," he said.

"I don't follow."

"I'm happy because you're going to take me to Arizona."

"I never said I was going to take you to Arizona."

"You said you were thinking about it."

"When did I say that?"

"Just a minute or two ago."

The realization came upon me slowly, accompanied by a sickening dread.

"Oh no," I said. "Oh crap. I'm supposed to be able to set that intercom so I can hear you but you can't hear me."

"Good luck with that," he said. "You haven't got it right yet."

"Well, if you heard me, then you heard me say I haven't decided."

"But you'll decide to do it. I know you will. Because it's the last wish of a dying man, and you don't know how to say no to the last wish of a dying man."

"You know what's interesting?" I asked him. "It's interesting how you've caught on that I'm a decent human being, and you have no qualms about using that against me."

"Whatever gets me to Arizona," Chester said.

—

I stood in the dirt parking lot of what appeared to be an auto body shop—or maybe a wrecking yard—about fifteen miles outside of town. It appeared deserted, and I was waiting for someone to notice I was there.

Chester was still in the passenger seat of my car, which was idling behind me, out of my field of view. Getting him in there had not been easy. Believe it.

The horn of my own car blared, causing me to jump.

I spun around to see that Chester had leaned over and was doing the honking.

"Stop that!" I shouted. "Try to behave for a minute."

I turned back and found myself face to face with a guy named Marshall. I knew his name was Marshall because it said so over the breast pocket of his work shirt. My life hadn't used to be filled with guys whose names were sewn onto their shirts. Clearly my life had changed.

"Oh," I said. "Hey."

"Hey," he said in return. He had short black hair, and he was wiping his hands on a blue shop rag. He looked past me to my car and waved at its inhabitant. "You a friend of Chester's?"

"'Friend' is a strong word," I said.

And he laughed.

He seemed young to own a place like that. I took him to be in his thirties. Maybe it was his father's place. Or maybe he just went after what he wanted young in life. Or maybe I just tended to spend too much time trying to dissect details like that when they clearly didn't matter anyway. How did I even know he owned that business? I didn't. He was just "walking around like he owned the place," which was a thought out of context, because I hadn't even seen him walk yet.

See what my brain does to me?

"I wanted to talk to you about Chester's Winnebago," I said.

He narrowed his eyes at me, as though he couldn't quite figure me out.

"Most people call on the phone to talk."

"I wanted to see it with my own eyes."

"Okay then," he said.

He turned away and started walking, and I followed.

Then he stopped suddenly, and I nearly ran into his back.

"*He* coming?" he asked, indicating my car with a flip of his head.

"Chester? No. I didn't bring his wheelchair. It was so hard getting him in there. No way I was going to try to get him out again until we're home."

He shook his head and walked again.

Over his shoulder he said, "Got bad, did it?"

"Very bad," I said, following.

He led me around back and into a massive metal building with an open front. Like a carport on steroids. In it were parked four motorhomes in various states of decay.

"It's this one right here," he said.

He pointed to the Winnebago, and initially all my eyes took in were the bumper stickers. There were two stickers on the rear bumper. They read, **CAUTION: I BRAKE FOR NOBODY** and **HORN IS BROKEN—WATCH FOR FINGER**, respectively.

"Well, those are coming off," I said.

"It's Chester," he said. "You know Chester."

"Yeah. I tried not to. But now I do. So how old is this thing?" I asked him, forgetting that Ellie had already told me.

"'Bout twelve years."

"Is it roadworthy?"

"Yeah, it's in pretty good shape."

"I mean for a long trip. He wants me to drive him to Arizona."

"Oh," he said, drawing the simple word out into multiple syllables. "Sue, right? He always did have unfinished business with her. That's not gonna be a fun reunion, let me tell you. But, yeah. I expect it would make the trip. The Winnie would be the least of your problems, most likely. It's been sitting for a couple years now, though, so I'm guessing you'd want me to change the oil and do a full safety check on it."

"Definitely."

"He put new brakes and tires on it about two years back, and replaced the engine. It was really high miles, and he knew it would be in for some trouble down the road. No pun intended. So he had me put in a rebuilt engine. Did it with my own two hands. He said he was going to see the country. See every damn thing. And then what should happen but his diagnosis? Damn shame. Real bad luck. I'm the one who got on him to go to the doctor and get a chest X-ray in the first place. I was like, 'Chester, every time you come in here you're about to cough up a lung all over my yard. Look into that.' Now I feel bad."

"Better to know, though," I said.

"That's how I was looking at the thing."

"So you're friends with him?"

"'Friends' is a strong word," he said.

And we both allowed sardonic smiles onto our faces.

"Look inside," he said. "I'll be right here."

The driver's side door was unlocked. I stepped inside and looked around. I had to keep my head down in the cab area, but as I stepped into the living quarters of the beast I was able to stand upright.

It was dim in there, because it was inside that big metal hangar, for lack of a better word.

There were two couches, one on either side, upholstered in a hideous orange plaid. I assumed they pulled out into beds. They seemed to be set up that way. The paneling and cupboards looked like a light wood, but might have been some sort of imitation. There was a tiny kitchen area, and a booth-style table. At the back of the rig I saw an accordion door. I opened it, and revealed a tiny bedroom that spanned the rear of the vehicle. It was pretty much all bed and nothing else.

Until I saw it, I was just about to say no to the whole trip. It was hitting me hard that I would be stuck in this little jail with the man for about a week, and that there would be no getting away from him and going home at night. But there was a door I could close. And I could always leave him in the Winnebago and go get my head clear elsewhere.

And maybe I could bring a tent. If he really got on my nerves, I could leave him inside this thing and go beyond earshot to sleep. Unless I couldn't do that for fear he'd need me, or take a fall. Maybe two cell phones. Mine and . . . did he even have one?

I made a mental note to tell Ellie it was a must.

I opened another door to find a miniature bathroom complete with a shower. It would be fine for me, but no way was I getting Chester inside it, because it wouldn't fit us both. We'd need to stop at gas station restrooms for him. Or maybe he'd just use the bedpan. And what about getting him a shower? Would he just get more and more rank as we traveled down the road?

So many questions. So much fear of the answers.

I stepped out again to find Marshall waiting for me.

"Good size for two people," he said. "But of course it depends on the two people. Think you could stand being cooped up in there with Chester for days?"

"I can't really stand being cooped up anywhere with him for days. Not sure this thing is any worse than his house. But those bumper stickers have got to go."

—

"Absolutely not!" Chester shouted. "I won't let you scrape them off!"

We were driving off Marshall's lot in the direction of town.

"That's nonnegotiable," I said. "I'll be driving. People will think those are my bumper stickers. They'll see it as a reflection of me."

"They're a reflection of *me*, and you can't scrape them off."

"Fine," I said. "Then we don't go. I was looking for an out anyway."

We drove in silence for several miles.

I could feel the air around his ears changing. The shift in his mood, the taming of his anger, was palpable. It felt disturbing to be so completely in tune with the likes of Chester Wheeler.

"Okay," he said too loudly, startling me. "Okay, fine. Scrape 'em. But the minute we get back you have to buy two more just like it and stick them on again."

"Not a chance in hell, Chester. No way. I'm not putting money in the pockets of people who make crap like that."

"I'll buy them, you stick them on."

"Nope. I'm not going to be any part of the system."

"Will you at least wheel me out there so *I* can stick them on?"

"I don't know, Chester. Maybe. Can we just focus on the task ahead for now? We have to get that boat all the way to Arizona and back. Can we worry about your horrible bumper stickers when we get home?"

"They're not horrible," he said. "*You're* horrible."

"Chester, how old are you? You sound five."

He grumbled. Mumbled something under his breath. But then he said not one single word the rest of the way home.

It was a tremendous relief.

—

Anna drove me out to pick up the horrible beast.

It was two days later, after Marshall had called and said he'd gone over every system of the Winnebago and would trust it on the road himself, even with his wife and baby in the passenger seat.

"Here's what impresses me," she said, her fingers tapping on the steering wheel. "You just decided. You didn't go back and forth, back and forth like you always do. Usually you—"

"Got it," I said, purposely cutting her off. "You made it painfully clear what I do."

"Oh, I'm sorry. Did I hurt your feelings with that?"

I opened my mouth to say, "No, not at all." But then I realized she was an actual friend, and I should tell her the actual truth.

"It stung a little, yeah."

"Seems like it helped, though."

"No, it was something a little different that helped." Then I watched the streets flash by for a few beats, in silence, wondering if this was a story I wanted to tell. "Remember when you said I tend to wait and try to find out where each decision will take me? But we don't get to know that in advance? Well . . . turns out that's not entirely true. I had this really vivid, realistic dream that Chester was dead and I hadn't taken him. And in the dream I knew I'd made the wrong decision."

She didn't exactly answer. Just nodded for a long time. As though she was thinking about what I'd said and approving of everything she was thinking.

"Here's a question," she began.

I expected it to be on weighty topics like knowing which road to take in a difficult world.

"Why are you carrying a paint scraper?"

I looked down at it, where it rested against the leg of my jeans.

"I guess I forgot to tell you about the bumper stickers," I said.

———

I scraped. And I scraped. And I scraped. And all I managed to do was scratch the damn things and break up their corners. The adhesive behind them was set like cement, and I didn't want to go too deep or press too hard because Chester would be furious—and more or less rightly so—if I gouged his bumper.

Both Marshall and Anna hovered over my shoulders like a cheering section.

"Damn, those are really on there, huh?" Anna said.

I said, "They're as stubborn as their owner."

Marshall jumped in with a potentially good idea. He said, "Wouldn't it be easier to put two other bumper stickers over them? You could find something both of you could live with."

I stopped scraping and stood up. The sun was hot on the back of my neck, even on a cool fall day. My back hurt from the squatting, and I stretched it out with both hands on it, accidentally poking myself with the scraper.

I said, "Something *Chester and I* could agree on? I'm not sure such a thing exists."

"He wants you to drive him," Anna said, "so maybe it's your call. Maybe he doesn't get a choice."

"But when Chester doesn't get a choice, I have to hear about it. Besides, I don't even want to drive it back to his house with these things on it."

"Oh, come on," Anna said. "Isn't that overdoing it a little?"

"I refuse to go through any portion of my life, no matter how long or short, being confused with Chester Wheeler."

"I got some duct tape," Marshall said. "I could slap some of that on just to get you home."

And he wandered off, presumably to do that.

"I'll go out and buy two bumper stickers," Anna said, "and meet you at your house."

"Wait. Where do you buy bumper stickers?"

"I don't know. I'll look it up on my phone."

"What are you going to buy?"

"I don't know. Does it matter?"

"Something fairly neutral," I said.

"You sure you don't want to take this opportunity to piss him off?"

"Positive."

"Okay," she said. "Trust me. I'll handle it."

She jumped into her car and started it up, and Marshall arrived with a roll of silver duct tape and taped over the offending stickers.

"Ever drive one of these?" he asked when he'd straightened up.

"No, never."

"Ever drive anything bigger than a car?"

"No."

"Then you better let me show you a couple things before you drive it off the lot."

———

I sat behind the wheel, and Marshall sat in the passenger seat, and I eased the huge boat toward an orange traffic safety cone he'd set up in the gravelly dirt.

"See, you can't turn when you think you can," he said. "You have to go way past that cone. Figure the cone is the curb and you're making a right turn. Pull left just a little. Because in a real traffic situation you won't have room to go left very much. Don't forget this thing is wide. Now, see how there's an inset mirror in the bottom of the right side mirror? That'll show you your curb. Or your cone in this case. Go farther past it than you think should be necessary, and then make your turn."

I eased forward again, watching the cone in the mirror as the land boat slid by it. I kept going. And going. And going. And then I swung the huge steering wheel right to go around it . . . and promptly hit it and knocked it over.

I stopped the monster and sat for a minute with my head in my hands.

"It just takes some practice," he said.

"It's more than that, though," I said through my fingers. "I thought I'd imagined every way this trip could be a nightmare. And now it turns out there was this whole other way I'd never even thought of. I have to drive a giant freaking Winnebago."

"It's mostly highway driving," he said. "Once you get it out on the highway it's a different deal. You just keep it in your lane and that's it. Try it again."

He jumped out and set up the cone, and I swung a wide arc around his parking lot and approached it again. This time I went even farther past the cone. Pulled even farther left. I made my turn . . . and knocked it over again.

Marshall opened the passenger door.

"One more time," he said. "You'll get it this time."

I took another quick tour of his lot and made another right turn around the cone, seriously exaggerating my tactics. It worked, though. I left the cone standing.

He came up to the passenger window and I powered it down.

"In a real-world situation," he said, "you'd never have that much room to swing left. But no worries. Go ahead and take it home. Nice and slow. People'll honk at you, but just let 'em. Just ignore it. By the time you get back you'll halfway have the hang of the thing."

I pulled out into the road, a knot in my gut the size of which nothing and no one but Chester Wheeler had ever caused.

—

Anna was waiting for me in front of the house. I assumed that meant she hadn't yet bothered to go bumper sticker shopping.

I pulled up to the curb and sighed out the most immense boatload of tension.

I turned off the engine, pulled on the parking brake, and stepped out.

"Jeez, Lewis," she said. "What could possibly have taken you so long?"

I stood in the street, staring at her, feeling the muscles in my thighs tremble—though whether their problem was physical strain or stress to my psyche remained unclear.

"Are you kidding me?" I asked her. "Have you ever tried to drive one of these things?"

"No. Why? Was it hard?"

"It was the most frightening time I've ever spent on a road."

"Well, you made it," she said. "Here."

And she handed me a small, flat paper bag.

"Don't tell me you actually had time to buy bumper stickers," I said.

"Wow. You really don't know how long you were gone."

I reached into the bag and pulled one out without comment. It was a "coexist" sticker. Most people have seen them, I think. They have all these religious symbols doing double duty as letters.

I narrowed my eyes at her. I opened my mouth to complain about what she was letting me in for. Then I closed my mouth and decided I should look at the other one first.

I pulled it out of the bag and burst out laughing. I couldn't help it. It might have been a release of tension. I'm not sure.

It said, **Better a bleeding heart than no heart at all.**

I looked up at Anna again.

"You call these fairly neutral?"

"Oh, come on," she said. "You must want to mess with him a little."

"You don't get it," I said. "You don't know how he gets when you mess with him. You'll be home where you can't hear it. I'm the one who'll catch it."

"Fine," she said. "Fine. Look. He's in a wheelchair, right?"

"I can't argue with that."

"So he can only go someplace if you wheel him there, right?"

"I suppose."

"So take him straight to the passenger door. Don't wheel him behind the thing."

"Interesting," I said. "You think I can get away with that the whole trip?"

"Who knows? But he wants to go. So he'll shut up about it. If he gives you a hard time about anything, just threaten to turn this ugly boat around. Now I'll put these on for you. You go inside and rest up and pack up for your big trip."

I walked into my house and threw the Winnebago keys on the hall table.

Then I more or less walked straight into the shower, peeling off clothes as I went along.

I stood under the scalding hot water for ages, trying to let my stress melt or wash away. I was resting up from my traumatic drive home from Marshall's, not for what lay ahead.

I was trying not to think about what lay ahead.

Chapter Eight:

What Lay Ahead

I was packing clothing and other such belongings into the horrible Winnebago when the FedEx truck showed up. All the kitchen and bathroom supplies lived in the rig between trips, and required no packing.

I stepped out to meet the delivery guy with my heart falling down around my ankles. I knew what the package was, who it was from, what was in it. It was literally the only thing standing between us and going.

Which meant now I actually had to go.

I signed quickly for the package and carried it into the house, tearing it open as I walked.

I found exactly what I expected to find. A credit card with Ellie's name on it, and a cheap cell phone for Chester.

Chester was sitting in his wheelchair, watching his soap operas on TV. I know. He didn't seem like the type, right? But Chester loved his daytime dramas.

His eyes came up to the package.

"Is that it?"

"Yeah," I said, sounding disappointed. "That's it."

"Let's go, then."

"Maybe in the morning."

He muted the TV with the remote and raised his voice into sonic boom territory.

"No, not tomorrow, Lewis! *Now!* We need to go *now!*"

"It's afternoon already."

"It's one in the afternoon. We could drive eight or nine hours before we have to stop and sleep."

"What's the big hurry, Chester? I honestly don't get it."

"Then you're incredibly stupid," he said.

"Stupid is when you talk that way to someone who's doing you a favor, and who could change his mind and not do it. Now adjust your attitude and explain it to me."

"I wouldn't think I had to."

"But you do."

He fell silent for a long time. He had his hands on the wheels of his chair, his elbows out, as if he were about to take off to someplace. As if he could wheel himself to the Southwest on his own power.

"The hurry . . . ," he began. His voice was entirely different. I had thrown him into that vanishingly rare humility mode. ". . . is that . . . I have no idea how much time I've got."

Then I felt bad because I hadn't known without forcing him to say it. It was so foreign to me, the idea that tomorrow was not a given. I couldn't make it stick in my head.

"Okay," I said. "Fine. Let me just double-check my packing list and then we'll go."

———

Unpleasant surprise number one for the trip: Chester wanted to chat.

It was funny, because around the house he had pretty much ignored me. Okay, "funny" is the wrong word. Considering his choice of subject matter it was damn near tragic.

To make matters worse, he hit me with the questions before we were on the expressway, while I was sweating bullets trying to navigate the land yacht through traffic.

"Here's the thing I never got about being queer," he said.

I instinctively put my foot on the brake and stopped right in the middle of a traffic lane. The guy behind me leaned on his horn.

"You have *got* to be kidding me, Chester," I said.

"Wrong word?"

"Wrong topic entirely."

I started up again just as the horn honker swung around me and blared his horn again for good measure. It was a nice wide street with two traffic lanes in each direction. I hadn't really been holding him back. Just one of those people who liked to express himself, I figured. A Chester type.

"Is that a word I'm not supposed to use, or what?"

"I would avoid it," I said, trying to balance driving and being irritated by him at the same time. "I mean . . . *I* don't have to avoid it. But *you* should."

"See?" he said. "That's just as prejudiced. You're just as prejudiced."

"How do you figure?"

"Because you get to do something and I don't."

"It's not prejudice," I said. I saw the expressway up ahead and breathed a sigh of relief. "It's that when *you* use it, it's an insult. When *we* use it, it's a reclaimed word."

"I have no idea what that means," he said gruffly.

"No, you wouldn't, would you?"

We drove in silence for a blissful couple of seconds. I kept scanning the mirrors, hoping there was no one right next to me. Because the damned vehicle was so wide. It made me edgy.

There was always someone right next to me.

"But back to my original question," Chester said.

"No. Not back to your original question. I'm trying to drive this thing, Chester. I've never driven anything this big before and I find it stressful. So could you please be quiet for a minute and let me drive?"

He imitated a motion of zipping his lips.

In my peripheral vision I watched him stare out the huge passenger window. He almost seemed hurt that I had shushed him—which made my head feel like it wanted to explode, because I'd been more polite in the asking than Chester ever was to anybody.

I pulled onto the expressway, set up camp in the right lane, and just drove. A lot of my tension eased out of me. Marshall had been right. Once you get it out on the highway, it's a different deal.

"Okay," I said. "I'm obviously going to regret this. But what *is* your big question about LGBT people?"

Call it curiosity. Call it stupidity. Or maybe I just knew him well enough to know it was coming out sooner or later, and I wanted to get it over with.

"I would never ask *that* question," he said. "I don't even know what all those letters mean."

"You know what I'm saying, though."

"Right. I suppose. More or less. You know, you can't just stay in the right lane all the way through to Arizona."

"Why can't I?"

"Because it's too slow. All that merging traffic. It'll add too much time to the trip."

"It'll add minutes to the trip. Stop being so damned impatient. I'm not changing lanes in this boat any more often than I have to."

"You'll get used to it."

"Probably. Now kindly leave me alone until I do."

He pitched right back in without missing a beat.

"Anyway, here's what I always want to know about . . . you people. You could already see it was going to be a much harder life. You know . . . your way. So why do it?"

85

At first I just drove for a few hundred feet with my mouth open. Then I asked, "You think it's a choice?"

"Oh, I know it is."

"You're saying you chose to be straight."

"No, you don't choose *that*. That's just normal. It just *is*."

"How can one sexuality be a choice and another be ordained?"

"I don't know how we got religion into this, but it's just what *is*, my friend."

"You're absolutely impossible," I said. "And I'm not your friend."

He had no immediate argument to that, so we just drove for several minutes.

The Winnie didn't have any kind of navigation, so I had my phone in the cupholder, open to the map app. I was glancing at it, trying to figure out how best to get to the 90 South toward Erie, Pennsylvania, without backtracking east.

"It sucks that I ask you a legitimate question," Chester said, "and you won't even bother to address it."

"There isn't much to address," I said. "When you grow up, you have attractions. You can't change them."

"You can change what you act on."

"Just live a loveless, celibate life? Is that your suggestion? Why would I do that?"

"Because it's so hard. You know. Being queer. Or whatever I'm supposed to call it."

"Here's another solution, then, Chester. There's nothing hard about being gay except homophobia. So how about you just stop being so damned homophobic and then my life is happy and easy and the problem is solved?"

"Jeez," he said. "You don't have to bite my head off."

"I really think this trip is going to go a lot better with a minimum of chatting."

Oddly, that worked.

We drove in blissful silence for hours.

———

Pleasant surprise number one—and possibly the only one—for the trip: the motion of the road put Chester to sleep.

We drove until after nine o'clock that night, Chester's head drooped onto his shoulder. Also he was snoring lightly and drooling.

By the time I used my phone to find an RV park where we could stop, I felt as tired as I had ever been in my life. And it was beginning to dawn on me that it wasn't really the driving that was the problem. Sure, the Winnie was a challenge, but I'd begun to adjust to it.

What I found exhausting was Chester. And not only on the road, either. He had been exhausting me for days, draining my energy, grating on my nerves, and wearing me down. I just hadn't allowed myself to admit it. I had put up a wall to keep him away from my tender inside places, and I'd been spending days pretending he hadn't breached it at will multiple times a day.

He sputtered awake when I stopped the Winnebago near the RV park office.

"What? Where are we?" he asked, wiping his drooly lower lip on the shoulder of his shirt.

"Barely past Indianapolis. As best I can figure, if I could've brought myself to drive another half hour or forty-five minutes, we'd have made it to Terre Haute."

He rubbed his eyes and looked around.

"What are we stopping here for?"

"To . . . sleep?"

"This costs money. They probably charge over fifty bucks for this place. You should've just stopped in a Walmart parking lot. They let you do that, and it's free."

"Ellie is paying for this trip, and I really don't think she'd argue with a night in a basic RV park. If nothing else, it'll be quieter."

"Pure waste of money," Chester said.

"Whatever. We're here. I'm too tired to go any farther. You stay here and I'm going to go sign in."

"Wait!" he shouted, before I could jump out.

"What?"

"I gotta pee like a racehorse."

"I never understood that expression."

"What's to understand?"

"How does a racehorse pee any differently than anybody else?"

"He pees a lot more, because he's a horse."

"Got it," I said. "How about I pull the curtains and bring you the bedpan?"

"You don't have to pull the curtains. It's dark out. So long as no lights are on inside the rig, no one'll see."

"Fine," I said. "Knock yourself out."

"But go out the side door. If you go out the cab door, the dome light'll stay on for a couple minutes."

I pulled the bedpan out from its storage in a hatch under one of the beds. I handed it to him and then quickly jumped out the side door and walked to the office. My legs felt rubbery from all the driving, and I could still feel the ghostly remnants of vibrations from the road.

I allowed my mind to touch briefly on the fact that, when I got back, the inside of the Winnebago would smell faintly of Chester's urine—which I knew from experience was not a pleasant odor. But it was too cold to open any windows.

Maybe there was a vent with a fan. I vaguely remembered seeing one.

If not, it was just another in a list of indignities to which I'd be subjected throughout this trip. All I could do was hold my nose—figuratively and possibly literally as well—and wait for the experience to be over.

—

We were lying in the dark. Chester was in one of the individual beds in the main body of the rig. I was in the bedroom in back, in that slightly urine-smelling atmosphere. I had left the accordion door open, in case he fell or needed help. I would not make that mistake again.

I thought Chester was asleep, until he said the following.

"I know you hate me. But you're doing this anyway."

I waited, in case he actually wanted to extend the thought to some kind of thank-you, but nothing else happened.

"I don't hate you," I said. "I dislike you. I find you disagreeable and unpleasant. There's a difference."

"No, you *want* to only dislike me. You want to *think* it's only that. Because you want to think I'm the hateful one and you're this perfect angel. But when I take a poke at your lifestyle, I feel the hate come up in you."

"It's not a 'lifestyle.' It's just what I am. And I don't have hate in me," I added into the dark, hoping against hope that it was true.

"Bullshit," he said. "Everybody has hate."

"Maybe you're just looking at the world through hate-colored glasses."

"No. You've got it. When I poke at you, I feel it come up."

"Then why do you keep poking at me?"

"I want you to see it for what it is. You think I'm a hateful man and you're not. I want you to see that we're not so different, you and me."

"Don't ever say that to me again," I said, my voice rising. I could feel my loathing for him start to come up and out. Then I realized he was drawing it out of me on purpose, and I tried to let my feelings settle again. "I'm nothing like you."

"Keep telling yourself that," he said.

We lay in silence for quite a while, though I knew neither one of us was sleeping.

"Even if that's true," I said without warning—without even warning myself—"even if we do both hate. You hate me for what I am. I hate you for the things you say and do. Huge difference."

"No difference."

"Totally different. You could behave better if you wanted to. You don't have to be a jerk."

"You don't have to be a queer. I told you, it's a choice and I know it. You might be able to fool everybody else, but you can't fool me."

For a moment I wrestled with the feeling in my gut. The despising of him. Somehow that seemed like an easier word to swallow.

I thought about going outside to set up the tent. But it was cold out there, and I'd probably need light to do it properly. And besides, I had just as much right to be warm inside as Chester, if not more. I wasn't about to let him chase me away.

"Stop talking and go to sleep now," I said.

"You're the one who brought it up the second time."

"Seriously, Chester," I said. My voice was a cold, hard warning. I could hear it. "Stop now."

He may or may not have gone to sleep. But he definitely stopped talking to me.

Chapter Nine:

Personal

When we woke the following morning, things felt different between us. And not in a good way.

Maybe our relationship was only what it always had been for him. How would I know? I wasn't inside that hard head of his, nor did I wish to be. But for me . . . it's hard to explain. It felt almost as though I'd been standing outside my loathing for Chester in the few days I'd cared for him. Treating it all like an irritating game.

Now it didn't feel like a game at all. Now it was personal.

I had been sleeping in my underwear for pure ease. I rose and pulled on pants, a T-shirt, and a heavy sweatshirt.

Chester stared at me the whole time.

"Now who needs a blindfold?" I said.

"I wasn't looking at you like *that*."

"What were you looking at me like?"

"Just trying to figure you out."

"The answer is not in my underwear."

"You sure? That seems to be a key puzzle piece with your people."

"Shut up, Chester."

It came out hard and cold. And strong. Even more so than I'd meant it to sound. He buttoned his lip immediately.

I got into the cupboard and took down a box of the cereal Chester liked. Basically crunchy sugar. I was just going into the minifridge for milk when he spoke up again, still in bed and under the covers.

"I don't want cereal," he said.

"What do you want?"

"Bacon and eggs and fried potatoes. And pancakes. And toast."

"We're in a Winnebago, Chester. We don't have anything nearly that fancy with us."

"I want to get out and go into a restaurant and eat."

My feet stopped moving, more or less of their own accord. My right hand instinctively came up to my forehead and began massaging. I had a mean headache behind my eyes.

"I thought you wanted to get on the road and get miles behind us."

"First I want a real breakfast."

"You do realize how hard it is for me to get you from here to the wheelchair and vice versa, right?"

"You have to get me down anyway. I have to take a dump."

"Chester . . ."

"What?"

"Could you please talk like a human being?"

"Oh, I'm so sorry, your majesty. Did I offend your delicate sensibilities? I need to do a number two. My bowels are moving. I have need of the powder room. People say 'dump,' Lewis. Deal with it."

"Fine," I said. "I'll get behind the wheel, and we'll find a coffee shop. And we'll have breakfast, and you can use their bathroom."

"Finally," he said. "You remember who you work for."

I got behind the wheel without comment.

I hadn't bothered to hook up any utilities the night before. The water hose, the sewer hose had stayed in their places. We had run on the cabin battery instead of plugging into power. Because it had been dark, I hadn't really been sure I knew how, and anyway the point was just to sleep.

I left Chester right where he was in bed and pulled out of our spot. I drove very slowly to the exit. Then when I got back to the street I turned east and drove.

Chester halfway sat up in bed and peered around.

"You're going the wrong way," he said.

"No I'm not."

"You're going east."

"Right. I know."

"We need to go west."

"No," I said. "We're not going west. We're going back to Buffalo."

"Wait," he said, his voice rising. "Wait, wait. Stop driving a minute."

I pulled over to the curb and put the beast in park. I sat a bit, waiting for him to start.

"What're you doing, Lewis?"

"I'll tell you what I *was* doing. I *was* taking a very disagreeable, very awful man to see his ex-wife, thousands of miles away. I was getting paid to look after him, but all I really had to do was sit at his house for ten hours and then go home. The rest of it was just a pure favor. Just me trying to be a nice guy. But then this terrible man, he decided he could order me around, and pretty rudely at that, just because his daughter is paying me a basic salary. So now I don't want to do it anymore. And it was always optional. It was never a job requirement. I make the same money whether I go or I don't. So we'll be back in Buffalo by nightfall."

I reached for the gearshift, but he shouted to stop me.

"No, wait!"

I waited.

"Yes?" I asked after a time.

"Don't go back."

"Why shouldn't I?"

"I won't say stuff like that again."

"I was looking for a little more."

"How do I know what you're looking for?"

"You will if you think about it. Because you're a human being. At least, I assume you are, deep down in there somewhere. And you'd better start accessing your decent human side if you want to get all the way to Arizona and back. Think about it, Chester. What do I need you to say?"

Silence. For several beats.

Then, "I guess . . . I'm . . . sorry?"

"Hmm," I said. "Not the most convincing apology I've ever heard. Might even be the *least* convincing. But I'm willing to consider the source. Now let's go get some breakfast before we head west again."

———

We stopped at a little diner somewhere in suburban Indiana, and I took Chester's wheelchair down from the bicycle rack on the Winnie's roof ladder and set it up near the rig's cabin door.

Then I almost dropped Chester getting him out.

I had made the mistake of getting behind him to take him down the two metal stairs. I should have gotten on the downhill side of him with my feet braced far behind me.

Also, he could have helped a little more. What possessed him to lean forward, I swear I didn't know. There was a safety bar next to the stairs—a sort of beefy handrail. I was holding it, and so was he. His grip on it was all that kept him from flying forward and landing on his face on the tarmac parking lot of the Good Morning Coffee Shop. My grip on that rail, and my other arm around his waist, was all that kept him from swinging out with only one hand anchored and having his feet come out from under him.

"Holy crap!" he breathed when he felt what he had done.

I pulled as hard as I could to try to right him, but he didn't right. His weight was too far forward. He was off balance and I was not strong enough to put him back onto it. I could feel the hand on the railing losing its grip. I could feel the arm around his waist begin to slip.

It would not be exaggerating the situation to say I experienced a miniature version of my life flashing before my eyes.

And then, just like that, two middle-aged men walked by, on their way out of the restaurant. They saw the situation immediately, and jumped right in, each bracing both of his hands against one of Chester's giant shoulders.

I breathed like I had never breathed in my life.

"Thank you," I said, my voice breathless. "I almost lost him."

The three of us eased him down the last step, turned him around, and lowered him down into his chair.

"Thank you," I wheezed in the general direction of my saviors. I was still deeply out of breath from exertion, or panic, or both. "Really. I can't thank you enough."

They just waved and walked to their car. As if it had been nothing. Because to them, I suppose, it *had* been nothing.

I walked around behind Chester's wheelchair and grabbed the handles with shaking hands. My heart was still pounding as I began rolling him toward the door.

"That was a boneheaded play," he grumbled.

"Me?" I shouted. And stopped pushing. "I'm not the one who leaned forward. Why did you lean forward?"

"I didn't do it on purpose. I lost my balance. Next time get down on the steps below me."

"Duh," I said.

By then I was pulling him backward through the diner's door, and there was a hostess right there waiting to seat us. We immediately stopped bickering and blaming each other.

I pushed Chester in the direction of the men's room, but the hostess said, "Staying for breakfast, gentlemen? Restrooms're for customers only."

"Yes," I said. "Staying for breakfast. Table for two. Two coffees and two menus. We'll be right out."

I wheeled Chester into the men's room.

It was a single, yet it had a small individual stall inside that only made it that much harder to maneuver. We left his wheelchair right outside it.

I was still shaky and a little weak, but I managed to get him on his feet and into the stall, and then turn him around. I held him in the dreaded bear hug while he tended to the dropping of his trousers.

Needless to say, I did not look.

I lowered him onto the toilet and then ducked out, closing the stall door behind me.

Then I slipped out of the men's room entirely and waited in the hall by the door, feeling the weight of the near disaster on my shoulders. I honestly think that was the first time it hit me that I was holding a man's life in my hands. Granted, I had known he could die at any moment. But I figured if he did, he would die of cancer, not my own inept mistakes.

I was responsible for everything. I was the one who would have to call the police, or call an ambulance. Or call Ellie and break bad news. I was the one in charge.

In time I heard the toilet flush, and I went back through the outer door.

"You ready?" I asked.

"Ready."

I went in with my eyes closed, and reached an arm out to him, and he grabbed on. I pulled him to his feet, then enveloped him in the aforementioned horrible hug.

"Damn," he said.

"What?"

"My pants fell down where I can't reach 'em."

"What do we do, then?"

"First of all, you keep your eyes closed."

"No problem there."

"You have to reach down and get them."

"How can I hold you up and reach down there at the same time?"

"Here," he said. "There's a bar. I'll hold the bar. And wait—let me brace my other hand on the side of the stall. Now go fast, because I can't hold myself up for long."

"But I can't see. How do I—"

"Hurry!" he shouted. "I'm already slipping."

I dove down there with my eyes still closed, groping near the floor. I touched Chester's hairy calf, which was disturbing enough. Then it dawned in my consciousness that my face was probably hovering dangerously close to his unmentionable bits.

"Hurry!" he shouted again.

I scanned the floor with my hands until I located his shoes, moved up until I felt a belt, then jumped up still holding it. I grabbed under his armpit with my other arm and he took the pants from me and pulled them partly into place. But he let go of the bar a split second before I could fully brace him, and we almost lost him again.

I had to lower him roughly onto the toilet seat with his pants half-on and half-off, and we had to start the whole thing over again.

"I am not getting paid enough for this," I said when he was finally clothed again.

"*You?* What are *you* complaining about? I'm the one who had your face in my nether regions."

"Not because I wanted it there, I can tell you that much."

We plunked him down into his chair. It happened a bit too roughly again, because we were both exhausted.

"Come on," I said. "We seem to have lived through all that some-how. Let's enjoy some breakfast."

But Chester was in no mood to enjoy. He was still barking com-plaints when I rolled him up to our table.

"You just don't appreciate what a slap in the face that is to my dignity," he said. "I mean, when you've got your pants down around your ankles like that, you want everything to go smoothly. No surprises, you know?"

I sat down and grabbed up my menu.

"I'm not the one who dropped your pants, Chester. That was you."

"Well, you're supposed to help me recover from stuff like that."

"I did what you told me to do."

"Next time just help me back down and I'll lean forward and get them myself, and then we'll go again."

"Fine," I said. "I wish you'd thought of it this time."

Before I could even finish my sentence, a young waitress appeared at our table. She looked about seventeen, with her hair worn up, and too perky for her own good.

"What can I get you fellas?" she asked.

Chester just completely lost it.

"Privacy!" he bellowed. "You can get us some privacy! This is a private conversation!"

The little girl shifted herself into reverse and more or less ran straight backward. As I watched her go I saw that everyone in the place was staring at us.

"Do not take it out on her!" I barked at Chester.

But it was too late. She had run back into the kitchen crying.

—

A few minutes later someone came to our table, but he appeared to be one of the line cooks. He was wearing a slightly greasy white T-shirt and a definitely greasy white apron.

"Was there a problem here, gentlemen?"

Chester only chewed on the inside of his lip in silence, which was a relief.

"My friend here lost his temper at a bad moment," I said. "I hope you'll give our apologies to the waitress. If you'll send her back here, I promise it'll go better."

"*I* don't apologize," Chester muttered in my direction. "And I'm not your friend."

"I can take your order," the man said.

It was a clear reaction to his having read the moment. It was a clear establishing of his role as the young waitress's protector, which I had already gathered.

Chester ordered exactly what he had threatened to order: three eggs over easy, home fries, bacon, a short stack, and white toast. I ordered an omelet, even though I had lost every last trace of my appetite.

I ordered apple juice so Chester could take his myriad pills. There was a glass of water sitting right in front of him, but he only pushed it away.

—

We drove in silence all the way through St. Louis and out the other side.

I was the one who broke the perfect stillness.

"So, listen," I said. "Chester."

I could see his jaw tighten, but he gave me the space to speak.

"Here's the thing, Chester. I don't think I can keep doing this."

"What're you saying?"

"I'm saying I think next time you get it in your head that you want something better to eat, I should phone ahead and get a take-out order and just bring it back into the Winnebago."

99

"Oh," he said. "I thought you meant . . ."

"Yeah. I know what you thought I meant."

The scenery that flashed by the window was very green. Very woodsy. Untouched, or at least it gave that impression. I had seen a sign a few miles back for the Mark Twain National Forest, but it's not like we were making side trips.

"It's because I yelled at that waitress," he said. "Isn't it?"

"No. Well. Yes and no. Yeah, you were horrible to her. But mostly . . . no. I know nobody likes to hear things like this said right out loud, and I don't mean to offend you, but you're not as mobile as you used to be."

He barked a sarcastic laugh.

"Nobody's as mobile as they used to be, Lewis. When you're not in your twenties anymore you'll learn that."

"No. I mean . . . you're not as mobile as you used to be when I first started helping you onto the toilet. And that was how many days ago?"

He didn't answer. I could tell he was having some kind of internal reaction to my observation, and it wasn't pretty in there.

"I don't mean to take away your autonomy or make you feel helpless or anything," I added. "I just don't want any injuries."

"Yours or mine?"

"I don't want either."

"And if I have to . . . use the facilities?"

"I was thinking I'd bring you the bedpan and disappear. I'm hoping that, given plenty of time and space, you can get yourself onto it."

"I was just trying to save you the unpleasantness. You know. Having to empty it and air the place out and all."

"I appreciate that. But I think it's better than anybody getting hurt."

We drove in silence for a minute or two as the green, green trees flashed by the window.

"When do you think we'll get into Phoenix?" he asked.

"Probably day after tomorrow. But if I really push for the miles, maybe not too late."

"Sure, okay," he said. "Whatever. Just so long as we get there."

"And back," I added. Because he didn't add it.

"If I can just get there," Chester said, "I'll be okay."

Chapter Ten:

Gobble Gobble Shine

I woke in the morning somewhere west of the Cherokee Nation in Oklahoma.

We had stopped at an RV park again, over Chester's objections, because RV parks have restrooms with sinks. I didn't want to wash the bedpan inside the Winnebago, for reasons I don't want to—and hopefully don't need to—explain in great detail.

The furnace was blowing hard, and underneath the roar of it I heard a strange noise that I couldn't identify and would find hard to describe. Maybe a sort of warbling sound? But with that noisy fan blowing it was hard to be sure.

I sat up in bed and raised the curtain.

The Winnebago was completely surrounded by a sea of wild turkeys. The RVs beside us were similarly engulfed. There were easily hundreds of turkeys, and though I can't claim I couldn't see to the end of their flock, if I just looked at the immediate area, I got the eerie sense that this part of the country had turkeys where most locales have dirt.

The toms were massive and fat, and displayed a short, even fan of raised tail feathers. They had bluish faces with brilliant red neck wattles.

The hens were thinner and more plain, with pale red heads and a beautiful crosshatch pattern at the ends of their wings.

They did indeed appear to be gobbling as a team, explaining the odd noise.

I was sleeping in the tiny bedroom at the back of the rig, and I leaned down past my feet and opened the accordion door to the main part of the RV's cabin.

"Chester," I said. "You've got to see this."

He groaned and lifted his head.

"What's that noise?" he asked, sounding mostly asleep.

He reached over and lifted his curtain. He looked out for a minute, grumbling slightly in his throat. Then he dropped the curtain and allowed his head to hit the pillow again.

"If I can't eat them," he said, "then I don't care."

—

We drank coffee and ate cereal quickly. I laid out the pills and poured the apple juice as efficiently as I could. All in an attempt to get on the road and get miles under our belt. But I had hooked up to the campground's water the previous night so I could take a shower, and before we could leave I had to get out and unhook and stow the hose.

The turkeys had gobbled on to greener pastures.

A guy in the next campsite waved at me. He was thirtyish, with long hair and a bushy beard. He looked like a throwback to the time of hippies. He was even wearing Birkenstock sandals.

"Love your bumper stickers," he said. "Really good."

I wanted to shush him, but I didn't want to be rude. Besides, it was already too late.

I coiled the hose and stowed it in the hatch under the living area, then climbed back inside. Chester was sitting on the edge of his foldout bed, and he watched me as I walked around raising all the curtains.

"Come on," I said. "We have to get you up in the cab so we can drive."

"Why can't I just stay here?"

"Because there are no seat belts here. Come on."

I reached out an arm. Chester did not take it.

"So? Drive carefully."

"I always drive carefully. Trouble is, I have no control over making other drivers drive carefully. And I'm legally responsible for an unbelted passenger. Now, come on, Chester. We need to get some miles behind us. Grab on."

He took hold of my arm, and I pulled him more or less to his feet.

It was only about three steps from his bed to the passenger seat. But it was a tough three steps, and getting tougher all the time.

As I was guiding him into his seat, halfway supporting him, halfway losing the battle and letting him drop, he said, "I thought you scraped off the bumper stickers."

"Yeah, that was the plan. But they were stuck on pretty tight, and I didn't want to scratch up your bumper."

I sat down in the driver's seat and buckled my seat belt, vaguely satisfied in the knowledge that everything I had just told him was technically true. Carefully selected to create a false impression, yes. But true.

I started up the engine and we sat a minute, allowing it to warm up.

"See?" Chester said. "People like those bumper stickers. They're funny."

"Whatever," I said. "I just want to get closer to Arizona."

"You and me both," he said.

So we headed out.

We drove slowly through the little town where we'd camped, because the speed limit was weirdly low. Fifteen miles per hour. I'd always figured a ridiculously low limit was probably a speed trap, so I obeyed it.

I had my phone propped up in the cupholder, open to the map app. And, according to Maps, we had driven completely through the Cherokee Nation. As I think I mentioned already. But maybe there was another sovereign nation right on the other side of it. In any case, it seemed as though every person we passed on the streets of that little town was Native American.

I was hoping Chester wouldn't say anything.

I did not get my wish.

"Injun country," he said.

I opened my mouth to tell him he was being offensive, but he never let me get that far.

"Oh, I know," he said. "You're offended."

"Yeah. But then I usually am around you. Are you saying that's some kind of problem to you?"

"I guess not. I mean, we licked 'em the first time."

"Are you suggesting they shouldn't be here?"

"Just saying it's our country."

"Actually this part of it is theirs," I said, acting more sure about the location of Native nations than I actually felt. "And the whole country was theirs before we beat them up and took it away."

"So? You just made my point for me. It's ours."

"So if some other country like Russia or China came over here and defeated our army, they'd own this country fair and square and we wouldn't belong here?"

"Nobody defeats the US Army," Chester said. "We've got the strongest, best-equipped army in the world."

"I think it would be better if we didn't talk," I said.

He fell silent, and within fifteen or twenty minutes he was fast asleep again, head lolling.

But that wasn't literally the last thing he said.

About an hour west of Oklahoma City, not too far from the Texas Panhandle, Chester spoke a very clear sentence in his sleep.

He said, "Of all the guys in the world, why did it have to be Mike?"
I waited, and listened, but he said nothing more.

———

Chester slept all day while I drove, which was a blessing.

In fact, it seemed to be a day full of blessings.

The main blessing was the pleasant surprise of the Southwest. I had
never seen red rock scenery before, and I was captivated by it. I wish I
could explain it better than that, but it's a tricky thing to put into words.
New Mexico found a place deep in my gut and satisfied it in a way that's
easier to feel than it is to describe.

I was tired of all the driving—tired in general—but I couldn't get
enough of that red rock scenery. And cactus! Or . . . cacti, I guess I
should say. And the deeply folded mountain ranges at the horizon. I
kept wanting to see what was around the next bend, so I drove straight
through Albuquerque and just kept going. And Chester just kept sleeping. Which was helpful, because this newly discovered landscape was so
much better experienced without him.

But soon it got too dark to see much anyway, and I worried about
road safety, so I pulled off the highway and parked for the night in a . . .
wait for it . . . Walmart parking lot.

Even in that least scenic of locations, I could see the faint outline
of a dramatic mesa over the insult of the big-box-store strip mall. It was
comforting somehow.

I consulted the map app on my phone, which told me we were
only about four hours outside of Phoenix. I briefly thought of driving
it through, but I knew I wasn't safe on the road in my exhausted state.

Chester never woke up, so I just powered his seat down until he
was lying more or less flat. I didn't want him to wake up with his back
hurting from sleeping too long in a sitting-up position.

I pulled all the curtains and locked the doors, ready to climb into the bed in the back and lose consciousness.

Then it hit me that Chester had been sleeping for an awfully long time, and more deeply than usual. And not snoring, either.

With a roiling feeling in my poor tired belly, I walked up front and held a couple of fingers underneath his nose. The air of his breath hit them immediately, and I sighed out my tension and put myself to bed.

—

I woke in what felt like the middle of the night with a bright light shining through my window curtain.

I sat up in bed and thought, *Right. This is why you stop for the night in an RV park, not a parking lot.*

I pulled the curtain up slightly to see what was causing the offending light.

It was the moon.

The minute I saw that it was the moon, it was no longer offending. Suddenly the light was beautiful. Another blessing.

It was hanging over that silhouette of the mesa, looking bigger than I could ever remember seeing it before. Full, or at least very close to it. The air was so clear that I could see its individual valleys, or craters, or seas, or whatever you call them. I'm not a moon expert. I just enjoy it as a layperson.

The light of it revealed a surprising amount of detail on that mesa, which was much more colorful and intricately eroded than I had realized in the dark.

It was so beautiful that I almost woke up Chester. I almost called to him and said, "You have to see this."

I didn't, of course. Even if we hadn't been talking about Chester, I wouldn't have done it. I knew the beauty of that moonlit night might be a personal thing, something that wouldn't strike anyone else quite the same way it struck me. And, after all, it was the middle of the night. It was . . . I felt around for my phone and then tapped its screen. It was a little after three in the morning.

And we *were* talking about Chester.

And you can't eat a full moon.

I lay awake for a while, watching it, as it gradually dawned on me that I was unlikely to get back to sleep.

I rose, stepped into my jeans, put on a fresh shirt from the mini-closet, and settled behind the wheel again, propping my phone up in the cupholder. I had put Chester's ex-wife's address into Maps, and I could see the virtual pushpin on my screen. It read "Sue's House."

Maybe I could even get there before Chester woke up.

Maybe he'd open his eyes and say, "Where are we?" and I'd be able to say, "We're there."

Speaking of Chester and awakeness, he sputtered up into half consciousness when I started up the engine. It was actually a relief. He'd been sleeping for an awfully long time again, and I'd begun to worry that he'd fallen into a coma or something.

"What?" he said. "What're we doing?"

"We're driving," I said.

"Oh. Good."

Then he was gone again.

Chapter Eleven:

There

I thought the red rock Arizona scenery would be lost in big-city ugliness as I got into Phoenix, but I was mostly wrong. Sure, the view outside my windshield quickly filled with buildings and traffic lights. But the house we were looking for was located in a suburb on the southeast end of the city—a sprawl of tract homes with all that southwestern beauty laid out behind them like a painted movie set.

I glanced down at my phone to see one amazing word showing large on the map screen.

"Arrived."

The house was a one-story ranch affair, made of stucco painted a pale green. It was surrounded by concrete walkways and a driveway, and sections of yard filled in with coarse gray gravel where my eyes expected to see green lawn. Maybe there was no such thing as green lawns in Phoenix, Arizona.

It was barely seven in the morning, too early to wake up the inhabitant—or inhabitants—of the house, and Chester was still asleep. I parked at the curb, pulled all the curtains down, and stretched out on one of the couch beds to see if I could finish a night's sleep.

—

I don't know how much later it was when Chester woke up. I had been sleeping, but not for long.

"What is this?" he asked, his voice sharp. "Where are we?"

"We're there," I said.

I was feeling pleased with myself, because crossing most of the country in an aging Winnebago with an aging Chester had been a massive undertaking, and I almost couldn't believe I'd pulled it off.

"That's it," he said, sounding increasingly panicked. "That's the house."

I sat up in bed and looked at him.

His seat was still laid out flat, but he was managing to raise his head slightly. He had the curtain on the passenger window up about an inch. Just enough to accommodate one peering eye.

"Yes," I said. "That's the house."

"Holy crap," Chester said.

He seemed to have descended into panic the way a person sinks into deep water. I pictured it closing back up over his head, swallowing him.

"You don't sound very happy that we're here," I said. "You did want to be here, right? I mean, wasn't that the point of this whole thing?"

"Yeah," Chester said. "Sure. But now we're here."

I sighed, and lifted my own curtain the tiniest bit.

A woman was sweeping the front porch. It was hard to see much detail in her face from that distance, but she didn't seem old enough to have been married to Chester. But she might simply have aged better—most people do—or maybe I would see things differently when I got face to face with her. If I ever did.

She kept glancing over at the Winnebago. I think she was wondering why it was parked in front of her house.

I dropped the curtain again, almost guiltily, though I have no idea what I thought I had to be guilty about. Well . . . that's not entirely true. I had brought Chester Wheeler back into her orbit. That's not exactly a helpful favor to do for anyone.

"Is that your ex?" I asked Chester.

"Not sure," he said.

"How can you not be sure? You were married to her. You had three kids together."

"But I haven't seen her in thirty-two years," he said. "People change. But, yeah. I guess that could be her."

I waited for several minutes to hear what he thought our next move should be, but he offered nothing.

"So are we going in?" I asked him.

"I can't go in," he said, still underwater in panic.

"Long drive not to go in."

"*You* should go in," he said.

"Oh no. Not a chance, Chester. That is *way* above my pay grade. This is your deal. You wanted to do this. The time has come, so do it."

"But it'll take so long to get me down out of here and into the chair, and she'll see me, and she'll go away or something."

"If she doesn't want to see you, we can't force her."

"She won't see me."

"I wish you'd come to that conclusion before we drove two thousand miles in this rust bucket."

"Hey!"

"What?"

"My Winnebago is not a rust bucket."

"Is that really what we're focusing on now?"

More silence.

I was beginning to realize that if anything was going to happen, I'd have to make it happen myself. At least get it rolling. It was an abhorrent idea, and no, it was not part of my job description. But I was the one who wanted to be sure we hadn't come all this way for nothing. The only one, it now seemed.

"Okay, I'll tell you what," I said. "I'll go talk to her and at least see if she's willing to come over here, or if she's willing to stay around while I get you down into your wheelchair. I'll feel out the situation."

No reply.

"Earth to Chester."

"Thank you," he said, his voice breathy.

It was a pretty stunning two words coming from Chester Wheeler. I'd never heard such a thing come out of his mouth before.

I opened the side door and stepped out.

The air was surprisingly warm considering it was only . . . well, I really had no idea what time it was. I didn't know how long I'd slept. But it was autumn, so I hadn't been expecting morning heat.

The woman looked up immediately.

I walked up her concrete path, and she walked to the edge of her porch to meet me.

As I got a closer look at her, I could see her as possibly in her sixties. Her hair, which I had taken for platinum blonde from more distance, was actually gray going to white. She wore it cropped into a stylishly short cut. She had lines around her eyes and mouth that let me know she had frowned, laughed, smiled . . . you know. Lived.

Oddly, as I approached her, she was smiling. Before I could open my mouth to speak, she let out a short bark of a laugh.

"What's funny?" I asked, thinking it was odd that we hadn't started with introductions.

"Oh, it'd sound crazy," she said.

Her voice was gravelly and deep like Chester's. As though she'd been a smoker all her life. But if she'd smelled like cigarettes, I was standing close enough to know it. She didn't. She smelled like some kind of light, flowery perfume.

"Try me," I said.

"Well. I've been staring at that big old Winnebago all morning. And some part of me half expected my ex to step out. Crazy, I know, but he always talked about getting himself a big Winnebago like that one. Then when I saw it was a total stranger, I just felt so relieved."

"Oh," I said. "Bad news about that."

She leaned on her broom, and her face went hard and dark in a hurry.

"Don't *even* tell me," she said.

"I'm sorry."

"It really is Chet in there, too?"

"I'm afraid so."

"What in the bloody hell did you bring him *here* for?"

I could have hedged around the thing. Eased into it. But I was worried about losing her, so I broke out the big guns immediately.

"It was his dying wish," I said.

She said nothing. Just leaned on her broom, with various thoughts and feelings—I'm not sure which ones, of course—flitting by behind her eyes.

So I said more.

"I realize it's not the biggest favor to you, and I'm sorry. Even more than I realized I should be before I met you. But a guy tells you he wants one thing to make his life complete before he dies. How do you say no to that?"

She narrowed her eyes at me, and we held each other's gaze for a few seconds. She seemed to be reading me in some way I couldn't quite pin down.

"You seem like a nice enough guy," she said.

"Thank you," I said, not knowing what else to say.

"He'll eat you for breakfast."

"He tries. But apparently I'm tougher than I look."

"You'd almost have to be," she said. "What are you doing with him, anyway?"

113

"Ellie is paying me to take care of him."

"Oh," she said. "Ellie. And Ellie never even told me he was sick. Then again, she knows better than to bring up his name around me. You sure he's really dying? It's the kind of thing he'd make up if he thought it'd get him what he wants."

"Oh, I'm positive. He's in bad shape."

"What's he got?"

"Cancer."

"Of the . . . ?"

"Of the everything. Started out in his lungs, but it's all over now."

In the silence that followed, I realized I had used Ellie's phrasing almost to the word, and that the double entendre still stung.

"What does he want from me?" she asked after a time. Her deep voice was set hard.

"Some kind of closure, I guess. I think he just wants to talk."

"Why didn't he come up my walk himself?"

"He can't. He's in a wheelchair. It takes some doing just for me to get him out of the RV and into the chair, and even then he can't wheel up the walk by himself."

I watched her eyes cloud over further. They were a deep shade of blue, those eyes. I found something in them that I liked, and that felt welcome. I'm not entirely sure what it was, but the feeling was pronounced and unmistakable.

"It's that bad, is it?"

"It's very bad," I said.

"Well." Then she didn't speak for a weirdly long time. "At least that makes him easy to walk away from. I don't really want him in my house. I'm sorry, but that's the way I feel about it. I suppose you could wheel him into the yard. But he has to behave himself. Any yelling, any abusive language, anything like Chet being Chet and you can just load him back into that giant rig and drive on."

"That sounds fair enough," I said.

114

"Okay. I know I'll regret saying this. But go get him."

I looked over my shoulder. I could see one of Chester's eyes peering out under the passenger window curtain.

Before I could get away she said, "You couldn't at least have let me know this was going to happen?"

"He figured if we asked, you'd say no."

"He figured right."

I trotted back down the walk to the curb and opened the side door of the rig.

"What happened?" he asked immediately.

"We're going in," I said.

———

"We only get to go into the yard," I told him as I wheeled him up the concrete walkway. "Not the house."

"That seems a little miserly."

Sue had disappeared from the front of the house while I was getting Chester down and into his chair, but the side gate to the yard had been propped open.

"Chester," I said. "You're supposed to be giving me a medal for getting her to agree to this at all."

"Oh. Okay. I'm sorry."

Another stunning statement from Chester Wheeler. First "thank you" and then "I'm sorry," both spoken as if they might even possibly be true. I would have marveled over the turn of events longer and more deeply if I'd had the time. But in that moment life just kept happening.

"And you have to behave yourself, or we'll be asked to leave."

"I always behave myself."

"Is that a joke?"

"What? No. What do you mean?"

"If you think you always behave, then we're in trouble, Chester. You never behave. Do you honestly not see that?"

"Okay, define 'behave.'"

"No yelling. No cursing. You have to be polite to her."

"Or else what? She'll kick us out?"

"Exactly."

"Okay. I'll try."

I stopped walking, and the wheelchair of course came to a stop. The path was slightly uphill, so I had to brace myself to keep it from rolling back on me.

"Don't 'try,' Chester. Just do it. Succeed."

"How am I supposed to know how to do that?"

"I guess we're about to find out," I said. "Say what you want to say right up front. Because this could be a very short meeting."

———

Sue came out into the backyard quite a long time later. Long enough that I'd begun to worry she'd jumped into the car and gone on a spontaneous vacation.

She was carrying an amber glass pitcher in one hand and three nested drinking glasses in the other. She set it all down on the glass-topped table between my lawn chair and Chester's wheelchair. We were sitting under an awning that provided some blessed shade.

"Thought you might like a cold drink of water," she said.

Then she sat down and looked at Chester. And Chester looked back at her. And the moment stretched out. Nobody said a word.

I thanked her, and reached over and poured two glasses of ice water. One for Chester and one for me.

It was something of an early litmus test. I already knew there was no love lost between Chester and water. How politely or rudely he received the refreshment might be a good indicator of how the next chapter of my life was about to go.

He took it from me and took a long swallow, then set it on the arm of his wheelchair. It was too narrow a resting place, and the patio was concrete underneath us, so I grabbed it up and put it back on the table.

He was still staring at Sue and Sue was still staring at him. And they were still not saying a word.

"How does it manage to be so hot here so late in the season?" I asked.

It broke the trance, and she looked away from Chester and turned those deep blues on me, which felt like a relief.

"You've never been to Arizona before," she said, "have you?"

"No. Never been west of Chicago."

"It shows."

A silence fell, but not for long. Chester opened his mouth and broke it.

"I know I look like crap," he said. "You might as well just go ahead and say it. I know you're thinking it. I know you were about to say it. Go ahead."

"I wasn't going to say that," she said.

"I know I've aged a hundred years since you saw me last."

"You've aged the same numbers of years as I have."

"You wouldn't know it to look at us."

She opened her mouth to speak, but Chester got there first.

"He in there?"

He indicated the house with a flip of his head.

She burst out laughing. "Is that what you think?"

"What was I supposed to think?"

"Honey, that man and I divorced in 1996."

"Oh," Chester said. I could see his face change as he digested the information. "Well, I can't say I'm happy to hear that."

"You're totally happy to hear that. Admit it."

"I'm not. I'm actually not. You blew up our marriage for that. I think it's even worse if it all went for nothing."

"I'm surprised Ellie didn't tell you at least that much."

"I don't ask her anything about you. And she doesn't volunteer anything."

"Good."

"Until I got sick, I barely saw her. It's not like I have a family anymore."

I could tell from her eyes and her face that she was losing patience fast. Whatever her good points, she was clearly not a woman long on patience. *They must have been quite the pair in their day,* I thought.

"Go ahead and say what you came here to say to me, Chet."

Chester stared down at his lap and said nothing.

"Seriously, Chet," she said, her voice rising. "You came all the way from Buffalo to say something to me. Now what is it?"

"I don't know," Chester said.

I felt, suddenly, as though all the air had been sucked out of the meeting, emotionally speaking. Had he really come all this way with no idea of what he wanted to say? Or was he just afraid to say it now that he was looking right into her face? With Chester it was almost impossible to venture a guess.

"You better be about to tell me you're kidding," she spat.

And that was it. The guardrails came down, the illegal holds were no longer barred, and it had become a fight, just like that.

"Well, it's hard," he shouted. "What am I supposed to say? You tell me I have to be polite or you'll kick me out again. How do you tell someone they ruined your life and be polite all at the same time?"

"You drove two thousand miles to tell me something you've told me a hundred times before? That doesn't sound right. Or at least it wouldn't with anybody else. With you I guess I'd be tempted to say it's par for your course."

"You haven't changed a bit," he shouted.

"Neither have you," she shouted right back, "except you look a hundred years older!"

"Okay, stop!" I bellowed.

I stood. And then I took a step and stood between them. And I held one hand out to each of them, like twin stop signs. It was a warning. And for reasons unknown to me, they heeded it.

"This is going south fast," I said. "So here's what we're going to do. I'm going to take Chester back to the Winnebago. And I'll see if I can't figure out what it is he's been wanting to say to you. And when we come back, he'll stick to that."

"I don't want him coming back," Sue said. "I don't want him here. I never wanted him here."

"Okay. Well. I'll try to get the message out of him and then *I'll* come back and tell you what it is."

So, there it was. Just like that, I had inserted myself into the process.

I'm sure it goes without saying that it was a decision I would soon regret.

Chapter Twelve:

The Disconnect

I loaded Chester back into the RV with great effort. I backed him up and sat him down on one of the couches. Tucked a couple of pillows behind his back.

Then, when I was sure he was nice and comfy, I let him have it with both barrels.

"What the hell was that, Chester? Oh my God. What is wrong with you?"

"Me?" he shouted back. "Don't put this off on me. She started it."

"She started it? Do you not get that I was *there*? 'I know you think I look like crap. I know you're thinking it. I know you want to say it. Go on! Say it! Say it! Say it!'" I got right up in his face and blasted it out one more time. "'Say it!'"

He pushed me back with one beefy hand.

"Get out of my damn face, Lewis!"

"I'm sure that's exactly how she felt. And then she asks what you came all this way to say. And you don't know."

"It takes time to get your thoughts together on a thing like that."

"It was a three-and-a-half-day drive!"

I had very much lost it by then, and it came out so loud it hurt my throat. I briefly pondered whether his ex-wife had heard me in the house.

"I thought I knew," he said, his voice uncharacteristically quiet. "I thought I had it in my head, but then I was there with her and my thoughts were just scattered all over the place. I couldn't think."

I sat down hard on the opposing couch. And it hit me, like the proverbial Sherman tank, that I was tired. But not a normal kind of tired. Seriously depleted. Really spent. Done.

"You're not looking at her now," I said.

"I guess I just want to know why."

"Okay. Fine. Let me go tell her you just want to know why."

"Wait. There might be more."

"You can think about that while I'm gone."

I turned on the generator and set the air conditioning to 72 degrees, so Chester wouldn't die of heat exhaustion in that metal roasting pan while I was gone.

I sorted his pills carefully onto the counter and then swept them into a little bowl with the side of my hand. Poured him a glass of apple juice. Handed him both.

"Here, take your pills," I said.

Then I trotted down the steps and out into the desert oven.

I marched up the walkway and rapped on her door.

She pulled the curtain back within seconds. When she saw it was me, her face softened and she let me in.

"I'm sorry about that," I said, stepping into her living room. "I realize that was quite a crap show."

"Now you know what it was like to live with him."

"I've pretty much been living with him for about a week now. So I think I already knew."

"Condolences."

She wandered away without comment, and I sat down on her couch and waited. The place was artificially cool and dazzlingly clean. It was decorated in a style that might have been retro or might not have changed since the actual sixties. Lots of white leather and turquoise. Still, whatever I thought of her decorating style, it was hard not to admire all that clean.

She stuck her head back into the living room and held up a large bottle of Jim Beam.

"You want something stronger than water?"

"It's still morning," I said. Even though I really did want it.

"I know it. And I'm not a day drinker. I don't want you to think I am. But every once in a blue moon you have a day that's an exception to the rule. Any day my ex-husband comes looking for me qualifies. And you—you look positively worn down."

"I'm . . ." I struggled for an apt description. ". . . tired right down into my bones. I can feel them buzzing with exhaustion. And not just physical exhaustion, either, though that, too. It's just been a really tough week."

"So is that a yes?"

"Yes."

She broke out two glasses and poured us each three fingers of whiskey. Sat down beside me on the couch.

"I'm sorry I helped ambush you," I said. I meant it sincerely, and I know that came through in my voice. I could hear it. "I thought if I didn't do it, I'd feel really bad after he was gone."

"I give everybody one pass," she said. "So we're good. But only one."

I took a long swallow of the whiskey. It hit me fast. It combined in a strange way with my exhaustion and made me feel as though I didn't actually exist.

"He said something after we got back in the RV," I said. "It felt pretty genuine. And that's so rare for him. Of course I want to tell it to you, but I'm not sure I can quote it word for word. This is somewhat paraphrased. He said he thought he knew what he wanted to say, but then he was actually there with you and it wouldn't come together in his head. He couldn't think in that moment."

"That makes sense, I guess. But you were back in the Winnebago with him. Could he think then?"

"I asked him. He said he thinks he just wants to know why."

She took a long swallow of her whiskey, her eyes far away. She seemed to be looking out the window, but in a half-focused way.

"Why's a hard question," she said.

"I guess you don't drive two thousand miles to ask an easy one."

She gave a long, slow shrug.

"I fell in love," she said. "People fall in love. Especially when they're not happy in their marriage."

We drank in silence for a couple of minutes. I was putting the whiskey away much too fast. I hadn't eaten, and I hadn't slept nearly enough. And when I looked down at my glass it was unexpectedly empty.

"Well," I said, and tried to rise. And almost fell down again. She reached out to steady me. "I need sleep," I added. "I'm going to go sleep. I'll tell him what you said. I can't believe this could really be it, but I'll tell him."

"Really be what?"

"I mean, he asks you one question and you give him a short answer. People don't drive most of the way across the country for that. Do they?"

"Depends on the people," she said. "But I doubt we're done."

She got up and walked me to the door.

"Get some sleep," she said. "And, look. I'm making a lamb stew. I was anyway. Even before I knew I was being invaded. What I'm saying is, you're invited. Come around seven. Chet is *not* invited, but I'll make him up a plate. He can eat it in the Winnebago."

"Okay," I said. "All things considered I'd say you're being pretty hospitable."

I stepped out again into the desert heat. Walked down that concrete path. Stepped up into the cool rig.

Chester jumped me immediately, verbally speaking.

"What'd she say?"

But I knew if I told him, it would evolve into a whole big thing, with more questions, and more answers, and more walks up and down that concrete path in the desert heat.

So all I said was "Tell you after I've gotten some sleep."

Then I told him briefly about our dinner plans and tucked myself into what had to pass for a bed. Because the air conditioner didn't work well in the actual bedroom.

And there wasn't a damn thing he could do about any of it.

———

Chester woke me at what I would later learn was 6:00 in the afternoon.

"Hey, nimrod," he called over from the couch bed on his side.

"What? Why are you waking me up, Chester?"

"Because you're about to sleep through dinner."

"Oh."

I sat up and blinked too much.

My head felt fuzzy and tightly packed, as if someone had stuffed it with cotton batting in my sleep. I was still tired.

I glanced at my watch and learned about the whole 6:00 thing.

"I could've slept another half hour."

"I figured you'd want to take a shower."

"For an hour?"

"You still need to tell me what she said."

"Oh," I said. I rubbed my eyes and tried to shift my brain into gear. "Right. It won't take half an hour, though. She said she fell in love. And that people fall in love. Especially when they're not happy in their marriage."

"Then ask her what she had to be so damned unhappy about."

"That seems pointless."

"What do you mean, 'That seems pointless'? And why do *you* get to judge? Just ask her."

"Fine. I'll ask her over dinner."

"No, now."

"No, over dinner, Chester. You can't order me around like that. This whole thing is miles outside my job description, and you're supposed to just be grateful I'm doing any of it."

Chester 2.0 did not hold. He expressed no gratitude.

I got up and stretched and tried to get myself into the shower, but he wouldn't let it go.

"Why did you say it seems pointless to ask that?"

"Because it seems pretty obvious to me what she was saying."

"So? Enlighten me. What was she saying?"

I stopped. Walked back away from the direction of the tiny bathroom. Sat down across from Chester. He was still sitting on the couch on the street side, still leaning on the pillows I had stuffed behind his back. I leaned forward with my elbows on my knees and leveled him with a serious gaze. Looked right into his face. He averted his eyes.

"Let me just clear something up here," I said. "Do you honestly not get it that you're a mean, thoughtless, difficult person?"

"Everybody's mean and difficult."

"Ah. So that's the disconnect."

"The what?"

"You think everybody's just as awful as you are."

"Well, they are."

"I'm going to take a shower."

"Wait," he said.

I was halfway between sitting and standing, but I stopped. And I waited.

"So you're saying I'm the reason she was unhappy."

"Pretty much, yeah."

"And you won't even ask her what she meant by it?"

"No, I'll ask her. Over dinner. I'm only saying . . . don't be surprised if it's what I just said."

I straightened up and headed for the shower again.

"Wait," Chester said.

I lost at least a good-sized chunk of my temper.

"Stop telling me to wait!" I shouted at him. "The world doesn't revolve around you trying to understand your former marriage, Chester. Now I want to take a shower."

"I was just going to tell you that you forgot to turn on the water heater."

"Oh," I said, and deflated like a balloon. "That."

"Yeah, that."

"How long does it take to heat up?"

"More time than you've got."

"Fine. Then I'll take a cold shower."

I took a cold shower. It was an unpleasant experience. But at least when I was done, I could honestly say I felt awake.

———

Just before I stepped out of the Winnie and left him for the evening, Chester dropped the following bombshell.

"I need the bedpan."

"Oh," I said. I realized, as I said it, that I'd been saying that two-letter word a lot.

Then I just stood there on the steps, with the side door open, wishing he didn't need the bedpan.

"Fine. I'll get you the bedpan."

"But then you need to come back and empty it for me. I don't want to just sit here with it. You need to empty it and open windows and turn on the fan."

I sighed out what felt like all the air I'd ever breathed into my lungs since I was born.

"Are you just doing this to sabotage my dinner? Because I get to go in the house and you don't?"

"No, I really do need it."

"But I just got all cleaned up. Why didn't you ask me before I showered?"

"I didn't know I'd need it then."

I sighed again, and walked back up the steps, and got the clean bedpan out from the hatch under Chester's couch bed. I handed it to him.

"You can call me on my cell phone when you're done," I said.

"How can I call you from the Winnebago?"

"By using the cell phone that Ellie bought you specifically for that purpose."

"I don't know how to use that thing."

"It's not brain surgery, Chester."

I walked the couple of steps up to the cab and got it. It was sitting in a little hatch where it could stay plugged in and charged. I unplugged it and carried it back to him.

"Look. I programmed my number in. All you have to do is hit 'Call.'"

"I don't like these new gadgets."

"You don't have to like it. You just have to hit 'Call.'"

"And what if I can't figure it out?"

"You might be able to reach the window behind you to open it."

"Fine. I'll use it and call."

I headed for the door again, but he still was not about to let me go.

"I really do need the bedpan, but I also think it sucks that you get to go into the house and I don't."

"It's an example of actions having consequences."

"I have no idea what that means."

"Why am I not surprised? It means that people who are kind and polite get more dinner invitations than people who are mean and rude. But try looking at it a different way. You blew your first chance with her. Now I'm going to go in and see if I can get you a second one."

"Oh. You're right. That does sound better. And you'll bring me some of that stew?"

"If she gives me some to bring to you. And she said she would."

"Knock before you come in. In case I'm on the bedpan."

"Well, I wouldn't want to walk in on that. So, will do."

I got out the door fast, before he could find another way to delay me.

As I walked up that now familiar concrete path, it struck me that between the time I woke up and the time I stepped out of the Winnebago, I had become thoroughly exhausted again. Chester had a way of draining off a lot of life energy. I briefly wondered where I could get more before I had to see him again.

Maybe his ex-wife had some she could spare.

Chapter Thirteen:

Honor

I stood in her kitchen, leaning back against one of her counters, watching her stir the stew. The oven had a glass door, and a light inside, and I could see a round loaf of crusty bread being warmed. The aromas were slaying me with their wonderfulness.

"You still look exhausted," she said. "Did you sleep?"

She was wearing a sort of loose, flowy kimono type of garment. Turquoise. Possibly to match the furniture, or maybe she just liked turquoise. Actually it was a pretty safe bet that she did.

"I slept. But then Chester got after me about this and that, and then all of a sudden I was exhausted again."

"He has that effect on people. Ellie probably thought you were young enough to bear up." She raised her eyes to me and looked me up and down. "Lordy, honey, you're just a baby. What are you? Twenty?"

"Twenty-four."

"The curse of getting old. Everybody looks like a child to you. No offense, please. I'm not trying to take away your right to adulthood when I call you a baby. It's more a jab at myself for being the opposite."

"No offense taken," I said. "Some days I feel like a baby. Like I don't know the first damn thing about life."

"Here's a news flash, honey. I'm sixty-seven years old and some days I feel like *I* don't know the first damn thing about life. Hate to break it to you. I hope you weren't counting on that wearing off over time." She met my eyes again with more of that Sue-style scrutiny. "Tell me again how you got roped into this job?"

"I needed the money."

She nodded briskly, as though I had satisfied her unexpectedly. "That I get. That's probably the only answer you could've given me that I could make sense of. Still. People will pay you to do various things that aren't this."

"I guess. I was having trouble finding those people. The job market was bad. I got laid off without notice, and I'd lost both my roommates in less than a month."

She clucked her tongue slightly, crossed the kitchen, and pulled that same big bottle of Jim Beam down from her cupboard.

"You've earned this," she said.

She gifted me with a generous pour, then poured some for herself.

"I just realized," she said. "I never asked you your name."

"Right. I guess not. It was a weird first meeting. It's Lewis."

"Lewis," she said, sounding almost approving. As though she had weighed the name and found it worthy. "Here's to your health, Lewis."

She raised her glass.

"I'm more worried about my sanity."

"To your health and sanity."

We clinked glasses and then tipped them back and drained them.

It helped some. Whether it was the good wishes or the whiskey, I'm not sure. Probably both.

She picked up a bowl from the counter. It was a Blue Willow china pattern, and big enough that I was left unclear as to whether it was for serving or eating. She began ladling stew into it.

"You can take this out to him," she said. "Oh, wait. I need to cut him a big hunk of bread. Chet loves his bread. But I need my bowl back."

"Of course you need your bowl back. It's a beautiful bowl."

I took it from her and held it by the edges because it was hot.

I watched as she slipped on hot mitts and took the loaf out of the oven. She cut off an end piece that looked to be nearly a quarter of the thing. I waited while she balanced it on the rim of the bowl. Then she took a soupspoon out of a drawer and buried it in the stew.

"I need the spoon back, too."

"You have my word," I said. "I will be personally responsible for making sure you get your bowl and spoon back."

She leaned in and patted me on the cheek in a motherly sort of way. It was unexpected, but not unwelcome.

"*You* I like," she said.

I noted that she put a strong emphasis on the first word of the sentence.

"I'll be right back," I said. "With any luck."

She opened the front door for me because I had no free hands. Then she followed me to the street, presumably to open the door of the Winnebago for me as well.

The evening was dusky, but still hot. The sky was steely blue and light behind a section of the mountains, which made them stand out in stunning relief.

"Nice of you to risk getting closer to your ex by helping," I said quietly.

"Purely selfish. I don't want my bowl getting broken."

She reached out to open the side door of the Winnebago, but I stopped her.

"Wait," I said.

"What?"

"Knock. He might be on the bedpan."

"Oh, jeez," she said.

She rapped on the door.

"Come on in, Lewis," Chester's booming voice called out to where we stood. "Coast is clear."

The curtains on the Winnebago were still down, and she was able to open the door while staying behind it, where she couldn't be seen from inside.

I made my way carefully up the steps and set the bowl down on the kitchen counter. When I crossed to the door again to close it, she was gone. In the mostly dark evening I could just barely see her stepping back up onto her porch.

I set up the portable table and served Chester his meal.

"So you didn't really have to use the bedpan," I said.

"No, I do. I just wanted to wait until I was really ready. You know. Till it was dying to come out. So I wouldn't have to spend too much time sitting and pushing."

"Holy crap, Chester."

"What now?"

"TMI."

"I don't know what that means."

"Too much information."

"You're such a cream puff. Did you get me another chance with her?"

"Not yet. We've barely started talking."

"What did you talk about?"

"Not you," I said.

And I let myself out.

He didn't just let me go that easily, of course. He was jabbing at me with words the whole way, but I kept moving, and fortunately I could barely make them out.

—

"This is incredibly good," I said. "I haven't had a home-cooked meal in . . . I honestly can't remember."

We were eating in her tiny nook of a dining room, with taper candles in the middle of the table, and silverware that actually was silver.

"What have you been eating?"

"Sandwiches. Pizza. Anything cheap. Although . . . my friend Anna treated me to a couple of restaurant meals. I felt guilty that she was paying, so I just had pasta."

"Restaurant pasta is not a home-cooked meal."

"I suppose not," I said. "But at least it's cooked."

I took another long sip of the whiskey. The combination of a lot of good protein followed by booze on a full stomach was changing the way I felt. Not making me feel any less tired, of course. But somehow I was starting to feel grounded and real in my exhaustion.

"Anna is your girlfriend?" she asked.

It didn't really sound like a prying question. She seemed just to want to know more about me. I told her more about me.

"No, Anna's not my girlfriend. Just a friend. I don't have a girlfriend. I had a boyfriend, but he left unexpectedly."

"You're gay," she said.

She sounded a little bit shocked, which shattered my sudden new calm.

"Yeah. Why. Does it matter to you?"

"Oh, hell no. Not me. I couldn't care less one way or the other. I was just thinking . . . I figured it would matter to Chet."

"Oh, it does."

"He gives you a hard time about it." It was a flat statement, not a question.

"Every chance he gets."

"I'm not surprised."

"So he was always like that?"

"Oh, no. Not always. When we first started dating, he didn't pay things like that much mind. But after the thing with Mike . . . well. You know how it is. You push something away that hard, you're going to want everybody else to push it away, too."

I dropped my spoon into my nearly empty bowl, and it landed much harder and more noisily than I had expected.

"Wait, wait," I said. "Wait. Back up. What thing with Mike?"

I watched her face redden slightly while I was waiting for her to answer.

"Oh, you don't know about Mike. Well . . . of course you don't. Now that I think about it, of course you wouldn't. Why would I think he would tell you a thing like that? Where's my mind? I wonder why I just did that. I just told on him about something without thinking twice. I wonder if I did it because I'm so damned mad at him."

"Are you trying to tell me Chester had an . . . experience with this guy?"

"Oh, no. No. It was nothing like that. Nothing *happened* between them. He just loved Mike so much. I think it scared him. Made him wonder a little about himself. I don't think it meant a damn thing myself. Sometimes you just love someone. Big deal. But he let himself get kind of obsessed over the whole thing."

We fell silent, and I scraped the bowl with my spoon to get up the last couple of bites and the leftover gravy.

In my mind I was remembering something that Chester had said to me.

It's a choice and I know it. You might be able to fool everybody else, but you can't fool me.

I looked up to see her watching me.

"Penny for your thoughts," she said.

"Oh, something was just coming together in my head."

"Up to you if you want to share it or not."

"I was just thinking how a couple of times he's let on that he thinks being gay is a choice. And he's really stubborn about it, too. Like he's just so sure, and nothing is going to change his mind."

"Because he feels like he made a conscious choice to move away from that. Right. But I don't really think that's what happened. Because if he'd really been gay, it would have kept coming up again and again."

"Of course it would have. If you can walk away, you're not gay."

"Ooh, that rhymes," she said. "That would make a nice billboard."

We smiled, and I finished my bread and my whiskey.

And then she told me a little more about Mike.

I was dying to know, but I wouldn't have asked, because it was clearly none of my business. I already felt guilty knowing the little bit I did about a subject Chester would so obviously want to keep from me.

"They were in the war together," she said.

"World War Two?"

"*World War Two?* Lordy, honey, exactly how old do you think we are? The guys who fought World War Two are mostly dead now, and those still around are in their late nineties."

"Sorry. Korea?"

"Keep going."

"Couldn't be Desert Storm."

"You missed one."

"Oh. Vietnam."

"Bingo. They were over there together, and Chet was more scared than he cared to let on, and Mike was more of the take-charge type, and he took Chet under his wing. Saved his life twice."

"Twice?"

"You can't make a thing like that up. Anyway, that's what I figured it was all about—the war stuff. It wasn't really a romance thing. When somebody saves your life twice, you look up to them. They take on this outsized importance."

"Right," I said. "It warps your feelings for them."

"That's all it was, I think. I didn't actually make any dessert, but I have store-bought cookies."

"I think I'm stuffed," I said.

We sat quietly for a minute. I couldn't stop my mind from going over the revelations about Chester's former life. Something about it was causing the world to make more sense to me.

We heard a horn honk out front.

We both listened without comment for a few beats. Then we looked at each other.

"Is that the Winnebago?" she asked.

"I don't know. I never heard the Winnebago's horn."

"Seriously? Are you kidding me, honey? You drove that thing from Buffalo, New York, to Phoenix and never honked your horn at anybody? You are nothing at all like Chet Wheeler, I'll tell you that much, young man."

"Thank you. That's the nicest thing anybody's ever said about me."

Another short blast on the horn sounded. We met each other's eyes again.

"Couldn't be him," I said. "I don't even think he could *reach* the horn." A couple more beats of silence. Then, almost instinctively, I added, "But I'd better go check."

I trotted out the door and down the concrete walkway, which had become overly familiar. It had begun to feel like a portal in space and time between the sane, comfortable world and the one I was forced to share with Chester Wheeler.

While I trotted, the horn blasted again, and it was definitely the Winnebago.

I threw the side door open, and the smell overwhelmed me immediately.

For the first time since I'd taken on Chester's care, I felt a little bit sorry for myself. It was hard not to wonder why I couldn't just stay in a clean, sweet-smelling world with lamb stew and taper candles and good whiskey, and people who weren't beastly.

Speaking of beastly, Chester was sitting right where I'd left him, right next to the now-unmentionable bedpan, his pants on but askew. He was holding one of those sticklike claw devices people use to get cans down from a high shelf. He was leaning over and using it to reach the horn. I caught him right before he honked a fourth time.

I grabbed the bedpan and flushed its contents in the bathroom, then set the dirty pan outside on the curb. I ran around and opened the two roof vents, turning on their exhaust fans as fast as I could manage.

Once that was done, I turned my foul mood onto Chester.

"Give me that," I said. And I took his stick away. "Where was that, anyway?"

"Right under the couch. Same hatch as you've been using for the bedpan."

"What happened to calling me on my cell phone?"

"I couldn't figure out how to work that damn thing."

"I'm going back," I said.

And I tried to duck out the door.

"Wait. Is she going to give me a second chance?"

"I don't know yet."

I tried again to leave.

"Wait. Is there dessert?"

"She didn't make anything, but she said there are store-bought cookies."

"Bring me back some cookies," he said.

I said no more to him, and left before he could say more to me.

I tucked the empty but unwashed bedpan under the body of the Winnebago. I just couldn't cope with it in that moment. Maybe later I could get Sue to let me use her hose, or I could use the Winnie's outside shower hose. After I'd changed out of my decent clothes.

Again I navigated the portal of the concrete walkway. But at least this time I was going in the preferred direction.

I opened the door and stuck my head in.

"Sue?"

I wasn't in the habit of entering people's houses without permission. It's just not the way I was raised.

"Come on in, hon. Everything okay?"

"Yeah. Pretty much. Everything except my life. Just a little bed-pan emergency. Now all I need is a place to wash my hands until they bleed."

"First door on the left," she said.

She sounded unfazed by the whole thing. Then again, I reminded myself, she'd had children. It made me feel better to remember that I was not the first to have to perform unpleasant and unsanitary jobs for helpless others, and I wouldn't be the last.

When I got back to the table she had poured me another stiff drink.

"You'll have to sleep at my curb tonight," she said. "You've had too much to drink."

"Says the woman who keeps pouring."

"You're too tired to be safe on the road tonight anyway."

"True."

"So you just do things like that for him no matter how he treats you?"

I sat down at the table again. Sipped. There was a plate of cookies in the middle of the table and I made a mental note to remember to bring some out to Chester.

"Well, yeah," I said. "It's my job. I knew who he was when I agreed to do it. I can quit if I want, but first I'd have to give Ellie enough time to find somebody else. That's just common decency.

Until I do that, I'm committed. And the way I do my job is about me, not him. He can be whatever he wants, but I'm not going to be someone who leaves a dying man without basic sanitation once I've made the commitment."

"And the part about playing referee between Chet and me?"

"Same thing, I guess. I said I'd do this thing for him. Help him get closure. So that's what I'm doing. It has to be more than just driving. Any idiot can drive."

She didn't answer at first. After a few beats I glanced up to see her watching me. It made me feel uneasy, so I reached over and took two cookies, even though I'd said I was too full.

"You're a good person," she said.

"Just like everybody else, I think."

"No." She sounded quite firm as she pronounced that word. "No, you're not just like everybody else. You have a greater sense of . . . responsibility? I almost want to say *honor*. It's inspiring. You've inspired me. If you can do all that for Chet, no matter how awful he is, then I can hear him out. Bring him by in the morning. We'll have breakfast out on the patio and we'll give the damn thing another try."

———

Chester was sleeping when I got in, but he stirred and struggled up into a half-sitting position immediately.

"How'd it go?"

"Fine," I said. "Here. I brought you some cookies."

I held them out to him wrapped in a heavy paper napkin.

"Oh, that's good. Thanks. But what I really want is for you to tell me she'll talk to me again."

"Tomorrow morning. Breakfast on her patio. She's prepared to hear you out. Don't mess it up this time."

"Oh my gosh," he said, which sounded a bit tame for Chester. "Lewis. You're a miracle worker."

I must admit I basked in the glow of that for a moment before brushing it away.

"She's a reasonable woman," I said. "It didn't take a miracle."

But somewhere in the back of my soul I questioned whether or not the second part of that statement was true. It was a little everyday miracle, if nothing else.

Chapter Fourteen:

Judgy

When I woke up and stepped out of the bedroom and into the main body of the RV, Chester was looking at himself in a hand mirror. It must have been in one of the drawers he could reach. I didn't know which one, and I didn't know why Chester had kept a mirror in the RV when there was one over the bathroom sink. I didn't know much of anything that morning. I think I wasn't fully awake.

"I want you to do me a couple of favors," he said when he saw I was up.

"Depends on the favors."

"I want you to set me up to shave like you did that first day at home. And then I want you to bring me a bowl of warm water and a washcloth and a towel, and a fresh change of clothes. And go away and give me some time to work all that out. I need to clean up as much as I can. I want to take what we used to call a navy bath in my day."

"Like a sponge bath."

"Yeah. Like that. I haven't showered for a really long time."

"That is so true," I said.

"And my toothbrush, of course. So will you do all that for me?"

"Absolutely," I said. "It would be my pleasure."

He seemed a little surprised by my good attitude, but he made no comment.

I laid a towel over his lap and brought him shaving cream and a razor. Filled a bowl with water and placed it on the portable table by his side.

"Do I have to shave with cold water?" he asked me, sounding mostly like Old Chester. "Or did you remember to turn on the water heater this time?"

"I remembered. That's not a mistake a person makes twice. Now I'll go shower and dress, and when I get out, I'll set up that navy bath and make myself scarce."

"Thank you," he said.

In my head I thought, *That's two.* I was definitely keeping a score-card for Chester 2.0.

As I was walking back to the shower he said, "Maybe you could go have coffee with Sue while I get ready."

"Kind of early, though. I don't want to wake her. But I'll take a walk if I need to."

"Thank you," he said again.

I marked the scorecard a second time in just minutes, thinking, *Wow. We are really on a roll.*

———

As it turned out, all the curtains had been opened in the house, and I could see Sue puttering around in the kitchen. I made my way up her walkway carrying her bowl and spoon, both clean, and she saw me and waved, and came to the door.

"You look rested," she said. "It's about time."

"I slept a lot."

"Coffee?"

"Yes, please."

I followed her into the kitchen and sat. There was a longhaired calico cat sitting on the table and he—or she—stared at me with a blank expression. I stared back.

"What do you take in it?" Sue asked.

"Black is fine."

She set a mug in front of me and shooed the cat off the table. Then she fetched her own coffee from the counter by the sink and sat across from me. She looked a little edgy. I didn't figure I blamed her.

"So are we taking bets on how this is going to go this morning?" she asked me.

"I'm betting on this session being less of a disaster."

"Where is he now?"

"He's in the RV getting ready. He wanted to shave and take a sponge bath, which is why I'm putting my money on less disastrous. It's unusual for him to think about how he's coming across to other people. Right now he's aware that he doesn't want to offend on a purely physical level. We'll see if that carries over into that dreaded moment when he opens his mouth."

She held up two crossed fingers and then sipped her coffee in silence for a minute or two.

It struck me that we were oddly comfortable with each other after only twenty-four hours of acquaintance. It felt like visiting a family member I hadn't seen for a long time, which was—let's face it—an odd way to feel about anybody from Chester Wheeler's past.

"Listen, that thing I told you yesterday . . . ," she began.

She didn't have to say which thing, and I didn't have to ask.

I pantomimed zipping my lip.

"Thank you," she said. "It's a personal thing to him, and I know he'd be upset that I mentioned it. I'm still not really sure why I did that."

"He makes you want to lash out and hurt him," I said. "You get so tired of being hurt by him and it's hard not to hit back."

"That's a good observation."

She sipped in silence for another minute, her mind seeming far away. After a time she shook herself back to the moment, as if trying to wake up.

"Well, anyway," she said, "I should get going on those waffles."

I watched her work for what might have been three minutes, or it might have been ten.

Then my cell phone rang.

At first I was surprised I had even remembered to bring it into the house with me. It was in my shirt pocket, but it had ended up there without any conscious thought on my part. I lifted it out and glanced at its screen.

The caller was one Chester Wheeler.

I had set up the new phone Ellie sent us so I could see him on the caller ID when he called. You know. Back when I thought he would actually call. When I assumed he'd be willing to use the thing.

"Well, look at that," I said out loud. "What do you know? Chester figured out how to use the cell phone."

"Is that hard?" she asked from the direction of the stove.

"Not for you or me."

I picked up.

"Well, look at you, Chester," I said in lieu of hello. "Using the cell phone."

"Come and get me," he said. "I'm ready."

———

When I had managed to get him into the chair and wheel him into the backyard, the glass-topped table was nicely set for three.

In the middle of it sat a serving plate with a stack of six homemade waffles. It was surrounded by syrup, honey, two kinds of jam, and what I took to be a pot of coffee.

I pushed Chester up to the table just as Sue stepped out of the house. She was carrying a bowl of sausage. I couldn't see inside the bowl, but I could smell it.

"Well, look at you," she said to Chester. "All cleaned up."

He only grunted in his throat.

Meanwhile I was mulling over that expression, because it kept coming up. *Well, look at that. Look at Chester. Look at you, Chester. Doing things.* It felt like we were spending the morning so far telling each other where to look. It also seemed a little like the way one handles a child—suggesting he be proud of himself for something that's really nothing at all by adult standards.

Meanwhile Sue was dishing up food onto plates.

"I was thinking," she said. "Maybe we just eat. First, I mean. And then talk after. So nothing spoils breakfast."

"Oh, so you just assume I'm going to spoil things," Chester said.

"Chester," I said in my most authoritative voice. "We're doing it her way. First of all, it's her house. And, for myself . . . just the tension of any serious conversation would be enough to spoil my appetite."

"Sure," he said, "because you're a big pansy."

Then he fell silent again, with a vaguely guilty look on his face. I gathered by looking at him that he might actually have been trying to be civil, and that the strain of trying to do something so unnatural to him had caused chaos.

Sue and I exchanged glances but said nothing.

We settled into our breakfasts.

After a couple of minutes of quiet chewing, I figured a little small talk couldn't hurt.

I asked Sue, "How long have you lived in this house?"

Chester answered for her.

"Thirty-seven years," he said, his voice low and gruff. "I know because I bought it. And then she took it away from me, along with my kids and my dog."

"Chester, I swear," I began. I was just at the edge of figuratively clobbering him and he clearly knew it. "I'll put you back in that RV right now. We can just drive home if you can't bring yourself to behave."

He fell silent. And, more remarkably, he remained that way.

In fact, we all remained awkwardly silent until every scrap of food had been eaten.

———

Sue rose and began clearing the table. I instinctively jumped up and helped her, following her into the kitchen with jam jars and syrup bottles.

"Still betting on less disastrous?" she asked over her shoulder.

"It's not going as well as I'd hoped, no."

"That's pretty understated."

"He crumbles under pressure."

"Yes he does," she said.

"I'll understand if you want to call this off."

"No, I'll try it," she said. "He's obviously on his last legs, so it's not like I'll ever see him again. Let's go ahead and give him one final chance to vent his spleen."

We left everything more or less in a heap on the counter and walked back outside to what felt like our own doom. At least, it felt that way to me. I was only guessing about her, but I think it was a pretty safe guess.

We sat down at the table with him, and Sue tore it wide open.

"Okay, Chet. You came all this way to tell me what's on your mind. Let's have it."

Oddly, Chester just stared at his legs for a moment and said nothing.

I thought, *Oh, bloody hell, he's doing it again. He's back to "I don't know."*

But then he looked up at her. Opened his mouth. The words that came out sounded surprisingly mousy and small.

"Why did you take my kids away from me when you knew how much I loved them?"

Sue sat back hard in her chair.

"First of all," she said, "they were *our* kids. Not *yours*. And you haven't seemed to love them very much since. Johnny and Danny say they haven't seen you in almost twenty years, and as best I can figure you didn't get back together with Ellie until you got sick."

A long silence fell. Chester did not fill it.

He did glance over at me with a desperate look in his eyes. I got the sense that he was in over his head and looking for a little assistance.

"With all due respect," I said in Sue's general direction, "you did sort of duck the man's question."

She turned her full ire onto me. It was considerable, even before she opened her mouth.

"Well, look at you," she said. "Getting right in the middle of this."

I thought, *Look at that. We're still doing it. Telling each other where to look.*

"Maybe I misunderstood," I said. "But yesterday I volunteered to be something like a go-between, which of course makes me the world's biggest blundering idiot. But at the time you both seemed willing enough to let me."

The moment just simmered there for many seconds. Possibly a full minute. I felt as though I was watching her process everything. She seemed to be trying to wrap up her irritation so it could be put away in a drawer and saved for some other occasion.

"Okay. Here goes. Why did I take the kids? I took the kids because I was afraid for them to be with you. We tried visitation, just in case you've rewritten history and are about to say we didn't. But you were bitter, and you were drinking heavily—"

He cut her off.

"I was bitter and I was drinking heavily because you ruined my life, leaving me for another man the way you did."

"I get that," she said. "But dangerous is dangerous and safe is safe. The story behind why doesn't change the odds of an accident."

"Great," Chester said. "You ruin a man's life and then tell him he can't have his own kids because he's upset about it."

Sue slammed her fist down onto the glass-topped table. Hard. Everybody jumped. She even seemed to have startled herself. I sat poised a moment, waiting to see if the glass was going to hold.

"Now, you listen to me, Chet Wheeler. You shut up and listen for one time in your mean little life. It was not a decision I made lightly. Johnny came home from a visit with you and told me you'd been drinking all day and then you loaded them into your car to go someplace. I don't remember where. And you drove right through a damn red light and almost caused an accident. He was terrified. You know how sensitive he is. He had nightmares for weeks."

"I hadn't had that many," Chester said.

"You'd had enough to drive right through a red light! And besides, you don't drive your kids around if you've had *any*!"

Silence. Chester was staring at his own legs again. That went on for a surprising length of time.

Then he said, in a fairly quiet voice, "You took my dog."

"She was not your dog," Sue said. And not quietly at all. "She was the family dog. The kids adored her, and they would've been heartbroken to lose her, especially in the middle of a divorce. And besides, she deserved to be safe, too."

"Great," Chester said. "That's great. That's just great. So I lost everything. And Mike got it all."

I noticed a tingling sensation around my ears. Then I noticed I was standing, but I wasn't clear on when I'd gotten up. I hadn't felt myself do it.

I turned my attention fully on Sue.

"You left him for *Mike*?"

I watched her face flush red while she wasn't answering.

"Wait a minute," Chester said. "Wait just a damn minute. What do you know about Mike? Sue, did you tell him about Mike?"

She ignored him and raised her eyes to me. I saw a sardonic twist to her mood underneath the embarrassment.

"Way to zip your lip, bunkie," she said.

"Right. Sorry. But . . . you left him for *Mike*?"

"You're being a little judgy, don't you think?"

"Right. Sorry. Maybe. *But you left him for Mike?*"

"Can we move on from this?"

"No. We can't. This is shocking news."

"Yeah, to *you*!" she shouted. "Everybody else at the table's known about it for decades."

I sat again. Plopped down, really.

"That's just so cold. Were you sleeping with him behind Chester's back?"

"Yes," Chester said. "She was."

"That's just . . ."

"Why do you know about Mike? What did she tell you about Mike?" Then, to Sue, "Why did you tell him anything about Mike?"

"Well," Sue said. "That was interesting while it lasted. But I think that concludes this episode of *Fun with Your Ex*. I think you guys need to leave now."

It was her house, and her decision, so I got up and wheeled Chester back to the RV.

"You got us kicked out," he said on the dreaded concrete walkway.

"Yeah. Sorry about that. It was just such shocking news. I didn't know what to do with it."

"And *that*," Chester said, "is probably the only thing you and I have in common."

Chapter Fifteen:

Grays

Chester and I sat in the RV for most of the morning, all the curtains down, the AC blowing a gale. I was vaguely thinking I'd need to drive the Winnie to a gas station soon, because even though we hadn't been driving, we'd been running the generator.

At first we didn't talk much at all.

Then I said, "Oh, you need to take your pills."

And I jumped up to get them all together and pour him some apple juice.

"I don't want them," he said.

"Take them anyway."

"Just the painkillers."

"You need all your pills."

"I really don't," he said.

I sat across from him and tried to look him in the eye. He wouldn't let me.

"Go ahead and answer me this, Chester. Do you want to live?"

"I don't get to live," he said. "Too late to change that."

"Do you want to live as long as you can?"

"I *did*. Because I wanted to get here. But now we . . . got here. So . . ."

It burned to hear him say it, because he was avoiding saying he'd actually done what he came here to do. Because he hadn't. And it was my fault that he hadn't. I'd gotten us kicked out.

"Look," I said. "I'm going to ask you to take them anyway. Because I promised Ellie I'd make you take your pills."

"So? She won't know."

"I'll know."

Chester only sighed.

I took that as a good sign, so I got up and got back to getting them ready.

He said, "Are we just supposed to stay here, or what? I don't know what we're doing."

"I'm not sure, either. But I think it might pay to give her some time to cool down. Maybe after a while I'll go in and see if she'll talk to me."

I swept the pills into their little bowl and poured him a glass of apple juice. I handed him both and sat on the couch across from him, watching him swallow one at a time. It seemed to require some effort. Swallowing was apparently getting harder for him.

"Thank you," I said when he'd swallowed the last one.

He set the bowl and the empty glass down on the portable table.

"I didn't take yesterday's pills," he said.

I scrambled around in my brain for some memory of the previous morning. I vaguely remembered handing him his pills and then leaving him alone. Why had I done that? Ellie had warned me. She'd said I'd have to stay right there and watch him take them, or he'd ditch them in the potted plants.

"You didn't take *any* of them?"

"I took the painkillers."

"What did you do with the rest of them?"

"They're under the couch cushion."

151

I wasn't quite sure how to respond to that. I wasn't sure if I should chastise him for ditching his pills or thank him for coming clean about it. I opened my mouth, but I still wasn't sure what I expected to come out of it.

Chester cut me off.

"What did she tell you about Mike?"

"Not all that much."

"No, seriously, Lewis. I'm asking you as a friend."

That made a bumpy landing.

I didn't think we *were* friends, and I wasn't sure if he honestly thought so at that delicate juncture or not. But I didn't say that. I didn't say anything.

"I really need you to tell me what she told you. Please."

Please. That was a new one. Another hash mark on the Chester 2.0 scorecard.

"She told me the two of you were in the war together, and that he saved your life twice. That you were more insecure about fighting a war than you wanted to admit, and Mike was more of a take-charge guy, and he took you under his wing. And that you looked up to him."

"That's all she said? I looked up to him?"

I got a bad case of the honests.

"No, not really. She said you loved him so much that it made you worry about your own . . . you know. Feelings."

At first he said nothing at all. We just sat there in all that blowing AC.

Then he said, "Why would she do that?"

"Out of anger, I think."

"Well, she got me again. I didn't think she could possibly hurt me any worse than she did all those years ago. But she just did it again. Go ahead," he said. "Go ahead and get it over with."

"Get what over with?"

"You know."

"I really don't."

"The part where you tell me I'm just as gay as you are and make fun of me for that."

"I don't think you're gay."

"Yes you do."

"No, I really don't."

I waited for some kind of response, but he was just staring at his legs the way he tended to do. Then he raised his eyes and turned his head like he was gazing out the window. But all the curtains were still down.

I thought it was interesting that when referring to himself he used the word "gay," rather than the mild slurs he used on me. I didn't say so, because I didn't think it would help. Because I didn't think he'd see the significance of it.

"Sometimes you just love somebody," I said. "Maybe it feels romantic and maybe it doesn't. Only you know that. But sometimes one person can just be an exception to the rule, and maybe it doesn't mean what you think it means. Especially when somebody saves your life and keeps you safe in a terrible situation like that. It's going to confuse your feelings around that whole thing. Did you ever feel that way about any other guys?"

"No. Of course not. Only Mike."

"Then I don't think you're gay."

"But maybe the reason I never felt that way about any other guy is because I made a conscious decision not to."

"No, it doesn't work that way. You can decide not to act on your feelings, but whatever you decided, the feelings would have been there. It does explain why you were so sure it's a choice, though. And I kind of appreciate knowing that."

I waited. But he didn't seem to have more to say. It felt as though the conversation might be over.

I stood to go.

"I'm going to go knock on her door and see if she'll talk to me."

"Here's what I still don't get," he said.

"What don't you get?"

"Why you didn't rag on me about it. You had a perfect chance to make fun of me and tell me I'm just like everything I criticized in you. And you let it go by."

"Yeah. I let it go by."

"But I did it to you."

"But I'm not like you," I said. "I've been trying to tell you that all along. Not everyone is mean and hateful. I'm not like that. And I hope I never am."

I moved for the door. Swung it open into the preheated oven that was Phoenix that day.

"Wait," Chester said.

"I'm losing patience with that."

"With what?"

"Being told to wait every time I try to get somewhere."

"I need to say something else before you go."

"What? We're letting all the cold out."

"I appreciate what you said just now, in a way. But I don't believe it. I think you just said it to seem like the bigger person. I think it was a lie."

"You think which part of everything was a lie? Except, even before you tell me, I can tell you it wasn't a lie. Because I don't lie to you."

"You lied to me about the bumper stickers."

"Wait. When did you see the bumper stickers?"

"Last time we stopped for gas. In my side-view mirror I could see their reflection in the convenience store window."

"Oh," I said. Which, as I think I mentioned, I'd been saying a lot. "Well. I didn't lie about them. Exactly. I said I didn't scrape them off. Which is true. These are just sitting on top of them. Okay, fine. I lied about the bumper stickers. But not about anything really important. What do you think I just lied about?"

"The part where you said what Sue told you doesn't make me gay. I think you think it does."

"You think wrong," I said, wilting in the heat. At that moment I figured if I never felt that kind of heat again it would be too soon. Maybe California had been a bad idea. "The reason I don't think so . . . you're going to find this hard to understand. I don't think so, because I don't see everything in black and white. Attraction is not a zero-sum game."

"I hate it when you talk in riddles."

"It's not all or nothing at all. That's what I'm saying. There can be shades of gray in a person's sexuality."

"You're right," he said, and just for a split second I thought I'd gotten through to him. "I find that hard to understand."

I shook my head and stepped out and closed the door behind me. He didn't tell me to wait.

I marched up the concrete walkway in the baking sun. It was something I was getting markedly tired of doing.

Sue was cleaning up the breakfast dishes. I saw her through the window. But, after laying eyes on me, she only turned her face away again.

I marched up to the door and knocked.

"What do you want, Lewis?" she called out.

"Are you speaking to me?"

"No."

"You just said, 'What do you want, Lewis?' And 'No.' That's a start. Maybe we can expand on that."

I saw her disappear from the sink. A minute later she opened the door. But only a crack.

"Remember when I said I give everybody one pass?"

"I do, actually. But what was my transgression, really? All I did was to be shocked."

"You were being judgy."

"But it was just my gut reaction. What was I supposed to do?"

"You could have kept your mouth shut."

"In hindsight, yes. I can see how that might have been a good plan."

She smiled just the tiniest bit. I could tell she was trying not to. It happened in spite of herself.

"All right," she said. "Fine. Come in."

———

"It was not my finest moment," she said.

Then we just left that sitting on the kitchen table for a minute while I decided if there were any words on the planet it might be safe to say.

"If he wants closure," she added, "he really should be having it out with Mike. Not me."

"I'm not sure why you say that."

"I'm not sure, either. I mean, I am. I know what I mean. I'm just not sure if I can put it into words. It's like . . . he thought so highly of Mike that he almost couldn't blame me for falling in love with him. It was just natural and believable to him that everybody would love Mike and nobody would love him. But he blamed Mike for not turning me away. For going ahead and taking me when I offered myself."

"Okay," I said.

"You're not saying much."

"I was practicing that 'keeping my mouth shut' thing we were talking about before. Do we even know where Mike is?"

"Yeah, I know where he lives. We keep in touch in a loose sort of way. He lives in LA. Venice Beach. Just what you need, right? Another long drive chasing another elusive bit of closure that he might or might not find."

"Yeah. Just what I need. Still, when you've got this much invested already . . ."

"Tell you what I'll do," she said. "I'll write out an apology to Chet. For every part of the thing that really was my fault. For all the stuff I look back on and see I could've done better. And I'll give it to you to give to him. And then I'll write out Mike's address and you two can move along."

"I think it would mean more in person."

"I'd get all tongue-tied."

"You could read it to him."

For a moment, there was no answer. No reaction.

Then she said, "Under one condition. If he promises to say not one single word the whole time."

I rose from the table.

"I'll go see if I can negotiate that," I said.

———

"We have to go get gas," I said as I stepped back inside the Winnebago.

I was leaving everything more emotionally complex off the table for the moment. Until I could catch my emotional breath.

"How much have we got?"

"It's getting down near a quarter of a tank. And you told me there has to be at least a quarter of a tank to keep the generator from shutting down."

"So we need to get me up?"

It really did seem like a huge undertaking when we were going maybe a mile.

"I'll just drive carefully," I said.

I plunked down in the driver's seat and pulled away from that curb for what felt like the first time in weeks. Right in that moment I almost couldn't remember my life before that curb, and what I could remember didn't feel real.

"So, you're going to tell me what happened in there?" Chester asked a block or two later. "Or you're just going to let me swing?"

"She's going to write you out an apology."

"For what exactly?"

"Everything she regrets, I guess. I talked her into reading it out loud to you so you hear the apology straight from the horse's mouth. I didn't think it would mean as much if it was just words on a page."

He didn't answer.

I pulled into the first gas station I saw, and filled it up with Ellie's credit card. It took forever, because the Winnie's tank was huge.

I watched shimmering heat waves rise off the pavement and felt the sweat trickle down my torso under my shirt. I vaguely wondered if it was hot enough to cause the gas to spontaneously combust.

Apparently not.

I climbed back in and fired up the engine, turning the dashboard AC up to full blast and training the vents onto my face.

Chester muttered something, but I couldn't make out the words over all that fan noise.

"What'd you say, Chester?"

"I said an apology would actually be nice."

"There's one big catch, though. You can't say anything."

"Should've known. There's always a catch."

I shifted into drive and headed back toward our curb.

"Is it worth it to you for the apology?"

"I think so. When are we doing this?"

"I don't know."

"You didn't ask?"

"I didn't figure she would know. She has to put her thoughts in writing. I didn't think she would have any idea how long that would take her."

"So what do we do now?" he asked.

He sounded like an impatient child asking if we were there yet.

"I guess we wait," I said.

"I hate waiting."

"I guess we wait . . . whether you hate it or not."

Chapter Sixteen:

You Want to Hear This

"I'm. So. Bored!" Chester shouted, nearly blowing out my eardrums on the final word.

"You don't have to yell," I said.

We were sitting across from each other in the Winnebago and I was reading an e-book on my phone. Granted, it was evening, and we had been waiting for hours. I didn't entirely fail to take his point.

"But I've just been sitting here for days. Doing nothing. How long do you think this damn thing is going to take her?"

"I think it's going to take as long as it takes, and I think you've been waiting for thirty-two years for an apology, so maybe you can just be patient a little while longer."

"But I don't know what to do with myself. I can't just stare at a phone for hours like you can."

"I'm reading a book," I said.

"No you're not. You're staring at your phone."

I sighed, and dropped my hands and the phone into my lap. The idea that I could read through his distractions was not panning out.

I reached over and showed him the screen of my phone.

"Oh," he said. "That's weird."

"Didn't you think to bring a book?"

"A what? You and your newfangled terms."

"I fail to see how refusing to read is something you should be joking about with pride. What do you do when you're at home?"

"Watch TV."

I looked around myself, sure I had seen one somewhere. I found it right where my eyes had left it, on a swinging bracket over the kitchen counter.

"What do you call that?" I asked, indicating it with a jerk of my thumb.

"It's a TV. But I can't watch anything on it because it's not hooked up to anything."

"Then what's it doing there?"

"When you stay in an RV park with full hookups, you can usually watch TV."

"You said RV parks were a waste of money and it's better to sleep in a Walmart parking lot."

"Unless you want to watch TV."

I sighed, and swiped the e-reader closed on my phone.

"What?" he said. "Why are you sighing and rolling your eyes at me?"

"Because every time I try to have a conversation with you I feel like you just take me around in circles."

His face took on a perturbed expression, and he opened his mouth to offer some sort of retort. I probably wouldn't have liked it, but I never got the chance to find out.

A hard knock came at the side door, and we both jumped the proverbial mile. I swear somebody could have shot off a gun next to the window and not gotten a bigger startled reaction from us. It struck me as odd, because we'd been waiting for hours for something to happen, and then, when it finally did, we were caught up in absolute nonsense and not expecting it.

I opened the door.

It was dark out on the street, but I could see Sue's face pretty well in the light that spilled out of the RV. She looked different than I was used to seeing her. More tentative and off balance. Not as though she were in charge of things in any way.

"Are you guys coming to *me*?" she asked, and her voice sounded just the way I described her face. "Or am I coming up there, or . . ."

"If you wouldn't mind," I said, "it would be really nice if you would come in here. It's an incredible project to get him in and out of here, and I feel like it gets more dangerous every time we do it."

She stepped inside without comment.

She looked at Chester. He did not look back.

I leaned over and hissed three whispered words into his ear.

"Not. A. Word."

"Where do I sit?" Sue asked me.

"You could sit next to me, but the light over me doesn't work. The light is good up in the cab."

I knew better than to suggest she sit close to Chester.

"Looking through the windshield, with my back to you guys?"

"No, those seats swivel."

I jumped up and attended to swiveling the passenger seat, but it wasn't as easy as the directions made it sound. The lever was finicky. There was grunting involved.

"There," I said when I had it more or less facing Chester.

She sat down.

She had a handful of papers in her grip, but I couldn't really tell how many, or if they were written or typed, one sided or two sided.

"I thought you said the light was good here."

"Oh. Sorry."

I leaned over her and switched on the dome light. It was positively blinding. I watched her blink too much for several beats.

"Yeah, that'll do it," she said. "Ready?"

"We've been ready for hours," Chester barked.

I caught his eye and warned him. Then I warned him out loud, for good measure.

"Chester . . ."

He dried up.

"Okay," she said. "Here goes.

"Chet. The first few sentences of this won't sound much like an apology. But before you get mad and decide I'm doing this all wrong, please try to bear with me until I can make my point.

"From the time we first started dating to the time our divorce was finalized, you hurt me every day. Little things, mostly. Little barbs, sharp things that came out of your mouth that made me feel invisible and small. And that's still on you. But it's my job to teach others how I want to be treated. Now I know that, but at the time I didn't know. I didn't know how to talk to you and you didn't know how to talk to me. There was no real communication between us. Then again, I knew your parents, and I knew my own, and I'm not sure who was supposed to be teaching us how to communicate. You can't teach somebody to do something if you don't even know how to do it yourself."

She stopped reading for a brief moment. Shifted uncomfortably in her seat. Scratched her head. I got the distinct impression that her discomfort had nothing to do with itches or seating.

She cleared her throat and continued.

"I didn't know how to say what I needed, or how to speak up for myself, so I just buried it all, over and over until there was no more room to stuff anything. And then, when I was ready to blow, I hurt you back. But my hurt was big.

"I want to say I didn't mean to, but that's only half true. I didn't start up with somebody else by accident. Then again I never woke up in the morning and thought, 'I think I'll rip Chet's heart out today.' I know I did, but it wasn't the objective.

"I know from personal experience that when somebody does you wrong, you can make yourself nuts going over and over it in your head.

163

And I'm not just referring to you when I say I've experienced that. It feels like the problem is that you know they did you wrong, but you can't get that confirmed outside your own mind. So you just keep making the case over and over again in your head. It can make you feel like you're cracking up after a while.

"So I'm going to validate your experience right now, for what that's worth.

"What I did to you was wrong. I couldn't help falling in love with somebody else, so I'm not really apologizing for it, but there's a right and a wrong way to handle a thing like that, and I handled it exactly wrong. I should have told you right up front, before anything happened, that the marriage wasn't working for me and I needed us to be apart. And there's really no excuse for my not doing that. It's just a scary conversation to have, and every time you think about having it, this little voice in your head says you can do it tomorrow. But I never did, and you had to find out the hard way on your own, and for that I sincerely apologize. It was pure cowardice on my part, and I hurt you by being a coward, and I'm sorry."

She paused, and glanced up at me, and I offered a deeply approving nod.

Then she looked back down at her letter again and I thought, *Wow. This was worth the wait.*

"As for the kids and trying to have any kind of amicable split, I didn't know how to deal with your rage, but that sounds like an excuse, and I'm trying not to make excuses. I was afraid of you. But again, if I could have been braver, I'd have saved you a lot of pain.

"It probably doesn't help to say it, but I do think I learned a lesson from all those mistakes. Nowadays I'm almost too brave and too outspoken for my own good, but of course that came too late to help your situation.

"I understand that you're reaching the end of your life, so I forgive you for all the small hurts, and I hope you can forgive me for the big one. I don't insist that you do, though. I offer you my forgiveness before you die whether I get any back or not, because it's my last chance, and if I decide I want to do it later, then that's probably going to be too late."

She looked up, but not directly at Chester and not directly at me. Her face looked, more than anything else, profoundly embarrassed.

She indicated the paper by holding it up and waving it.

"And then it says on here, 'Sincerely, Your ex, Susan.' But I guess I don't need to read that part, because you're sitting right there in front of me and you can see me with your own eyes. It's not like you don't know who the letter was from."

She fell silent, and the moment grew very still and very long. I didn't speak, because it wasn't my place to do so. Chester didn't speak, presumably because he'd been firmly instructed not to.

He was wringing his hands, looking down at them the whole time, as though it was an activity that required intense concentration.

"I'll go," Sue said.

And she jumped up.

"I'll walk you out."

Which was a silly thing to say to someone when the door is less than three steps away from any conceivable direction.

We stepped down onto the dark sidewalk together, and I closed the door behind us. The air was still surprisingly warm.

"You think that was okay?" she asked me.

"I think you did great."

"Thanks. I like this non-judgy side of you better."

"But it's not non-judgy at all. I just judged your performance and decided you did great. Isn't it funny how we never object to that kind of judgment?"

"Humans, am I right? It wasn't the reaction I expected from him."

"In what way?"

"He didn't say anything."

"Is that a joke?"

165

"No. Why would it be a joke?"

"You specifically told me to tell him that under no circumstances was he to say a word."

"Oh, that's right," she said. "I did, didn't I?"

She held a small scrap of paper out to me in the dark.

"What's this?"

"Mike's address in Venice Beach."

"Oh. Thanks."

I took it from her and stashed it in my shirt pocket.

"You going there?"

"I don't know. I actually haven't broached the subject with him yet."

"But you will. Broach it. Right?"

"Yes. I will. And if he wants to go, we'll go, and if he doesn't want to go, we won't. But do me a favor and don't call Mike and warn him, okay? Let us ambush him like we did to you. It's so much more fun that way."

"Yeah. Fun. Big fun. Okay. You'll sleep and drive in the morning, right?"

"I think that's best."

"Maybe call me when you get home. Let me know everything's okay."

"I don't have your number."

"Give me your phone."

I slipped it out of my pocket and handed it to her, and she keyed her information in and handed it back.

"There. Now you have it. Drive safe."

Then she walked up her path and disappeared into the house.

When I got back inside the RV, Chester was still speechless. Still wringing and twisting his hands and watching himself do it.

"You okay?" I asked.

"No."

"Want to talk about it?"

"No."

But then, a handful of seconds later, he did anyway.

"I made her feel small," he said. Purely on a volunteer basis. His voice was . . . something I'd never heard from him before. I don't really know how to describe it. "I never thought she was small. I thought she was everything. But I didn't tell her that. I didn't make her feel like she was everything. I only told her things that made her feel small. And I scared her. And I didn't even get to tell her I was sorry. She got to apologize, but I wasn't allowed to say anything."

"Hold that thought," I said. "Wait right here."

Which is a ridiculous thing to say to someone who couldn't move far if you begged him. I was being silly and ridiculous a lot that night. Even more so than usual.

I ran down the steps into the night and sprinted up to Sue's door. I rapped hard, and breathed hard while I waited.

When she opened the door, she looked peeved.

"Now what?" she barked. "Okay, sorry, but you must admit that seemed like a perfect ending a minute ago. This is becoming the visit that wouldn't die."

"Chester has something he needs to say to you."

"I thought we agreed—"

"Sue," I said, cutting her off. "I've heard this. You want to hear it. Trust me."

She sighed deeply.

"If you're wrong," she said, "I will literally punch you."

Then she followed me back out to the curb.

When we stepped inside, Chester was still staring at his hands and wringing. But when he saw she was back he looked up, right into her face, and she didn't look away.

"Tell her exactly what you told me just now," I said to him. "No ad-libs. No tangents."

He still was staring straight into her face. She still was not averting her gaze.

"I didn't think you were small," he said to her. "I thought the sun rose and set in you. I thought you were everything. But I didn't make you feel like everything. I made you feel small. And I scared you. I think I scared you because I was so scared all the time. I'm not sure why those two things go together, but it feels like they do. I just think they do."

"I think they do, too," she said.

He looked down at his hands again, and I got the strange sensation that he was trying to disappear. Maybe even that he was succeeding.

We hung there near the door together, she and I, in case there was more. He hadn't actually explicitly said "I'm sorry." But no more words seemed forthcoming. And the tone and intention of the message had been pretty clear.

When it was obvious he planned to say nothing more, she leaned in, took hold of him by both temples, and kissed him briefly on the forehead.

"However much time you've got left," she told him in a quiet voice, "pack as much living into it as you can."

She patted me on the cheek as she passed by.

Then she slipped out the door and she was gone.

Chapter Seventeen:

Chester 1.0

Morning found that Chester was not a changed man. I guess that kind of transformation is always asking too much of the world.

At first he seemed quiet and almost chastened, if a bit complainy.

"I'm tired, Lewis," he said when I moved him up to the passenger seat.

I wasn't quite sure how or why, since he'd barely moved for days, but I didn't question the statement, since I've never had cancer.

He seemed to read my mind anyway.

"It's the moving me around," he said.

"We can do less of that."

I belted him in, sat down in the driver's seat, and started the engine. I let it run awhile to warm up.

"And the lifting myself onto the bedpan."

"I'll lift you if I have to."

"I hate to ask you to do that."

"We'll do what we have to do," I said.

I pulled away from the curb and followed directions on my map app through the city to the I-10, even though I knew he had a big decision to make before we got there. We were actually already headed west, away from home. But there was no need to bring that up.

"I hurt," he said.

"The painkillers will kick in soon."

"They don't give me enough of them. If you would let me take more, it would help."

"First of all, I can't let you take more without permission from one of your doctors. Second, if I let you take more, you'll run out before we get home."

"Maybe Dr. Walker would phone in a prescription to a pharmacy on the road. If you called his office."

"It's not out of the question, but let's see how you feel after your morning dose kicks in."

"Yeah, I guess. Okay. Such a long drive home. How long do you think it'll take?"

"Depends. We have some choices to make."

"At least three days, though," he said.

"Probably more like four."

"Maybe we should have flown after all."

"You said people with lung cancer can't fly."

"Oh. Right."

He turned his head and looked out the window at Phoenix proper flashing by. We were on the 60 West, and I peered at the map on my phone and watched the I-10 approaching, knowing we still had to decide on our direction before we got there.

"That actually wasn't true," he said. "I don't know that people with lung cancer can't fly. Maybe they can't, but I don't know. Nobody ever told me I couldn't."

"If you want to fly home, I'll put you on a plane. Say the word. I'll drive home by myself."

"No, I can't do that. I can't make you drive all that way on your own."

I wanted to laugh out loud. I wanted to tell him he overestimated the value of his own company. I didn't.

"I would be absolutely fine," I said.

"Besides. How would I get home from the airport?"

"Car service? Shuttle? If it was some kind of bus, it might even have a wheelchair lift."

"Okay," he said. "Okay. I'm lying again. I'm afraid to fly. And you just shut up about it, too. Don't even start with me. Everybody's afraid of something."

I pulled off the highway at the last exit before the I-10 and onto a side street. I found a spot at the curb. Shifted the Winnie into park. Unfortunately he seemed to think I'd done that to give him some kind of dressing-down, and that only made him more combative.

"You lie too," he said. "Don't even try to tell me you don't. You shouldn't have put on those bumper stickers. They're ridiculous. I shouldn't have to ride around in my own RV with those on the back. It's embarrassing."

"If you want, I'll go peel them off right now."

"Well, it doesn't really matter. You're driving. It's a reflection on you, not me. I'm just saying you were wrong to do that."

I could have been detail oriented and overly specific and said *Anna* was wrong to do it, not me. But I hadn't stopped her. So that mostly would have been a weaselly dodge.

"You're right," I said. "I was wrong to do that."

He seemed to struggle with that for a minute, but then he came up fighting. To say my admission of guilt didn't mollify him would be an understatement.

"See, that's what's so weird about you, Lewis. It's just completely abnormal. When somebody gets on you for doing something like that, you're supposed to defend yourself. It's supposed to be a fight."

"I don't want to fight."

"I know," he said. "It's weird. There's something about you that's not quite right."

We sat quietly for a minute while I tried to think how to phrase my important question.

"Why aren't we driving?" he asked.

"You have to decide on a direction before we get to the I-10."

"Wow, you're really losing it, Lewis. It's east. Home is east."

Speaking of losing it, I noticed that he hadn't caught on to our direction by the angle of the morning sun, which would have been easy. When the sun is behind you in the morning . . .

"Right, home is east. But you have to decide if you want to make one other stop first. You came out here for closure, right?"

"Yeah, and I got it."

"With Sue. But there might be more closure out there for you."

He pondered that statement for about the count of three, his forehead furrowed.

Then he said, "You better be talking about my kids."

"I'm not."

"I don't want to talk about him with you, Lewis. It's none of your business. When are you going to get it through that thick skull of yours that it's none of your business?"

"We don't need to talk about it. I just want to know if you want me to drop you there for a visit before I take you home."

"Drop me where, Lewis? Use your head. We don't even know where he is."

I pulled the slip of paper out of my shirt pocket. I didn't hand it to him or show it to him. Just let it dangle there in the fingers of my right hand, which was draped over the steering wheel.

"I know where he is," I said.

That simple statement brought on lots—and I do mean lots—of silence.

He turned his face away and looked out the window. I turned the dashboard AC up high and aimed the vents at us, because I sensed we'd be there for a while.

—

Six minutes later I decided that if the silence was ever going to be broken, I'd have to break it myself. And I was glancing at my phone at regular intervals, so when I say six minutes, I seriously mean six minutes.

At four minutes I had picked up the phone, keyed in the address in Venice Beach, and hit "Directions." It was almost four hundred miles and about six and a half hours away.

"So, what are we thinking?" I asked Chester. "I figure it's time to get on the road one way or the other. I worry about the engine overheating if we sit here idling and running the air conditioner much longer. And if I turn it off, we'll roast. Time to know what we're doing."

"Where would we have to go?"

"Venice Beach."

"Where the hell is that? Italy?"

"Not that Venice. Greater Los Angeles area."

"How long does it take to drive there?"

"Maybe seven hours with a stop for food and gas."

After that brief discussion of logistics he fell silent again.

I opened my mouth to encourage some mode of action on his part, but he beat me to it.

"I'm guessing you have some kind of ulterior motive for suggesting this."

"What possible kind of ulterior motive could I have?"

"You know."

"I don't know."

"Encourage me to explore my feelings so you can tell me they're just like yours."

"Chester," I said. "Listen up. I couldn't care less how you feel about what person. I'm offering to drive you there. Nothing more. You don't have to tell me what happens or how you feel about what happens. I won't make any comment. I'm just asking if you want me to take you there. Yes or no. It wasn't even my idea."

"What do you mean it wasn't your idea? Then whose idea was it?"

"Sue suggested it. She said she thought you needed closure with him more than with her."

"Why would she say that? Did she say why she said that?"

"She said a little bit about it, yeah. She said she thought you blamed him more than you blamed her. She said you figured everybody would love Mike, so you hardly blamed her for it, but that you blamed him for taking her up on the offer."

"That's . . . actually true," he said. "But I can't go there. I can't see him. I can't talk to him. I wouldn't know what to say. And it's wrong of you to push me to do it."

I popped my cap over that. I raised my voice at him.

"I'm not pushing you to do anything, Chester! If you say you want me to take you there, I will. If you say you want me to take you home, I will. The only thing I'm pushing you to do is make a decision while we still have a functioning engine!"

In the silences, including the one that followed my tirade, we could hear the cars rushing by on the freeway, reminding us it was where we needed to be. Whether the I-10 westbound or back the way we'd come, we needed to get on the road.

"What would you say to him if you were me?" he asked.

Which of course was a serious departure from the whole Mike situation being none of my business and something I was not permitted to talk about. I didn't point that out, because it felt like he was making progress.

"I guess I would handle it the way you did with Sue. But, you know. More levelheaded. Less yelling. Ask him why things happened the way they did. Try to be honest about how it felt to you."

"I can't tell him how I felt."

"Actually I meant how you felt about his taking your wife away from you."

"Oh. That kind of feelings. Well. I'm not sure. Maybe I could do that. But I don't know. It sounds hard."

"Most of the best things in life are," I said.

I was hoping that would wake him up. Why did I still hope? I had no idea.

"I still don't know."

I remembered Anna exploding at me in that Italian restaurant because I couldn't make a decision. I finally understood how frustrating that can be.

Instead of responding in words I shifted into drive, made an awkward three-point turn on that side street, and headed for the freeway. Chester watched in shocked silence.

I followed the signs for the I-10 West.

"What are you doing, Lewis?"

"I'm driving."

"So now you're forcing me to go?"

"I'm not forcing you to do anything. Tell me to turn around at any point, I'll turn around. But somebody had to do something, and it didn't feel like it was going to be you."

Chester apparently had nothing to say in reply.

I watched the mile markers, because I was curious to see how far we'd get.

A little past the eleven-mile mark, he piped up.

"Turn around."

I was disappointed, but I did nothing to express that.

There was an exit coming up in just a couple of hundred feet. I moved right and kept my right-hand turn signal on.

Just before I was about to actually swing right to follow the exit, more words burst out of him. They were loud words, hovering just at the edge of panic.

"No, don't turn around! Keep going."

I switched off my turn signal, and we kept going.

———

We didn't talk at all until we reached the Colorado River, which marked the transition from Arizona to California. The state line was actually in the middle of the river.

I think that's when I was finally willing to believe that he wasn't going to tell me to turn back.

"I think you made a good decision," I said.

Chester only grunted in reply.

"I'm glad if I said anything that helped."

"You didn't," he said.

It was pure Chester 1.0, and I shouldn't have been disappointed. I should have been used to it by then. But it's hard to usher in a little progress and then watch it fly away again.

"Whatever," I said.

"No, not whatever. It was something Sue said that helped me decide."

"What did she say?"

"You don't remember?"

"She said a lot of things, Chester."

"Right before she walked out of the RV for the last time. She told me however much time I had left, I should pack as much living into it as I can."

"Right," I said, watching the river slide by underneath the highway. "I do remember that now. I think that was some pretty sound advice."

———

I didn't push him to talk. I didn't talk much myself.

But there was this long, barren stretch of California desert between Blythe and Indio. Not so much like New Mexico or Arizona. It wasn't red rock scenery and, although I found it pleasant, it wasn't all that visually arresting. It was just sand colored for the most part, with low, scrubby brush.

The driving had taken on a serious tedium.

About halfway through that landscape, he just seemed to split open.

"What if he's horrible to me?" he asked.

I opened my mouth to speak, but he kept going.

"What if he tells me I'm just a giant piece of crap and he never gave a damn about me one way or another?"

"Well. That would sting."

"Ya think?"

"I think that would weigh heavily on you for the rest of your life. How many weeks d'you figure that'll be again?"

Surprisingly, he didn't get indignant. One corner of his mouth twisted into a sarcastic half grin.

"Yeah, I guess I see your point," he said.

"Here's how I see it, Chester. Since you asked my opinion." *Mark this day on your calendar,* I thought. "Even if he hurts you, I think that's going to hurt less than lying on your deathbed thinking, 'Damn it, I didn't even try.' One way you're disgusted and disappointed with him. The other way you're disgusted and disappointed with yourself. Disappointing yourself is the worst."

"I'm used to it," he said.

It was a surprising admission coming from Chester. And I found myself not wanting to let it go by. Not wanting to coddle him with false pity or convince him it wasn't true when we both knew it was.

I got a little heated up about it.

"Then get *unused* to it, Chester. Just damn well get *unused* to it."

He snorted dismissively.

"Little late for that. Don't you think?"

"Yeah. It is, Chester. It's a little late. But it's not *too* late. Know how I know? I'll tell you how I know. Because you're not dead yet."

I waited for him to dismiss me and ridicule me. And argue back at me.

He never did.

Chapter Eighteen:

Watching You

I want to say I didn't know the I-10 went straight through the heart of downtown LA. The truth is I did know—sort of. I'd seen it on my phone map, but I hadn't really registered it, because I saw no reason why it mattered. I was a newbie at LA driving. I didn't realize that you never go through the city proper if you can possibly avoid it.

It was before one o'clock in the afternoon. One would tend to think, if one didn't know the territory, that it wouldn't be rush hour. Surprise! It's always rush hour in LA. Every damn minute of every damn day.

We were just sitting there in bumper-to-bumper traffic, holding perfectly still. Then rolling forward a few feet. Then holding perfectly still.

My world was an endless sea of brake lights.

And that kind of motion did *not* put Chester to sleep, which was unfortunate to say the least.

Now and then the traffic would move forward and I'd be a little slow to start up, and another car would simply *materialize* in front of me, its driver cutting me off to take the space I'd left open only for a brief second. And I mean with inches to spare.

After the third time it happened I said, "The drivers here are insane!"

Chester said, "They're just doing what they have to do." As if he were an expert on LA traffic. As if he'd lived there all his life.

"What kind of attitude is that?"

"It's *my* attitude."

"I can't argue with that, actually."

"It's like this . . . ," he began.

And I said, "Oh good. More mansplaining."

"More what?"

"Never mind."

"It's like this," he began again. "It's a dog-eat-dog world on the freeways out here. And so you have to do what you have to do. Otherwise they'll roll right over you. You can't be soft."

I opened my mouth to tell him he was an idiot, and that people like him were the whole problem. But what would that do to improve anything? That would just have been him pulling me down to his level again.

"You would have found out soon enough," he said. "Since you and your fruitfriend were going to move here."

Speaking of moving, we weren't. Not even an inch. So I got to turn my head and glare at him.

"How did you know Tim and I were going to move here?"

"I heard you talking about it on your front porch with some of the other members of your extended fruit bowl."

The barbs were sticking under my skin, but so far I was letting them go by.

"We weren't going to move *here*. We were thinking about Santa Barbara. Or possibly San Francisco."

"San Francisco!" he cried.

Of course, I was not surprised. I'd known as soon as it was out of my mouth that I'd given him the opening, and that I should have seen it coming.

"Mecca!" he fairly sang. "The holy pilgrimage for your people!"

I slammed my palm down hard on the dashboard and he jumped.

"All right, that's enough, Chester! What is wrong with you, anyway? You sat right in this Winnebago and told me you ribbed me and ribbed me and ribbed me about being gay, but then when I got a shot at you, I let it go by. And now you're still doing it?"

He drew back into himself then, and got quiet. Needless to say, it was a blessing and a relief.

About twenty minutes later, when we'd managed to crawl three or four miles, he meekly spoke up.

"What time do you think we'll get there with all this traffic?"

"At the rate we're going," I said, "it should be sometime next month."

———

An hour later we had managed to move west of the heart of the city, and traffic thinned out some. We were doing thirty miles per hour and it felt like flying.

I took the cutoff for the 187, which was really just another way of saying Venice Boulevard. From there it was a straight shot to the beach. My map app said it was less than seven miles.

"How much farther?" Chester asked.

"Not far. We're almost there."

"Maybe we should turn back."

"You've got to be kidding me. Please tell me you're kidding me."

"You told me you'd turn around anytime I asked you to."

"After everything we just went through to get here?"

He didn't answer, and I didn't stop driving.

A minute or two later he said, "I'm scared to do this, Lewis."

"I know you are. I don't blame you."

"You don't?"

"Of course not. I'm sure I would be, too, in your situation. But I think you need to do it. I'm not going to force you to do it, but I'm going to drive you to this guy's house, and we're going to sit there for a while and see if you can manage it."

No reply.

By then I'm pretty sure we were in Venice, and the scenery had begun to change. There was an atmosphere to it. Something I hadn't experienced before. It was . . . I'm not sure how to describe it. It was like this informal circus, performing spontaneously on the street.

The streets were crowded with people on foot, on inline skates, on skateboards. Walking dogs in costumes. Riding bikes one handed, holding surfboards under the other arm. The buildings were covered with brightly colored graffiti and murals, and it was almost hard to tell which was which. If you raised your eyes, you saw palm trees everywhere. If you lowered them, you saw homeless encampments. Everywhere.

"Mike can't live here," Chester said.

"He does, though."

"But this is like a hippy place. Mike's not a hippy."

"I got the address from Sue. She said they keep in touch."

"I didn't need to know *that*," he said.

I turned left onto a small street because my map directions told me to. But it didn't seem to have an outlet, and I was uneasy about turning the boat around on it, because it was so narrow.

"Your destination is in three hundred feet on the right," I told Chester. Because that's what my phone told *me*.

"No, this can't be it."

"But it is."

We rolled up to a fence. Probably there was a house behind it, but I couldn't see anything but rooflines. The fence was about six feet high, made with vertical wood boards. They were painted with a complex mural that was very purple and contained multiple pairs of eyes, along with some orbs that seemed to depict outer space. It was a long fence, covering most of the block. I figured there must be more than one house behind it.

"You sure this is it?"

"Positive."

"I don't think I can do this."

"Sit awhile and decide."

I turned off the engine and pulled on the parking brake. Then I walked around inside the Winnie, opening all the windows. The ocean was close by—I could smell it—and the air that blew through the RV was cool. It was such a relief.

I sat down on the couch on the driver's side—what would normally be considered Chester's side—and closed my eyes.

A minute or two later I heard Chester say, "What? I can't hear you."

"I didn't say anything, Chester."

"Not you. I was talking to *that* guy."

I saw no one. It worried me slightly, thinking Chester was literally delusional. But I stepped up into the cab to see, and there was a small, balding man pressing his face up against the driver's window, his breath fogging up the glass. It startled me, but I tried not to let on.

I dug the key out of my pocket, slipped it into the ignition, turned it to accessory, and powered the window halfway down.

"Can I help you?"

"I know who you are," he said.

"I doubt that."

"Oh, but I do. You're those people who come around in a moving van and rob people's houses. The neighborhood watch folks warned us about you."

I just stared at him for a moment, wondering. Wondering . . . so many things.

I turned my face to Chester, who only shrugged.

"That's not him," I said. "Right?"

"Oh hell no."

I turned back to the small, odd man.

"This is not a moving van. It's a Winnebago."

"Then what are you doing on this street? You don't live here."

"We're here to see Mike."

"You're here to rob Mike's house?"

"No. We're not here to rob Mike's house. We're not here to rob anybody. We just want to talk to him."

"Oh, you're cops."

By that time I was getting irritated.

"No, we're not cops. What kind of cops show up in a Winnebago?"

"Undercover cops. Cops who don't want you to know they're cops."

"We're not any kind of cops. It's not illegal to park on a street even if you don't live there. And it's not unusual. We just came to see Mike."

"Mike's not home," he said. Then he got a desperate look on his face, as if he'd just accidentally handed the keys to Mike's house over to burglars. "But he'll be home any minute now."

He did that gesture. That "I'm watching you" thing. Two fingers out wide like a peace sign, pointing first to his own eyes, then in the general direction of mine.

He slithered away, looking once over his shoulder and repeating the watching gesture. Then he disappeared through a gate in the crazy fence. I hadn't realized there was a gate there, because it was so much a part of the mural.

"I think I should go see if Mike's home," I said.

"That guy just said he wasn't."

"Right. I'm thinking that guy might be an unreliable narrator."

"Jeez, Lewis. Half the time when you talk I have no idea what you're saying."

"I'm saying he might've told us Mike wasn't home because he thought we were cops."

"But then he said he'll be back any minute."

"Because he thought we were burglars."

"We can't very well be both."

"Don't tell me. Tell him."

I opened the driver's door to step out.

"Wait," Chester said.

This time it didn't surprise me in the least. I'd finally gotten used to it. I just paused there, half in and half out, trying not to sigh.

"What will you say if he's home?"

"Probably just that I brought somebody he used to know, and that you were hoping for a visit."

I waited there in the silence for a fair amount of time. Possibly a full minute. Because technically he could still say, "Turn around." I'd promised him that.

He said nothing, so I stepped out into the street with my phone in my hand, found the crazy hidden gate, and stepped through.

There were three houses behind it. All wood, all ancient and funky. A simple dirt path branched out in three directions. I checked the house number on my phone, then looked up again. The little man was watching me out his window.

I followed the path up onto Mike's porch.

The house was weathered unpainted wood. The windows on the porch side were small and round, like portholes. Mobiles of driftwood and shells hung from the porch roof, and a wet suit hung on a hanger in the corner. It was not currently dripping wet, but there was a wet spot on the dry-rotted porch boards underneath it.

I looked for a doorbell before realizing I was standing next to an Asian gong, with a striker on a stick. I took hold of the striker and rang the gong, and it was much louder than I'd expected. It vibrated my eardrum in waves.

I waited. And I waited. And I waited.

Mike was not home.

I walked back to the RV. All the way through the gate the little man was still watching me.

—

"What time is it?" Chester asked.

He was still in the passenger seat because it would have been so hard to move him. We'd been waiting for close to an hour.

I pulled my phone out of my shirt pocket and tapped it awake.

"A little after four."

"How long are we going to wait?"

"I don't know. I would think at least till six or after. He probably works a regular day job."

"He's old enough to be retired."

"Not everybody can afford to retire."

"You should call my doctor's office and see if they'll give me more painkillers."

"It's too late. I'll have to do it in the morning."

"It's not too late. It's not even four."

"Here in California it's not even four. Back home in Buffalo it's nearly seven."

"Oh," Chester said. "I forgot about that."

"I'm not sure they'd talk to me anyway. I mean . . . they'd *talk* to me. But I'm not sure if they'd prescribe on my say-so. What I should do is call Ellie and have her call your doctor and ask."

I waited for some kind of reply, but nothing came back to me. So I took out my phone and searched for Ellie's number.

"Lewis," Chester said. He was speaking in a half whisper, and his voice sounded positively iced over with panic.

"What?"

"That's him. That's him, Lewis. I'd know him anywhere."

I sat up quickly and looked out the window. But I couldn't see anyone. So I opened the side door and stepped out.

I was feeling a little shocked, as though I'd just been wakened from a sound sleep. Somehow I hadn't been expecting Mike to show up. I

186

know that's silly. I should have been expecting it. Of course I should have. But I'd been stuck in that endless waiting mode, and somehow I only expected more waiting.

I found myself face to face with a man who seemed to have been headed for the gate before I'd cut him off. He stopped, and we just stood there on the narrow sidewalk considering each other for a few beats.

He possibly could have been Chester's age, but I would have made him to be in his late fifties. His hair was collar length, curly at the ends, and barely even gray. Just a few threads of silver in otherwise darkness. He was wearing jeans faded nearly to white, and a crisp white shirt. Its cuffs were rolled back two turns, and his forearms were thickly hairy. His face was aggressively tanned and deeply lined. He was several inches taller than me. Well over six feet.

"Mike?"

He tilted his head slightly, the way a dog might do if he failed to understand.

"Do I know you?"

"No. You don't. But I brought someone here to see you. Someone you know. You haven't seen him in a long time, but I think you'll remember."

I walked him up to the passenger window where Chester sat frozen in panic. Really classic "deer in the headlights" stuff.

We just stood there for a couple of beats.

Then Mike said, "I'm sorry. I don't . . ."

I made a cranking motion to Chester, to get him to lower the window, but he only threw his hands into the air. I'd forgotten that he couldn't do that without the keys.

I ran around the front, digging the keys out of my pocket as I went. I jumped into the driver's seat, fumbled the key into the ignition, and turned it to accessory.

I waited for Chester to power his window down, but he never did. He was frozen.

I did it for him.

"I'm sorry," Mike said through the open window. "You have to help me out here."

"Mike," Chester said. He sounded breathless and quiet. "It's me. Chet."

"Chet?" Mike asked. It was clear from his tone of voice that he considered what he'd just said to be impossible.

Then he said nothing. And did nothing. And made no move. He was frozen now, too. Everybody was frozen. Time was frozen. The whole world was frozen.

"Chet?" he said again. "Chet Wheeler? Is that really you? I can't even recognize you. What happened to you, man?"

I could tell by his face that he regretted that last question. That he was speaking on autopilot. I could see him wince as it came out, but it came out all the same.

"Cancer," Chester said.

I thought he sounded like he was trying not to cry, but it was only one word, and I could have been wrong.

"I never thought I'd see you again."

"Well I never thought so, either."

"You want to come in? Are you gonna try to kill me?"

"It's really hard for me to get down from here," Chester said. "I'm in a wheelchair, and getting in and out of it is hard."

"Maybe we could both get you down," I said.

"Or I could just come up there," Mike said. "Since you obviously couldn't kill me even if you tried."

He disappeared from the window and tried the side door, which was still unlocked. He stepped up into the rig.

"You have to go, Lewis," Chester said. "This is between me and Mike. You can't be here."

"Fine. No problem. Just call my cell when you want me back."

I started to step down to the street, but he did it again.

"Wait."

"What?"

"Turn my seat around. Otherwise I can't see him."

"Or I can do that," Mike said. "Just show me how."

"Yeah, okay," Chester said. "Go away now, Lewis."

I stepped down and headed out on foot.

I did not take offense.

Chapter Nineteen:

Cool

I walked down to the beach, which was not far, and took a stroll along the boardwalk. Except it wasn't really a boardwalk. Not the way I think of a boardwalk. I mean, boardwalks should have boards, right? This was just a wide, flat concrete street with no cars.

Shops on one side. Informal vendors on the beach side, under umbrellas or square awnings. Tents and impromptu dwellings made of blue tarps everywhere. Palm trees as far as the eye could see.

And there were street performers. Dancers and jugglers and acrobatic tumblers. A guy playing guitar who probably belonged in his own living room. A woman playing violin who might've played in a symphony orchestra if life had been more fair.

I walked out onto the sand and just stood there, looking at the Pacific Ocean—which I had never seen before—and listening to the rhythmic sound of the flat, shallow waves coming in. Then I plunked down with my butt in the sand and just sat for a time.

I pulled my phone out of my pocket and called Ellie.

She picked up on the second ring.

"Lewis," she said, sounding a little breathless. "Thank goodness. I haven't heard from you for days."

"I'm sorry. Should I have called more often? We're on the road."

"Well, I know *that*," she said. "I knew you made it to Phoenix, because I could watch the charges come in on the card. Besides, I talked to Mom."

"I'm sorry if I worried you. You could always have called *me*."

"Not worried, exactly," she said. "I'm just glad for a progress report. I trusted you to let me know if there was anything that needed knowing."

As she was finishing up that last sentence, I heard a voice over my left shoulder.

"Hey buddy?"

I looked around and up to see a battered young man standing over me. He looked to be maybe seventeen, and probably hadn't shaved or gotten his hair cut for a year.

I pointed to the phone, so he could see I was busy. He nodded and said no more. But he didn't go away. He just hung there, making me uneasy.

"So is my dad doing okay?" I heard Ellie ask.

"He's getting by."

"Is he there? Can I talk to him?"

"He's not here. Exactly. He's in the Winnebago. I'm sitting on the beach."

"The beach? What are you doing at the beach?"

"Getting out of his hair so he can talk to Mike."

A long silence.

I could feel that guy still hanging over me, so I whipped my head around and glared at him, hoping he'd get the message. He didn't. Or, at least, he didn't act on it.

"Mike . . . as in, my stepfather Mike?"

"Yeah," I said. "That Mike."

"That's unexpected."

"It was your mom's idea. She didn't tell you that part, huh? They're talking in the Winnebago and I took a walk to get out of the way."

"Sounds like a good plan. You might want to get out of the state."

I let that go by.

"So, listen. Here's what I called to ask you. He wants to increase his pain meds. And that's not a decision I can make on my own. But I've got to tell you—in my opinion, he's not faking. I really do think the meds aren't touching his pain at this point. He's having a tough time. He wanted me to call his doctor, but I can't imagine his doctor prescribing anything on my say-so. I'm not blood family. I thought you could call and see if he'll send a prescription to a pharmacy on the road."

"Why can't he just take more of the ones he's already got? If the doctor says it's okay, that is."

"If we do that, he'll run out before we get home."

"Okay. Yeah. Okay then. I can do that. I'll call in the morning and let you know how it goes."

"Thanks, Ellie."

"Any idea how it's going with him and Mike?"

"None at all. I'm staying clear."

"Probably best. I'll call you."

We said our goodbyes and ended the call, and I jumped up to face the guy behind me, which I'd been wanting to do for a long time.

"What?"

"Got any money, buddy? Even a dollar or two would help."

"No," I said. "I'm sorry. I'm not carrying any cash at all."

It was a flat-out lie. I was carrying some cash in my wallet. It was everything I had left from my final paycheck and my rent party, and when I got home, I'd have to make rent, and I wasn't giving any of it away.

"Nobody carries cash anymore. It's too bad. But there's an ATM right by that yogurt shop. You could *get* some."

"No, I can't. It's not even my credit card."

"Oh, you stole somebody's credit card?"

"No, I didn't—"

"It's cool. I'm not judging."

"I didn't—"

"Don't worry about it, buddy. I get it. You're in need, too. It's cool." He moved a few steps off, which felt like a relief. Then he turned and waved at me. "Be cool," he said.

I stood there watching him go, thinking, *Does anybody really say "cool" anymore?* Well, one person still did, anyway.

I sat down in the sand again.

I people-watched until nobody seemed interesting. Or until everybody seemed equally interesting, which made them uninteresting. Then I read a book on my phone until I started worrying about running the battery down.

I got up and bought a falafel from a storefront shop, and ate it standing up so I couldn't get sand in it.

Then I sat on the beach again.

I was feeling more than a little bit adrift.

My mind went back to Tim in that moment. Was he somewhere nearby, enjoying his new life in California with our shared funds? Was he seeing someone new? Would I ever wrap my mind around what went wrong with him? Would the part of me that had driven him away, the failing I had yet to identify, ruin my next attempt at love as well?

And then, the hardest question of all.

Why was I crossing the country helping somebody else find closure with his past when I barely understood my own?

It was not a fun evening inside my head.

———

Hours had passed. Literally hours.

The sun had dipped closer and closer to the ocean horizon, then disappeared completely. Lights came on in the streetlights along the boardwalk, and glowed in the shops behind me.

I checked my phone to be sure the ringer wasn't turned off. I checked the "Recents" list. Nobody had been trying to call.

I started worrying that Chester didn't know where I kept that new cell phone, or had somehow unlearned how to use it.

I started worrying that it was all going very badly and it was my fault for pushing him into it.

I decided to walk back and see if I could tell how things were going without getting intrusively close.

When I turned the corner onto Mike's street, I could see inside the Winnebago perfectly. The curtains were up, just as I'd left them, and all the interior lights had been turned on. I could see the back of Mike's head. He was sitting on the couch on the passenger side. Chester's face was blocked from my view.

I was tired, so I sat with my back up against a light pole, faced away from the RV. I closed my eyes, which it might not have been safe to do in that neighborhood.

One of two things happened.

Here's what I know for sure: I heard a car door slam, and I whipped my head around to see Mike walk out of the Winnebago and through the strange gate in the strange fence. Here's what I'm not sure of: whether Mike stepped out of the vehicle mere seconds after I closed my eyes, or whether I'd fallen asleep without really feeling it.

My phone rang in my pocket. I pulled it out and saw Chester on the caller ID.

I picked up.

"Hey, Chester," I said.

"I need the bedpan. You need to hurry. Are you far away?"

"No, not far at all."

"Good. Hurry. I told him to go. Because I needed to use the bedpan. But I didn't tell him that was why. That would have been humiliating."

"I'll be right there."

I trotted down the street and stepped inside.

"Oh good," he said. "You're here. You need to drive someplace."

"I thought you—"

"Not here. It can't be here."

I started up the engine and tried to get us out of there.

The following minutes were deeply stressful for me. I'm guessing they were for Chester as well. But, in that moment, I had to concentrate on me.

The street was narrow, as I think I mentioned. More people were home from work, and there were cars parked on both sides. I had to make a thousand-point turn in that unwieldy boat, creeping at a mile or two an hour, half expecting to hear a crash on each round. Worrying that someone would need to drive through while I was blocking the street. Worried that Chester could only hold it for just so long.

Meanwhile his face was growing whiter and more strained.

When I finally cleared the cars and could pull out, I swung around the corner and stopped at a red curb. If parking enforcement came by, I'd throw myself on their mercy. I jumped up to get the curtains, but he stopped me.

"No time for that," he said. "Just help me."

I had to help him get his pants down and then help him lift up enough to get the pan under him. At first I tried to close my eyes.

"Don't," he said. "Don't look away. It'll only slow you down."

As I lowered him down on the pan he said, "I know you're not looking like that."

"Is that it? Should I leave you?"

"Paper," he said.

I flew into the bathroom and pulled the roll off the wall, possibly breaking the holder in the process. I pushed it into his waiting hand and then stepped out the side door, because opening the side door wouldn't cause the dome light to come on.

I stood leaning on the Winnie, waiting, trying to get my breath again, as the Venice nightlife teemed by me.

I didn't have to wait for long.

A minute or two later I heard him knock on the window.

I won't go into great detail, but I emptied the pan inside the Winnebago's bathroom and washed it with the outdoor shower hose.

Then I washed my hands for a long time, and we drove off into the night with both cab windows wide open.

"Thank you," he said.

"No problem. It's my job."

"I couldn't do it right there on his street. What if he'd come back to the window for something? Maybe to say one last thing he forgot."

"I understand."

"It's humiliating. Not even being able to take care of my own toilet needs. I don't even feel like a man anymore."

"Well, you still *are* a man."

"I don't feel like one."

"Maybe you need to ease up on your definition of the word."

We drove in silence back to the I-10.

"Should we go back through downtown?" I asked him.

"How would I know?"

"Can't possibly be all that traffic at this hour."

"No idea. But I *would* like to get out of LA now. Before we stop and sleep."

"Yeah. I can do that."

I got on the I-10 East. It felt good to really move again. Especially toward home.

I powered my window up.

"Ellie's going to call your doctor in the morning. You know. About the pain meds. She'll keep us posted."

"Thank you," he said.

He still hadn't powered up his window. The air was rushing in, battering his face. Flapping his jowly cheeks. Blowing his hair around. But he just leaned into it, like a dog happy to take a ride in the car.

"So did it go okay?" I asked him.

"I don't want to talk about it," he said. Actually, he shouted it. But I think that was to be heard over the sound of the wind. "I thought I made it really clear that I don't want to talk about it."

"You don't have to," I said. "All I was asking—and you don't have to answer if you don't want—is if you're glad you did it."

He powered his window up. The silence felt stunning.

"Yeah, I think so."

"Good."

"Thanks for pushing me so hard. I thought you were being an insufferable jerk about it, but now I'm glad you're such a pain in the ass."

"It's my special talent," I said.

Then we got closer to downtown, and hit an absolute brick wall of bumper-to-bumper traffic.

—

We spent the night in a Walmart parking lot in what might have been El Monte or might have been West Covina.

We didn't try to move Chester. It just would have been too much for both of us. I unbuckled his seat belt, powered his seat down until it was reasonably flat, and covered him up with a blanket.

I was exhausted, and went straight to bed without showering or undressing. Without even brushing my teeth. I stretched out on the driver's side couch so I could see him, in case I needed to check on his well-being. You know. Without getting up.

I think I fell asleep in seconds.

I woke up because he said something.

He said, "He agrees with *you*."

I assumed he was talking in his sleep again, so I ignored it.

A minute later he said, quietly, "Are you not speaking to me, Lewis? Or are you asleep?"

I sat up on my couch bed and blinked, waiting for my eyes to adjust to the faint light.

"I was asleep," I said.

"Oh. Sorry."

"It's okay. What does he agree with me about?"

"Lie down again, so I don't feel like you're staring at me."

I stretched out on my back and laced my hands behind my head. The light above my head was off, but it had a little red LED light that helped you locate the switch in the dark. I stared at that as he spoke.

"He doesn't think it meant anything about me. He didn't act like it was any big deal. He said it was just the war, and my thinking he would keep me safe the way he did. He said he's had a couple of guys in his life he really loved. Probably not me, though. He didn't really say, but I figure not me. But he said he just didn't worry about it. He knew he liked women, so he didn't worry about it."

"Wow," I said. "You talked about some pretty brave stuff. I'm impressed."

"So here's what I want to know, Lewis. Why did I spend my whole damn life worrying about it?"

"Sorry," I said. "I'd help if I could, but I honestly don't know the answer to that one."

We lay there in the dark for a time without talking.

Then I asked, "Did he shed any light on why he hurt you so badly?"

"The Sue thing, you mean?"

"Yeah. That."

"He kind of did. He apologized up and down for what happened with that. He said after he got back from 'Nam he was doing a lot of drugs. Hard drugs. Serious stuff. And he said he just kept getting more and more cut off from his own conscience. Which was a weird thing for me to hear, because I thought he was this totally brave guy and what happened overseas didn't affect him at all."

"Nobody's that brave," I said.

"Some people do a damn good imitation."

"That's true," I said. "Some people do a damn good imitation. But it's still an imitation."

I lay awake for a while longer, in case there was more he wanted to say. But he didn't speak again that night, and in time I drifted back to sleep.

Chapter Twenty:

The Win

When we woke the following morning, Chester was quiet, and moving slowly. Then again, so was I, and I felt fine in general. I figured he was emotionally drained. *I* was emotionally drained, and it wasn't even my past that had been so rudely cracked open and spread out for display.

"How about a nice big breakfast?" I asked him.

It was after morning meds, and just before we pulled out of our parking lot.

He appeared underwhelmed.

"I could deliver it to you right in your seat," I added.

"Ask me again in an hour," he said. "My digestion's a little off. But *you* can stop and get something."

"Nah, it's okay," I said. "I've got granola bars and peanuts in the glove compartment. I think my goal today is just to make miles. Lots and lots of miles. I think we're both ready to get home."

"Amen."

"I may go through a Starbucks drive-through, though."

"Oh, you think so?"

I didn't get what he was driving at.

"Yeah, I think so."

"I don't think so."

"Explain yourself, Chester. I'm too tired for riddles."

"You know those little sticks they make you drive under to check your clearance?"

I suddenly knew what he was driving at.

"Oh. We're too tall."

"They're generally about seven feet tall. We're over twelve feet."

"Fine. I'll park and go in. You want something?"

"Yeah, get me a black coffee. No. Get me one of those fancy coffee things with foamy milk, but the kind that taste like chocolate. What do you call those again?"

"A café mocha?"

"That's the one. Get me a giant one of those."

"You only live once," I said.

I was remembering Sue's advice, and I figured he was, too.

"And I have to hurry," he added.

———

I took the turnoff for the I-15, to get us going farther north.

He noticed immediately.

"This is not the way we came," he said.

"No, it's not. I didn't think you were paying close attention."

"I notice everything," he said.

"Good to know."

"Why are we going back a different way?"

"Because Phoenix is out of our way. It's too far south. Shortest way home is to cross the country on the diagonal, starting right about now."

"Does this take us through Las Vegas?"

He didn't notice everything, I noted. He'd been giving himself too much credit. Because the sign for the I-15 had very clearly said **I-15 North, Las Vegas**.

"It absolutely does."

"I always wanted to see Vegas."

"By day is not ideal, but anyway, we're going right through."

"I don't really care," he said. "I just want to be able to say I've seen it." He looked out the window for a few beats. Then he added, "I'm not sure who I'd be saying it to, though."

More silence. For some reason I expected it to last.

"I was going to see the whole country," he said. "Every damn thing worth seeing. I even got a rebuilt engine put in this thing."

"I know. Marshall told me."

"Oh. Marshall. Right. I forgot you met Marshall. I kept coming in and looking over his shoulder. I wanted to watch my new engine go in. And I was coughing up a storm, and finally he said to me, 'Damn, Chester. You'd better get that looked at before you cough up a lung all over my yard.' And that was the beginning of the end. I never got to see a damn thing."

"You got to see some things on the ride to Arizona. And then to Venice Beach."

"Yeah, but I slept all the way through New Mexico, and I used to live in Arizona anyway. Don't let me sleep through Vegas, okay? Wake me up if you have to. I might just close my eyes for a few minutes."

He powered his seat back a foot or so and sighed. Closed his eyes.

I drove all the way through Victorville and Barstow, and was coming up on the Mojave National Preserve, and he hadn't said a word. I just figured he was asleep.

Then, without even opening his eyes, he said, "I'm sorry for what I said to you."

He might have left his eyes closed on purpose. Maybe for the same reason he'd told me to lie back down the night before so he didn't feel like I was looking at him while he spoke.

"Much as I appreciate the sentiment, Chester, you're going to have to narrow it down tighter than that."

202

"Taking shots at you about being gay."

"You were tired after the whole Phoenix thing," I said.

"Not just the last time, though. I mean all the times."

I felt more than a little stunned. I wasn't quite sure what to say.

"Oh. Well. That means a lot, Chester. Thank you."

I did not say "coming from you" or "considering the source." I only thought it.

Seriously, though. It was a moment.

———

When I saw the towering hotels of the Las Vegas Strip, I leaned over and shook his arm.

He came up sputtering, as always.

"What? What're you doing, Lewis? I wanted to sleep."

"You said to wake you up for Vegas."

"Oh, Vegas," he said. And his tone utterly changed. He sat up and looked around for a moment, his eyes wide. "Look, there's the hotel that's shaped like a pyramid. And there's the New York–New York one with the Statue of Liberty and everything. And the Eiffel Tower one. Damn, Lewis. I really wanted to come here. This is my kind of town."

Funny, but he said it just as it hit me that Vegas was *not* my kind of town. Then again, it was Chester Wheeler and yours truly. Where exactly was I expecting all that commonality to be hiding?

"Pull off the highway, Lewis. I want you to do something for me."

I wasn't thrilled with the idea, but I took the next exit.

"What do you want me to do?"

"I'm going to give you a quarter, and I want you to play a slot machine for me."

"It's going to be awfully hard to park this boat in one of those lots, though, don't you think?"

"Some of them have RV parking. Some of them actually have RV parks."

"Yeah, but which ones?"

"I know the Circus-y one does. It's one of the places I was going to go. Before I got sick."

We were sitting at a stoplight anyway, so I keyed the hotel—at least, the one I thought he meant—into the map app and it brought up directions.

Driving through Vegas was crazy. Everything was moving, everywhere you looked. Neon lights flashed and rolled, even by day, and bright, kinetic video scenes flashed by on LED screens. I wondered why traffic didn't constantly pile up while drivers took in all the distractions.

Then, while we were waiting for that forever-stoplight to turn, three drivers got tired of waiting and just drove right through the red.

I glanced over at Chester, wondering if I dared say it.

"The drivers here are crazy."

"Yeah," he said. "This time I agree with you."

—

I hooked up the Winnie to power in the RV park by the hotel, so the air conditioning could run while I was gone. You know. Without wasting gas.

"You sure you don't want food?"

"Not really. Not yet. You could bring back a sandwich and put it in the fridge. I might want it later. Or not. Just if you pass something. I don't really care."

It wasn't like Chester to be lackadaisical about food, but I didn't bring it up. He'd said his digestion was off. Why push?

He handed me the quarter.

I stepped out and walked across the parking lot through a hot Nevada day.

When I stepped into the hotel casino, I was overcome with light and noise—flashing neon and video arcade–type sounds. The place had no windows, so you couldn't tell if it was day or night outside, and it smelled like cigarettes, booze, and unwashed humanity.

I didn't bother to seek out any food. We had food in the Winnebago. I could make Chester a sandwich later. I wanted to get out of there. I wanted to get back on the road and get home.

I stopped at the first row of slots. They almost blinded me with their blazing, rolling, flashing lights. It was nearly enough to induce a seizure, if I'd been prone to them.

I dropped in Chester's quarter and pulled the handle, then watched the symbols roll into place. Seven. Seven. Lemon.

So, that was that. The quarter was gone, and it had gone for nothing. But that's gambling for you.

I was about to walk out again, but then I saw a change machine between me and the door. I pulled my wallet out of my pocket. Took out a twenty. Part of my precious rent money. But it didn't really matter. When I got home, Ellie would pay me, and I would still make rent.

I put the bill into the machine and it spit out quarters. Eighty quarters. I collected them in one of the little paper buckets they provided, with ads for their steak house on it.

I carried the change back out into the baking heat and walked back to the Winnie. I unhooked the power, stowed the cable, and let myself in through the driver's door.

"What's that?" Chester asked, trying to peer inside the paper bucket.

I handed it to him.

"I won?"

"Everything you see in the cup," I said. "It's not a ton. But it's a win."

"I can't believe I won."

"Well, it's right there in front of your eyes," I said.

"I needed a win."

"I know you did. Now let's get ourselves home."

———

We were in Utah before we really talked again.

"I like Utah," he said. "It has hills and mountains. It's not flat. I hate flat."

"Well, you're in the right place, then."

"Does this highway go over the Rocky Mountains?"

"Yes and no. We do, but it doesn't. The 15 goes north into Idaho and Montana. When we get a little deeper into Utah, we fork off onto the 70, and that goes through Colorado. And then there will definitely be Rockies, yes."

"Good," he said. "I've always wanted to see the Rockies. Don't let me sleep through them, okay?"

He had been holding that little paper change bucket in his lap for many miles. He stashed it in the map pocket of the passenger door. Then he put his seat back and closed his eyes.

"Still can't believe I won," he said. "I never win."

"Now you don't get to say that anymore."

"Oh, right. I guess that's true."

He was snoring and drooling within minutes.

———

Ellie called at around one o'clock. I put her on speakerphone so I could just keep driving.

"So I did call his doctor," she said, "but he hasn't called me back yet. He usually calls at the end of the day, and by then the pharmacies will mostly be closed. Unless you could find an all-night one. Anyway.

If my dad asks for a little more, give him a little more. We'll sort it out before you run out of them. I'll take responsibility for the dose change."

"Define 'a little more.'"

"Maybe three instead of two?"

"He actually didn't mention it this morning."

"Okay. But if it comes up tomorrow, give him three."

"You sure it's safe?"

"I'm sure if they prescribe two, then three won't be fatal, yes. He doesn't have time to get addicted. And besides, what's safe? He's dying. He needs pain relief."

I glanced over at Chester, who was drooling on his own shoulder and not waking up.

"Hospice uses tons of meds when people are on home hospice care," Ellie added. "A whole cocktail of them, and if it's a fatal dose, well . . . they were terminal patients."

"We should look into that when we get home."

"Agreed. I think it's time. I'll call you in the morning."

"Thanks," I said.

And we ended the call.

Chester still did not wake up.

———

I shouldn't have tried to drive so far that day, but in the great scheme of things I'm glad I did.

I drove until very late afternoon, with the sun on a long slant.

We were in Colorado, but I'm not sure exactly where. Past Grand Junction. Not nearly to Denver.

Then the Winnie came around a long curve in the road and I got my first good look at them. The Rocky Mountains. Their tops were white with snow, standing out like gems against a deep navy afternoon sky, with a more shadowy portion down below, and scrubby foothills. And I had to find a place to pull over.

A mile or two later I found a rest area that also seemed to be a vista spot. It had bathrooms and everything.

I gently shook Chester awake.

"I'm tired, Lewis," he said.

"I know you are. But you wanted to see the Rocky Mountains."

"Oh, are we there?"

He seemed to be exerting great effort to pull himself back up into consciousness.

"Not *there*, exactly. But we're where we can see them."

He opened his eyes and looked around until he saw.

For a long time he just stared at them, saying nothing. It might literally have been five minutes. I don't know. I wasn't checking the time. I was looking at the mountains, too.

Then he said, "That's the most beautiful thing I've ever seen in my life."

And, with that, he sank straight back down into sleep.

I didn't try to drive any longer. I'd been driving all day and I was spent, and probably unsafe on the road.

I pulled all the curtains down and made myself a sandwich. Sat on one of the couches and ate it, lifting the curtain slightly so I had a view of the mountains while I ate.

Then I brushed my teeth, slipped out of my shoes, and stretched out. It wasn't even dark yet, but I fell asleep immediately.

—

Because I'd gone to sleep so early, I woke very early the following morning. Before four a.m.

Chester did not. And I don't mean Chester didn't wake up early. I mean Chester did not wake up.

I opened my eyes in the dark, and waited a moment for them to adjust. There were lights in the parking lot of the rest stop, and they glowed through the curtains.

Chester's head was lolling over toward the driver's side. As though I were sitting in that seat and he was staring at me. His eyes were open. His mouth was open.

And I knew. I just already knew.

I got up and held two fingers under his nostrils. No breath touched them. I placed a palm on his forehead. His skin was unnaturally cool.

But I'd already known. Like I said.

"So long, Chet," I said out loud.

It was an odd sensation, to be so surprised.

I'd known all along that he was dying. And yet, in that moment, at that Colorado rest stop, sitting there with what he'd left behind, I realized I had not expected Chester to die.

A human brain is a very odd place to have to live your life. And that's really all I have to say about that.

Chapter Twenty-One:

It's Okay, Honey

I stood outside, on a hill overlooking the rest area, in the dark. I'd had to hike up to the top of it to get cell phone reception.

I had no idea what time it was where Ellie lived, because I'd never asked her where that was. I'm not sure why not, but I hadn't. I'd just always called at safe times.

This was not a safe time. Even if she lived in the eastern time zone, it would only be 6:00 in the morning there.

I called anyway.

She picked up on the first ring, which seemed odd.

"Lewis," she said. "What's wrong? What happened?"

I think everybody knows that phone calls at rude hours are nothing but trouble.

"I have some bad news, Ellie."

"My dad died."

Before I could even open my mouth to confirm, I heard her talking to someone else in the room. Her husband? Did she have one? I'd never even thought to ask. There were so many things I'd never thought to ask.

"It's okay, honey. Go back to sleep. It's my dad. No, it's not my dad calling. It's Lewis. My dad died. That's why he's calling now. No, I said my dad died. But it's okay." Then she seemed to come back and speak directly into the phone. "Sorry, Lewis. Now what were you saying?"

"I don't really know what to do."

"He's in the Winnebago?"

"Right."

"Well, I'm not much of an expert on it, either. Or maybe I'd have an idea if this hadn't just happened, and I wasn't feeling . . . But I think if I were you, I'd go straight to a hospital. Maybe go right in the emergency entrance? And just . . . tell them what happened. They should know what to do, right? I mean, people die at hospitals, so they have morgues at hospitals. Right?"

"I guess," I said. "I've never really had to think about it before."

There was a bright moon hanging over the mountains, to the east. Several days past full, but big. My eyes had adjusted to the darkness, and I could just barely make out the white glow of the snowcapped peaks. They really did seem to glow, as if they owned their own light source. It was beautiful and kind of spooky at the same time.

I'll never forget that. I can still see it when I close my eyes.

"As soon as you get there with him, call me. Tell me where you are so I can call them. Or give them my number and have them call me. I'll take care of all the details and everything. I'll get the body cremated and then shipped home."

"To you? Where do you live?"

"No, not here. My daughter and I live in Akron, but he wants his ashes buried in Buffalo. He has a plot next to Grandma and Grandpa. Are you okay? That must've been upsetting for you."

"Honestly? I'm not sure how I feel. I think it hasn't hit me yet."

"Where are you?"

"Colorado. Somewhere west of Denver."

"Can you handle driving home by yourself? Because if you wanted, you could take that monstrosity to a used car lot and dump it and use the money to fly home. I wouldn't care."

But Chester wouldn't like that, I thought.

"I'll drive it back. I don't mind."

"I'm going to tell you something now, Lewis, something I've been wanting to tell you for a while, and it might not be something you want to hear. You might want to reject it. But please just listen."

I squeezed my eyes closed, causing the faint mountains to disappear. I braced, thinking she was going to say something hurtful.

"You're good at this," she said. "I know you probably don't want that to be true, but it is. You're good at taking care of difficult people. It's like a talent, and most people don't have it. It was a real blessing to this family, and I'm sure there are other families out there who would be grateful for it. It's just something to think about."

I opened my eyes. I had to let them adjust again before I could see the Rockies.

"Most families would want a certified aide."

"So? Get certified."

"I wouldn't even know how to do that."

"Shouldn't be too hard to find out."

I shook the whole thing off again, because she'd been right. I wanted to reject it. It was something I didn't want to hear.

"I have to go now," I said. "I have to find a hospital. You'll hear more soon. Sorry about your dad."

She seemed surprised by that last part. She seemed to fumble for a reply.

"I didn't know him very well," she said. "You might have known him better than I did."

I could hear the subtext in those sentences. She was telling me, in the most polite way possible, that she had no feelings about it. Or very few, anyway.

212

It wasn't my place to tell her to have feelings about it. Just like it wasn't her place to tell me not to.

Maybe it would catch up with her later, and she'd be surprised.

Maybe we both would.

"I have to go now," I said again.

"Thank you for everything, Lewis. I'll mail you a check. You really pulled my chestnuts out of the fire. You did my whole family a real service."

All I said was "Bye."

Then I began the long hike down the hill in the moonlight, to do something I'd never in my life imagined having to do.

———

I had to drive him all the way into Denver.

I instinctively wanted to rush. I'm sure I don't have to explain why. At least, I hope I don't. But I forced myself to drive the speed limit because I was afraid of being pulled over.

Can you even imagine? The state police pull a guy over for speeding and he has a dead body in the Winnebago with him? I mean, I'm sure it's happened. But I didn't want it to happen to me. I set the cruise control and took it slow. It took about an hour. A very uncomfortable hour.

There were details to this morning of my life. Lots of details. Lots of conversations. Lots of red tape. All uncomfortable. All dull, I'm sure, to anyone who hadn't been there. I doubt it would be worthwhile to relate every single minute of it, even if I thought I could remember it all.

I'll touch on a few important points.

I parked fairly close to the emergency entrance, walked inside, and two guys in scrubs agreed to come get him out of the rig. I thought I'd made it abundantly clear that he was actually dead already, but it all happened very fast. Looking back, they might have been initially unclear on the point, though I imagine they figured it out soon enough.

While I was waiting for them to put him on a gurney, watching from an emotionally safe distance, I called Ellie and told her where I was. Gave her the address and phone number of the hospital. Begged her to call them so I wasn't in this alone.

Then I followed Chester's body inside. And I took a seat in an outer waiting room with blinding fluorescent lights. And I waited. And waited. And waited. And waited. Possibly because it was off hours and only the night crew was on staff.

After about an hour a nurse came and stood over me and told me I'd done it all wrong.

"This is not really what we do," she said.

She was big like a mountain, especially to someone sitting below her like that. She had her gray hair back in a braid.

"I didn't know what to do. I've never had a person die around me before."

"You should have taken him to the nearest mortuary or funeral home," she said.

"Are there any open at this hour?"

"Probably not."

"So what do I do? Please tell me you're not going to give him back to me."

"No. He's here now. He was brought in. He shouldn't have been brought in, but he was. So now I think you'll have to arrange to have a funeral home pick him up from here."

I breathed for the first time in the conversation. Or it felt that way, anyway.

"Someone is talking to his daughter right now," she said.

"Oh. Good. So I can go?"

"Oh hell no," she said. "You most definitely can't go. When a person presents a deceased body, there has to be a confirmation of how he died. Someone has to confirm whether or not it was an expected death."

"It was an expected death. He had terminal cancer. The doctors had given him less than three months to live."

"So you say. But we need a confirmation of that to avoid the police coming in and turning it over to the coroner to establish a cause of death. If there's no confirmation, then an autopsy will need to be performed."

"Hopefully someone is doing that confirmation thing with his daughter right now?"

"Let's hope. You'll need to speak with a hospital administrator. But no one will be in until nine."

So I waited quite a bit longer.

———

What felt like several weeks later, a woman came and got me. She was a striking woman in her forties, wearing a neat gray suit, with beautiful dark skin and hair shaved to just a shadow.

"Mr. Madigan?" she asked.

"Yes."

"Come with me, please."

I followed her down a long hall. And then another. And then another. Then we stepped out into the cold, bright morning and walked outside to an entirely different wing of the hospital.

She led me into her office and indicated a chair, and we sat on opposite sides of her desk. She had a nameplate sitting right in front of me. It read, PAULINE FISCHER.

She looked right into my eyes with a very determined attitude.

"Well," she said, "you've certainly complicated my morning."

But it was the way she said it. It wasn't really a complaint. She said it almost as a private joke. The way you tease someone when you know the person well enough to get away with it.

Her phone rang.

"This might be related," she said, holding up one very-long-nailed finger.

She picked up the receiver and listened for a few seconds.

"Yes, put her through."

Then she just listened again.

After a time, she said, "Before I say anything else, please let me say how sorry I am for your loss."

I breathed deeply then, knowing she was talking to Ellie.

For a time all the conversation happened on Ellie's end. I just sat there listening to the silence.

Then Pauline said, "Here's what I need you to do, darling. I need you to call his doctor and get those documents sent here. That will enable a death certificate to be issued."

Another bit of silence.

"Oh, you did. That's good. Now you'll need to call a local mortuary or funeral home. Local to us, I mean. Not to you. I can email or text you a list. They'll pick up the body and arrange to get it shipped home to you. Which, I'm sorry to say, is not inexpensive."

Silence.

"Oh. That won't be bad, then. Cremated remains are fairly straightforward as far as shipping goes. Let me just confirm that we have everything his doctor sent, and that it's all that's needed. And then poor Mr. Madigan can get back on the road."

She put Ellie on hold with one long, apparently strong fingernail, and pressed a couple of other buttons on the phone.

"Yes," she said. And, "Good." And, "What did he send?"

A longer silence.

"All right, then."

And she clicked back to Ellie.

"I think we're all set on the hospital end," she said. "We just need you to arrange getting the body picked up. And, again, very sorry about the loss of your father."

I wanted to say, "She doesn't care. She barely knew him." Of course I didn't. It was unnecessary and rude, and in the fullness of time it might not have proved to be true.

She hung up the phone and leveled me with a gaze. She might have been relieved, too. Not nearly as relieved as I was, but likely more than I would have expected.

"Do you know how to find your way out?"

"Not even close."

We rose, and she walked with me to her office door, where she pointed to thin lines of walking paths on the hall floor that seemed to have been made with colored tape.

"The blue line will take you back to reception."

"I'm parked near emergency."

"Ask at the front desk. They'll direct you."

I started to walk away, but I stopped when she spoke again.

"Just one question," she said. "And I'm not asking this in any official capacity. I hope you'll excuse my curiosity. What were you and he doing seven states away from home?"

I remember thinking that was some pretty good math for someone not even looking at a map. If she was counting correctly, that is. I figured I'd probably check her on it when I was off on my own.

"He had a couple of things he wanted to do before he died."

"And did he get to do them?"

"Yeah. He actually did."

"Well, good for you, then."

She retreated into her office, and I followed the blue line toward the people who could direct me back to the place I'd parked, and that was the end of my hospital experience.

And yes, that really was the short version.

—

217

When I stepped outside, the morning was cool and clear. I could see the tall buildings of downtown Denver in the distance, backed by snowy mountains. I could feel the altitude in my lungs.

Just outside the main lobby there was a circle set into the driveway that had been planted with grass and sturdy decorative vegetation, with a bench right in the middle of it.

I sat down on the bench, suddenly not ready to drive away. Which was funny, because I'd wanted nothing more for hours.

I sat there, leaning forward with my elbows on my knees, staring at those mountains. I could feel the sun warming the back of my neck.

I was wondering if Chester was going to have any kind of memorial.

I figured probably not. Clearly his sons wanted nothing to do with him. Ellie was a new grandmother, and not wanting to travel. And who else *was* there? Obviously no one, or I wouldn't have been roped into taking over his care.

It felt like the best possible advertisement for kindness. Treat people well, otherwise you might die and no one will notice or find it especially relevant to their life.

I decided to give him a tiny send-off, right there on the bench. It seemed only right.

I wasn't a religious guy, though I did think there was something going on in the universe that was bigger than us mere mortals. So I addressed the universe in general. Out loud.

"Hey, universe, we just sent you Chester Wheeler," I said. "Those of us down here on this little blue speck of Earth just turned him over. I'm guessing almost every single person on the planet would probably say, 'Good riddance. You can have him.' I might be the only person bothering to mark the occasion at all."

Then I stopped and tried to decide if that was enough. It didn't feel like it.

"He wasn't the best person who ever lived. He wasn't even in the top fifty percent. Hell, he probably wasn't even in the top eighty-five percent."

This is going badly, I thought. *Bring it home.*

"He wasn't a great person. But he was a person."

It felt sad to think that was the best I could come up with.

"He was a difficult guy, but I don't think he started out to be. I don't think he meant to be. It probably wasn't what he had in mind. I guess he just got kicked and pounded into that condition."

I sighed, feeling I had done poorly. But, honestly, that was my best. Maybe I should have added that he had apologized to me. But the moment seemed to be gone.

—

After I got back into the Winnebago but before I drove away, I leaned back against the driver's door. With my head tipped back against the window glass and my eyes closed, I called Sue.

"Hey, Lewis," she said when she picked up. "You home already?"

"No. I'm in Denver."

"So you *did* take him to see Mike."

"Yeah. We did that."

"How's he doing?"

"Which he?"

"I meant Chester."

"He died."

"That's weird," she said after a breath's worth of pause.

"In what way?"

"It's weird the way you totally know something's going to happen, but then when it does, you feel like it was unexpected. Like you really didn't think it would happen."

"I know," I said. "I think that's weird, too."

She didn't say anything for a long time, and neither did I.

"What did you see in him?" she asked after that very long silence.

"I'm not sure I understand the question."

"I know you said you took the job because you needed the money. But you offered to drive him across the whole damn country. And you would've gotten paid either way. You must've had some indication that there was something good in there somewhere."

While I wasn't answering, I had a flash of a memory. Standing alone in the dark on the top of that hill, overlooking the rest stop where Chester had died. Talking to Ellie on my cell phone. She'd said something. Not even to me. But it had reminded me of another something . . . Oh, I'm sorry. I'm being vague, I know. My mind was frazzled. She'd said to someone in the room, "It's okay, honey. Go back to sleep." At the time I hadn't bothered to explore why that sentence felt so familiar. There had been too much else going on.

That had been a few hours earlier, that hilltop conversation, but when I thought back on it, it felt like something that had happened months ago.

"He talked in his sleep," I said.

"Oh yes, he did."

"Oh, okay. I didn't know if he always had."

"Always. How do you think I knew about the whole Mike thing? It's not like he was freely sharing that kind of information. But I'm sorry. Go on."

"Anyway, the first night I was taking care of him . . . I think it was the first night . . . Ellie'd had an intercom installed. And he mentioned your name in his sleep."

"Uh-oh."

"No, it wasn't bad. It was . . . ordinary. It was like this . . . ordinary moment. This is probably not word for word, but he said something like 'No, it's okay, honey. Go back to sleep, Sue. I'll get him. He probably just wants a drink of water.' It sounded like a situation with a child waking you up in the middle of the night. He said they'd shine a flashlight under the bed and in the closet, so he'd know not to be afraid."

"That would've been Johnny," she said. "He was scared of the dark. Saw monsters everywhere for years. Or maybe not *saw* them, I don't know. But he just knew they were there."

More silence fell. I wondered if I was making her feel bad for separating Chester from his kids.

"So that's what you saw in him," she said.

"I think it *was*, yeah. Not only because it was a glimpse into a regular husband and father, but also that it still came up in his sleep all those years later. That ordinary little moment from raising a kid was still there in his subconscious to bubble up after all that time."

She didn't answer, so I added, "I can't tell Mike that he died. I don't have his phone number."

"I'll tell him if you want."

"Yeah, thanks. Tell him I said thank you. He was nice with Chester, I think. I mean, I wasn't there. But it seemed like he was honest with him and made him feel better instead of worse."

A pause fell, and she did not fill it.

"I'd better get back on the road. I've got a long drive in front of me."

"You okay, honey?"

"It's a weird experience. You know. Waking up with a dead body."

"I can only imagine."

"I'll be okay, though."

"I know you will, Lewis. You're good at this."

"At what? Waking up with a dead body?"

"No, all of it. The care thing. It seems like the role you were born to play."

"That's what Ellie said, too. But I think you're both wrong."

"Call me when you get in safely."

"Will do."

We ended the call and I fired up the engine and let it warm up for a bit.

While I was waiting I used my fingers to shrink the map app on my phone, so I could see the whole country. I counted states. Seven. I was seven states from home. Just like Pauline had said. *Pauline is good,* I thought.

Then I headed east, alone.

Chapter Twenty-Two:

Weenies

I picked up the 76 on my way through Denver and veered north toward Nebraska.

I knew I wasn't destined to achieve a lot of miles that day.

It was after ten o'clock in the morning, and I was physically, mentally, and emotionally taxed. Just completely drained. But I had to try to get closer to home. I just had to.

Anna called on my way down out of the mountains. I put her on speaker.

"Hey," I said.

"You're welcome."

"What am I thanking you for?"

"For introducing you to the perfect guy."

"When did you do that?"

"The minute you get home."

I sighed. I was hoping it wasn't loud enough for her to hear it.

"What's with you?" she asked, apparently having heard it.

"Mostly tired."

Also the prospect of a fix-up was making me feel even more exhausted.

"Chester driving you crazy?"

"He's dead."

"I give up. What are you going to kill him for this time?"

"No, he's dead, Anna. He's actually, physically dead."

A brief silence while she—I guess—took that in.

Then she said, "I know some tricks to make it look like an accident."

It hit me very badly.

"It's really not so damn funny, Anna." Then, before she could answer, I said, "Oh, I'm sorry, I didn't mean to bark at you. It's just . . . I've had such a damn day. I mean, I woke up this morning and he was dead in the Winnebago four feet away from me, and I've been dealing with it ever since."

"I'm sorry. I had no idea it would be so hard for you. I actually thought you'd be relieved."

I opened my mouth to try to explain that I wasn't exactly the same person I'd been when I first drove that land boat out of Buffalo. But I knew she wasn't ready to hear that, and I wasn't sure I was ready to say it. I certainly wasn't ready to try to explain it.

"Turns out you only think that when you don't know the person at all."

"When're you coming home?"

"Day after tomorrow if I'm lucky. But, Anna. Come on. You know how much I hate blind dates."

"Brian. Will change. Your mind."

"No, but there's more to it than that, Anna. It's more important than just hating blind dates. Tim is gone and I've been so wrapped up in Chester's life that I haven't even processed that. How can I start a new relationship when I haven't even figured out the old one?"

I thought, *I did something wrong. Or I was something wrong. And I don't even know what.*

But even as I said it, I heard her likely reply. "Figuring things out is overrated." She said that to me every chance she got.

This time, not so much. She simply repeated her previous announcement.

"Brian. Will change. Your mind."

I opened my mouth to answer, but the call had been dropped. Either that or Anna had already hung up. It was not out of the question. She didn't always hang around for the word *goodbye*.

———

I made it into and mostly through Nebraska, but I didn't make it out the other side that day. I was just too tired.

I found an RV park near the Platte River and set down roots for the night, even though it was only five or six o'clock in the afternoon.

I wanted to hook up to water so I could shower for about a year without draining the tank. Or, anyway, until the small water heater—which I had turned on nearly a whole state earlier—was tapped out, whichever came first. Well. Running out of hot water was obviously going to come first.

I stepped down and unlocked the storage hatch under the body of the Winnie with my small key. Pulled out the water hose and began uncoiling it. I hadn't done a good job putting it away, so it had a few snarls.

I just stood there for a minute or two, half looking at the river and half looking at the hose as I worked.

There were four ladies sitting outside in the space next to mine. They looked to be in their sixties, with pastel sweat suits, and hair more deliberately styled than one might expect of campers. They had a fire going in the ring firepit provided with the sites, and they were roasting weenies over it on long barbecue forks with wooden handles.

I heard one of the ladies say, "He's one of them communists."

I looked over, curious as to whom they were talking about. They were all staring right at me.

"Who, me?"

"We're talking amongst ourselves, honey."

I decided to let it go by. It seemed the better part of wisdom not to ask any questions.

I set about hooking up the hose between the provided spigot and the water fitting on the Winnebago.

"But yes," she added. "If you must know, we were talking about you."

I straightened up and tried to get all of this information to work together in my brain. It did not go especially well.

"I'm not a communist," I said. "I'm definitely a small cog in the capitalist machine."

"Which is exactly what a communist would say. Who else talks like that? I ask you."

A different lady said that. She had a high, squeaky voice, like a doll suddenly come to life.

"Where's all this coming from?" I asked.

"We were reading your bumper stickers," the original lady said.

Ah. My bumper stickers. That explained a lot.

I opened my mouth to say something. I didn't know exactly what it would be, but I had a general idea. I assumed it would be the same sort of something that would have come out of my mouth at any other juncture of my life. One, I would be clever. Two, I would stand up for myself. Three, I would put their meddling to shame. And fourth but not least, I would clearly show myself to be right, whether they were able to see and accept my rightness or not.

"You ladies have a nice evening," I heard myself say.

Then I stepped back toward the driver's door of the rig.

"What in hell's that supposed to mean?" the doll-voice lady squeaked.

I didn't turn around and engage them. I didn't even look back to gauge their reaction. Over my shoulder I said, "It means I hope you ladies have a nice evening."

"See? He won't tell us," another one of them said.

I laughed out loud. I couldn't help it. It was one of those dark comedy moments that come through a life now and again. But I more or less kept it to myself.

I retreated into my own private space.

I showered until the hot water ran out, made and ate a sandwich, and put myself to bed. I did not dwell on the exchange, or argue with my temporary new neighbors in my head, or feel any lingering sense of having been ruffled over it.

It was their objection, so I let it be their problem. It really had nothing to do with me.

I slept well, and for a good long time.

———

The following morning I woke up early and drove all the way home.

I shouldn't have. Every mile of the second half of the drive, I knew I should be giving up and finding a place to stop and sleep.

It was about sixteen hours of driving, all told, and the road hypnosis set in hard. The lane markers became like a hypnotist's pocket watch, figuratively swaying back and forth in front of my face.

I stopped for coffee six times, and drove with the windows open, blasting cold air into my face. I purposely put on music I hated, that I found grating and jarring, and turned it up to full volume.

Now and then other drivers would pull level with me, and try to peer in to get a look at me, which is hard when you're so many feet higher off the road than they are. Either it had something to do with my bumper stickers, or it was complete and total paranoia on my part, brought on by exhaustion, and the whole thing didn't exist outside of my head.

After sixteen hours on the road it gets harder to sort these things out.

I can't even explain why I did it. I had just completely lost my will to continue driving a Winnebago through flat and uninteresting states. Home had become a magnet with an irresistible pull.

When I finally, finally pulled up in front of Chester's house, I sighed out a boatload of tension I hadn't even known I was holding. In that moment, I knew I'd risked a lot by driving through so much fatigue.

I should be able to look back and say it wasn't worth the risk, and, in a purely cerebral sense, yes. I can say that. But I was so relieved to be back that it *felt* worth it. It felt worth anything.

I let myself into my house and fell straight onto the bed with all my clothes on. I didn't even take off my shoes.

That's the last thing I remember from that day.

—

I woke at about three o'clock in the morning, and holy crap, was I awake. The kind of awake that you just know will never fade and let a person get back to sleep. I'm sure the six cups of coffee played a role.

I kicked off my shoes and lay awake in the mostly dark room, just the slight glow of a streetlight shining into the living room and barely making it through my open bedroom doorway.

I realized I was supposed to call Sue and tell her I'd made it home safely. But probably not in the wee small hours of the morning I wasn't supposed to. I tried to make a mental note to do it later in the morning, but it seemed so ripe for failure that I gave up and set a notification on my phone.

Then I rolled over and tried to go back to sleep, even though I knew full well it was hopeless. I lay awake for hours, and found myself plunged into the middle of a very strange sensation.

It started when I thought, *I'm back in my life.*

That's when it all caught up to me.

Because "I" was not the "I" I'd been when I left. And my life was not the life it had been. So who was I, and what was this life I'd just rejoined?

I knew I would find out fairly soon, but, as I lay there in the half dark, I literally didn't have so much as a guess. It felt like opening a door with not even the faintest hint of what I would find on the other side.

Suffice it to say I was not a fan of the experience.

Chapter Twenty-Three:

Sentimental

Ellie called at nine o'clock–ish, which was too bad, as I had just gotten back to sleep.

"Where are you?" she asked.

And I thought, *Great question. Existentially speaking.*

"Home," I said.

"Already?"

"Yeah. I really put on the gas. So what do I do with the Winnebago?"

"You know . . . ," she began, and I could "hear" a sort of internal sigh from her end of the line. ". . . I honestly don't care. Keep it, sell it. Really, whatever."

"But if I sell it, I'd give you the money, right? It would be part of his estate and you'd split it between you and your brothers?"

I heard a kind of braying noise that I realized after the fact was a forced laugh of some sort. Probably of the sarcastic sort.

"What estate? He really didn't have anything. If he did, I wouldn't share it with my brothers anyway, because where were they when all the care workers were running out on us and somebody needed to deal with things?"

"What about the house?"

"Mortgaged to the hilt. I'll sell it, but what's left over will be a pittance if there's anything left over at all. Hey, speaking of money. I did something, and now I'm unsure . . ."

I sat up in bed, because she sounded uncomfortable and that made me edgy as well.

"What did you . . ."

"I sent you a check."

"Thank you."

"I sent you two checks, actually. And now I'm not sure. Maybe I shouldn't have. But you can just tear up the other one if you don't want it."

I'm not sure I understand, I thought.

"I'm not sure I understand," I said.

"I went online to a couple of community colleges and found out what they charge for a certification course. And I sent you a check made out to the closest one near where you live. I put a note in there saying you can just tear it up if you don't want to do it. But now I'm thinking you'll be mad."

I got up and walked to the window. I think I was trying to wake up more fully to deal with this conversation. I was still completely dressed. I drew back the curtain, and the light was searing in my eyes. And I was looking at Chester Wheeler's house, which somehow looked unavoidably sad. How a house can be sad, I'm not sure. If I'd had to guess, I'd say I was anthropomorphizing, and the sad was in me. That seemed like a reasonable bet.

"I'm not mad," I said, flopping back down on the bed. "It was thoughtful, and generous, and I know it came from a good place. But it's out of the question, because I have to find work that pays. And I need to find it more or less right now."

I knew as I said it that I could probably work a job and complete the certification course at the same time, but I forcefully put it out of my head, because I didn't want to know it.

"I actually have a temporary job you could do. But I'm not sure if you'll want it."

"Don't tell me you have more difficult relatives hiding in the woodwork."

"No, I'm fresh out of those. But I need someone to clean out my dad's house. And I'll pay well."

"There are people who do that."

"Yeah, there are. But the problem is, they work on a sort of commission. They sell everything that's worth anything and take their pay out of that. Nothing in my dad's house is worth selling. It mostly has to be hauled to the dump."

I lay there without talking for a moment, seeing if I could wrap my head around the concept, not to mention the task. It was hard to imagine that a man's entire life could be garbage.

"What about things that are just . . . you know . . . useful? Flatware. Plates. A coffee maker or a blender. His TV. Why take all that to the dump?"

"You can donate stuff like that to a thrift store."

"And what about sentimental things? Mementos?"

She let out one of those braying laughs again.

"Seriously? My dad? Sentimental? He doesn't even have pictures on his walls. So does this mean you'll do it? You're talking like you'll do it."

I opened my mouth to say "Let me think about it." But then I remembered Anna blowing her stack with me in an Italian restaurant because I couldn't make a simple decision.

"Yeah, I suppose I'll do it," I said.

I thought it was interesting how she had managed to successfully draw the conversation away from the community college money. I also thought it was good that she had. Because I needed more time to decide how I felt about that.

—

By 10:00 a.m. I was over at Chester's house, opening the door with my key.

When I stepped inside it was dim, and slightly odorous, which of course I had known. But somehow in the process of all those days on the road I'd managed to put it out of my mind, and it struck my senses as something almost new.

I decided the best plan would be to walk around and make a plan.

There would be furniture and large appliances, and beds, and other things too big to carry. I'd have to get a hand truck. I'd have to ask Ellie where to leave those heavy items pending pickup. I'd need a couple of boxes of big, strong garbage bags for the smaller items. Maybe a recycling bin for paper and plastic.

And the items of some limited value, the ones I'd be donating to a thrift store—I'd have to think where to gather those in the short run. Maybe it would be best to put them directly into my car?

I walked around and opened cupboards and closet doors, feeling my mood sink lower and lower with every area I examined.

Finally I collapsed in the living room in all that horrible shag carpeting. I sat cross-legged for a long time and just let myself be overwhelmed—just tried to accept the fact that I was emotionally unable to begin.

I think I can at least point a finger in the general direction of what had me so down.

I was dismantling a man's entire life. Going through everything that had ever meant anything to him, and deeming it all unworthy of keeping. In most cases, unworthy of keeping by *anybody*.

I could already picture the late Chester looking over my shoulder as I worked. Saying, "No, no, not that. Don't throw that away, Lewis. I love that." And then, when I did anyway, he would think what? And, to really stretch a point, feel what?

I tried to shake such thoughts away again, as they were only going to tank my ability to do the work.

My phone rang in my pocket.

I picked up the call, assuming it was Ellie. If I had looked, I'd have ~~'~~, ti. ~~" ID~~ that it was not Ellie, but I was lost in thought, and I didn't look. I just assumed.

An unfamiliar male voice said, "Lewis?"

"Yes."

"Brian Kennedy."

I said nothing at all. My mind had been a hundred miles away, and I was having trouble bringing it home again. And I didn't know anybody by that name. It was hard to think of a reply more tactful than "Who?"

Since I didn't speak, he kept going.

"Anna's friend. Well, not friend, really. I just met her one time at an office party. She works with my mom. Don't ask me why I went to a party with my mom. I just now realized how that must sound. Such a party boy, right? It's a long story why I was there."

"There's nothing wrong with being close to your mom," I said.

My mom lived in Kansas with her third husband, and we were not close. I would have liked more of a relationship with her, but I'd been forced to accept, at some much earlier point in my life, that it was simply not in the cards for us.

Of course, I didn't say all that, except in the privacy of my own head.

Meanwhile I was feeling vaguely resentful toward Anna for giving the guy my number without permission.

"Anna's told me a lot about you," he said.

I was just opening my mouth to explain that I was staunchly anti–blind date when he said more.

"And . . . listen. I get it. I know fix-ups are awful. Just the absolute worst."

"I'll say."

"That's why I thought I'd just call you and say hi. None of that unbearable nonsense where Anna pretends to be having a little get-to-gether at her house and we have to pretend we don't know it's a set-up. That's so weird."

"So very weird," I said.

I realized I was not helping myself much, but I was off balance, and my mouth wasn't working well. Or maybe I should have been blaming my brain, as my mouth did seem to be doing a fair job pronouncing the wholly inadequate words it had been sent.

"So here's what I was thinking," he said. "If you're up for it, that is. What if we just met for a cup of coffee? One cup. Could be twenty minutes. And if we're not feeling it, then we're just not."

I opened my mouth to say no. That there was just too much going on. My life was too far out of balance to meet somebody new. What if he asked me what I did for a living? I wouldn't even know what to say. What if he asked me if dinner fit into my schedule that week or the following one? I didn't even have a schedule, or, if I did, I wasn't privy to it yet.

And beyond and underneath all those concerns, I was still sorting out the emotions of the previous days. Trying to get them to drop into some kind of slot of understanding, so they would go away and leave me alone. Allow me to function.

"Sure," I heard myself say. "Why not?"

As if I hadn't just thought of a number of reasons why not.

———

I walked back to my house for a few starter trash bags. Then I walked back to Chester's, and began discarding the man's life. I didn't even spend a lot of time stewing about the wisdom—or lack of same—behind my coffee date later that afternoon, because I was too wrapped up in listening to the things Chester said over my shoulder as I threw his belongings away.

At first it was mostly silly little things I was discarding, all firmly and inarguably in the trash category.

There was a drawer literally full from top to bottom with bottle caps. He had either saved every bottle cap from every beer he ever drank in that house, or he had saved the ones from beers he drank on occasions that felt special to him for some reason. Without knowing how much beer he drank, it was impossible to guess. If the latter, the man had lived out a lot of significant occasions, at least in his own mind.

There was a stack of newspaper sections, all the same section, and all open to the crossword puzzle. The puzzles had been done, though some not completely. They had been filled in with pen, and had lots of cross-outs and scribble-overs.

There were a few books sitting on a plain metal shelf, a surprising number of which were corny joke books from the 1950s.

Then I opened his bedroom closet and things got decidedly less silly.

On a high shelf, above a dozen Hawaiian shirts and a blazer with slightly frayed cuffs, I found an old-fashioned scrapbook with black paper pages, and a shoebox.

I opened the shoebox first.

In it were dozens of letters, all in the same handwriting, and clearly very old. The paper of the envelopes was discolored, and just at the borderline of disintegration. They were all addressed to Chester Wheeler in Phoenix, Arizona. All from Mike Erikson in Los Angeles, California.

I sat there on Chester's bed for a minute, sorting through them in my hands. Counting them. There were sixty-seven letters.

So what would Chester want me to do with all of his letters from Mike? I imagined his horror if I loaded them into a plastic bag and put them out on the curb for the garbage collection truck, treating them like just more trash. On the other hand, I knew nothing would horrify

Chester more than the idea that they could fall into the wrong hands—that somebody might read the words that felt so personal to him.

I thought about it for a few minutes. And felt about it.

Then I took them into the kitchen, turned on the gas burner, and lit the corner of one of the letters on fire. I carried it to the fireplace, the box under my left arm, and threw the burning letter in.

I opened the flue and started the next letter on fire, using the flame from the first one to light it. Then I just kept feeding them in. Letter after letter curled and browned and turned to ash, and the smoke rose up the chimney and joined the sky, the ether. It felt as close as I could get to giving the letters back to their rightful owner.

When the letters were gone and I was sure the fire was safely out, I walked back to Chester's bedroom and opened the scrapbook. I paged through it with half-squinted eyes, prepared to close the cover and look away if there was anything inside that I felt I was not meant to see.

It was all mementos of his children.

He still had all of Johnny's report cards from the third grade. Crayon drawings of houses and families and cows, signed by "Ellen." A handmade Father's Day card from Danny. As I got deeper in, there was apparently a long gap of time, followed by newspaper clippings. Ellie's wedding announcement in the Akron newspaper. Johnny—now John—in an article about a court case in which he was the lead attorney.

I closed the cover again, having seen enough to help me know what to do.

I called Ellie, and she picked up on the second ring.

"You don't want to do it anymore," she said in place of "hello." "I was afraid of this. What can I say to change your mind?"

"I'm doing it," I said.

Then I just sat there on the edge of Chester's bed for a time, breathing into the phone. And she just waited for me to tell her why I'd called.

"Turns out," I said, "there's something sentimental here after all."

"What was he sentimental about?"

"You. And your brothers."

"No, that's impossible."

"I'm holding impossible in my hands," I said.

And I told her a little bit about what I'd found.

"But . . . ," she began.

The thought apparently had no ending, though.

"I'm going to send this to you," I said. "I need your address."

"But he didn't . . ."

Again, no apparent finish.

"What didn't he?"

"He didn't pay any attention to us. After Mom threw him out of the house, he never paid any attention to us at all."

"Actually . . . he paid attention to you, Ellie. Just not to your faces, where you would know about it."

A long silence on the line.

"Ellie? I just need your address."

"I'll have to call you back," she said.

It was clear from her voice, and from her enunciation of the words, that she was crying.

I opened my mouth to try to say something helpful and supportive, but she had already ended the call.

I sat on the bed for a few minutes, trying not to think of my own lost father. Trying not to wonder if, on his death, someone would find proof that he had kept tabs on me in some unexpected way. Also, failing at that.

Chapter Twenty-Four:

Serve

I walked down to my favorite coffee place, and sat out on the patio, and waited. I was a little early. The weather was cool, and I was wearing a light jacket, which felt good after sweltering for so long on that overheated trip.

For a second, I had a pang of regret. Maybe I was wrong to do this—to try to meet somebody new when I hadn't even sorted out the somebody old.

And then it hit me. Just all at once like that. Like the proverbial ton of bricks.

I was taking Tim's treatment of me personally.

Maybe I wasn't wrong, or bad, or defective. Maybe I was just wrong for Tim.

It left me reverberating inside, wondering why I hadn't thought to extend my Chester Wheeler lesson just a little bit further. At least, until that exact moment. I just sat there for a time, feeling the echo as it passed through. Feeling the inside of me return to stillness.

There was an umbrella above the table, casting shade. I almost got up and moved it, to get some sun on me. I was feeling a trifle chilled. Instead I got distracted by wondering if it was 2:00 yet.

I turned over my phone and glanced at it. It was 2:01.

When I looked up again, he was standing at the other side of the table.

"Lewis?" he asked.

"Brian," I said.

"You don't have coffee."

"I was waiting for you."

"I'll get us something. What do you want?"

He wasn't exactly what I'd call handsome—he wasn't a head-turner—but he was pleasant enough to look at. His hair was brown and just that perfect amount of tousled. I wasn't sure if he rolled out of bed with it looking that way, or if he spent hours working to achieve the impression of "natural." But if it wasn't effortless, he certainly made it look that way. His eyes were dark brown and just the tiniest bit askew. It was so slight that I almost wasn't sure if I was imagining it. He wore jeans and a plaid flannel shirt with no jacket.

"Let's see," I began. "I'll have . . . the largest café mocha they've got." Like Chester, living it up. "Nonfat," I added quickly, because unlike Chester I would still be around in a week or a month to regret my excesses.

He went off to get them.

I could see him through the coffeehouse windows the whole time. I could watch him without him watching me watch him. He seemed at home in his own skin, but that was just a first impression. He had a slightly oversize nose, but it worked with his face.

He was older than I was—fairly significantly, I decided—but definitely not old. Maybe thirty, or even in his early thirties. He had a young energy, so it was hard to tell for sure.

He ordered and paid, then came back out and sat across from me.

"Well," he said.

And I said, "Well," too.

"Sorry if it's awkward."

"I thought it would be," I said. "But now that we're here doing it, not so much."

It's possible I was lying, though. Or at least exaggerating. Because I immediately opened my mouth and asked a question I would not have asked if I'd been able to think of a single better thing to say.

I asked, "So what do you do for a living?"

Ironic, huh? The one thing I truly feared *he* would ask *me*.

"I'm a registered nurse," he said.

"Huh. That's interesting."

I thought, *The universe is having its way with me.* I didn't say so out loud.

"Interesting how? I know it's interesting to *me*, because it's my livelihood. It's my calling. I'm curious as to why it's interesting to you. Unless you just said that to be polite."

"No. I didn't. It really is interesting."

"That's how it seemed."

"Interesting how?" I repeated. "Okay. Where to begin?"

There was a massive and very old maple tree growing up right through the middle of the patio, and a big wind shook its branches and sent red and golden leaves flying and spinning in the air. One of them landed on the table between us. Another got caught in my hair and I had to brush it away.

I can't entirely explain why, but in that moment my life felt like a better place than it had been for as long as I could remember.

"I'm at this intersection in my life," I began, "where I have to decide if I want to go into a health-care-related job. Nothing as fancy as being a registered nurse. Just a home health-care worker."

"Don't say 'just,'" he interjected.

"You're right. Sorry. I just got done doing end-of-life care for a man. I wasn't certified or anything, but he just needed something like a babysitter. So, right, I'm still saying 'just' a lot. I hear myself doing it. But I guess that's different. Anyway, now both his daughter and his ex-wife have been trying to tell me I'm good at this. That it's something I should consider. You know. Going forward. Right at the moment I still don't think I agree. But it just keeps coming up. I don't want to be too quick to dismiss it, you know? The daughter even wants to pay my way through a certification course, but I still don't know how I feel about that."

"Okay," he said. "Try this. If you're willing, of course. Tell me the thing you liked best about the job you just finished. And then tell me the part you liked least."

"Oh. I'd have to think about that."

The coffees came, and we thanked our server and then pulled ourselves back to the conversation at hand. I sipped at my mocha, but it was prohibitively hot.

"What I liked best," I repeated. "I liked who I was on the job. Even though I didn't like who *he* was. He was pretty awful, actually. Mean and callous and thoughtless. Homophobic. But when he needed something, I put that aside, because it was my job to be there for him. I'd agreed to do it, and I took that responsibility seriously. So I guess I liked what I saw in myself, or I might even say what I saw come up and out of me, during that time."

Another swirl of autumn wind sent maple leaves flying. Brian had to hold a hand over his cup to keep one from landing in his coffee.

He didn't interject any thoughts. We both knew I hadn't completed the assignment, so he only waited.

"Least. I guess what I liked least was having to clean up after someone's . . . you know . . . bodily functions."

"Felt degrading?"

"A little."

"It's really not, though. Not in my opinion, anyway. But I don't mean to discount your experience."

"No, go on with that thought. If you have a way to reframe bedpans, I'd honestly like to hear it."

"Here's how I look at it," Brian said. "And you have to believe I've come in contact with a lot of unpleasant things that come out of a person's body. I don't find it degrading. At all. I think it has the definite potential to be degrading for the patient, but it's in our power to defuse that, which is a huge service to do for someone who's dying. Look at it this way. Think about a baby. A baby pees and poops and vomits. A parent cleans it all up. And a parent's job is not seen as degrading. They care for that baby out of love, and it's noble. And nobody blames the baby. The baby feels no shame, and nobody tries to shame babies for having no control over their bodily functions. Somehow we see the adults differently, the elderly and the dying, but I'm not sure why. I'm not sure how different it really is. A human body is a fragile, messy undertaking. There's a time in the middle of our lives when we tend to have it under good control, but coming into the world and going out of the world, we're much more vulnerable. We need help. And being willing to be that help for someone is a very high calling, in my opinion. It's really the purest definition of the word *serve*."

He fell silent. We both did. I got the sense that he was embarrassed at having said so much.

"You think that was daft," he said. "Don't you?"

"I think it was brilliant. Absolutely beautiful."

A few more beats of silence.

Then I said that thing I'd been so careful not to say before.

"The universe is having its way with me."

"Not sure I follow," he said.

"I feel like it's pushing me."

"Don't push back," he said. "That never pans out."

———

I talked about Chester for a really long time. Really. Long. Longer than I realized while I was doing all that talking.

Then I sort of . . . simply . . . came up out of it, the way a person might drift up toward the surface of water for a long time and then suddenly break free.

Having broken the surface, I felt more than a little bit embarrassed.

"But I'm not sure why I'm talking about him so much," I said.

"Oh, I know why," Brian said. No apparent doubt or hesitation. Then he backpedaled slightly. "I mean, I think I do. I don't mean to sound like one of those people who think they know you better than *you* know you. But you just said you're not sure, and it seems pretty clear to me."

"Okay," I said. "Hit me with it."

"He was the first person to die in your care. That's a pivotal moment. It leaves a mark. It brings death very close to home and makes it feel real in a way we're not used to. It requires some time for digestion. And this was pretty recent, right?"

"Oh, hell. *So* recent. I'm trying to think, but the days are all stretched out of shape in my head. I want to say it was four or five days ago, even though it feels like a month, but when I go over the details in my head, I think it might actually have been three or three and a half. Or two and a half! But I totally could be wrong."

I felt awkward and embarrassed, what with not being able to tell time properly, but I hadn't even caught up on my sleep since arriving home.

"For the purpose of this discussion," Brian said, "three days or five days is really all the same. The point is that they're both no time at all in the great scheme of things. It affected you, and you haven't had a chance to process it yet."

"No, I know I haven't. I can feel that."

"So you're talking it out of your system as a way of making peace with it."

"Yeah. Sorry."

"Don't be sorry. I've gone through this. Just about everybody I work with has gone through it. It's a natural process. Even if there wasn't much of a bond with the patient. I know you said the guy was unpleasant. But your first close brush with death will shake you, whether you had much rapport with the person or not."

"The weird thing is, I sort of did. Have a rapport, I mean. I was starting to. I didn't like him, but I was beginning to understand him. Like . . . the more I found out about his life and his past, the more I empathized with his situation. And the whole experience of dealing with him . . . it was . . . I don't know how to describe it. I'm not sure I've managed to package it up in words yet. But it was . . . I keep wanting to say *freeing*. I don't mean his dying. Not that part. I mean the part about learning enough about him that I started to understand him. Because somewhere along the line . . . somewhere down the road in this process I *got* something. All the way down to my gut I *got* something I'd never gotten before. I got that when a person is rude and abusive to me, it's not about me at all. They can say something terrible to me or about me, but they're revealing themselves, not me. It has nothing to do with me. They're just showing me the landscape on the inside of themselves as they project it out onto somebody else. Does that make sense? It's the first time I've tried to put it into words."

He was only silent for a beat or two, but it felt longer. I bent myself into a pretzel trying to guess how those words had struck him.

"His daughter and his ex-wife were right," he said.

Oddly, I made no immediate connection that would help me understand what he meant.

"About . . . ?"

"You should think about caregiving as a life's work. You have a spark for it."

His pronouncement made me uncomfortable, and I think I might've squirmed in my seat a bit.

"I'm pretty sure that was more than twenty minutes," I said, referring to our original deal for the meeting.

"I think so, too," he said, "but I'm not wearing a watch and I left my phone in the car. What time is it?"

My phone was lying facedown on the table, half-covered by a truly spectacular red and orange maple leaf. I turned it over.

"Holy cow," I said.

"Late?"

"Ten after four."

"I should go."

He rose, and I rose.

And I thought, *I blew that. I chased him away. I mean, it was nice of him to talk to me as though he had no objection to being my sounding board. But who wants to listen to Chester Wheeler stories for over two hours?*

"I'll call you," he said.

I didn't respond, because I wasn't sure if he meant it, or if that's just what you say to get away from the table.

"That is," he added, "if you want me to."

"I do," I said. "I want you to."

And he gave me a comfortable little smile and walked to his car.

I bussed our cups into the tray provided near the coffeehouse door, and then I headed for home on foot.

I called Anna on the way.

When she picked up, I said, "I'm about to thank you for something, but don't say 'You're welcome,' because you already did."

"Told you so," she said. "Brian. Changed. Your mind."

———

I let myself back into Chester's house and did a lot more work, even though I was much too tired.

At about seven in the evening I got a text from Brian.

It said, Accept or discard, as you choose. You might think about volunteering with hospice. Care for another couple of people, maybe easier ones this time. It might help you decide how you feel.

I sat with that for a minute or two. Then I texted back, Easier ones? Where would be the challenge in that?

He returned a little smile. Not one of the emojis people usually send, but an old-fashioned and simple sideways smiley face made from a colon, a hyphen, and the second part of parentheses.

:-)

Then I remembered I'd never called Sue. Somehow I had managed to ignore the reminder on my phone. I must've dismissed the notification without even thinking.

So I did that, but she was not picking up.

I left her a voice mail that said, "Full disclosure. I got home last night and forgot to call. But I'm fine. I'm cleaning out Chester's house because Ellie is paying me to do it, and it feels weird. So, so weird. But other than that, I'm fine."

I opened my mouth to tell her about the scrapbook, but I realized it was the last thing she would want to hear. The only possible outcome would be to fill her with guilt.

"Okay, then. Bye."

I hung up the phone and worked long into the night. Well past the time I should have done myself a favor by sleeping.

Chapter Twenty-Five:

Calling

In the morning I woke up early, despite having gone to bed late.

I dressed quickly and made myself a coffee for the road, with the goal of doing important errands.

Before I left, I let myself in over at Chester's house and opened all the windows. Every damned one. I figured Ellie would have a real estate agent showing the place soon. And I knew it would be nice if every potential buyer didn't have to start their tour by doing that vague sniffing thing with their nose working the air.

Just as I was leaving again, I stopped, and questioned the wisdom of going away and leaving the place wide open like that. The window screens certainly offered no protection at all from a break-in.

Then I laughed out loud at my own foolishness.

Force-of-habit thinking on my part. I should have been so lucky as to have someone break in and clean the place out. They'd be saving me hours of labor.

I jumped into my car and drove.

I rented a hand truck from an equipment rental place, for furniture moving. Then I stopped at a big-box store and bought a silly number of garbage bags, and some miscellaneous cleaning supplies.

Back in my car, I picked up the phone to see if anyone had called or texted.

And then, just like that, I was looking at a web page for my local hospice. And I swear I couldn't even remember the thought process behind it, not to mention keying the word into the browser on my phone.

I decided now would be as good a good time as any to drop in and say hello to the folks at my local hospice.

———

Their office was a big old two-story house in what clearly had been a high-end residential neighborhood in the distant past.

I stepped inside.

There was a youngish woman doing some kind of paperwork in the front lobby, but she didn't look up. I sat down with my now stone-cold coffee, feeling awkward.

A minute or two passed, and I was just getting ready to change my mind about the whole thing and slip out the door.

Right at that moment she looked up.

"Oh," she said. "I'm sorry. I get wrapped up in what I'm doing."

"No worries," I said, even though it had nearly sent me back out the door.

Well. That and so many other things.

"What can I help you with?"

"I wanted to talk to someone about what's involved with being a volunteer."

"Oh," she said. She sounded surprised, as though that was the last thing she had expected me to say, but I had no idea why. "We have a training course. You'll want to be sure it's something you really want to do, though, because it's thirty hours."

"Just the training course."

"Right. Then we ask that you commit to at least four hours of volunteer work a week. But you're more than welcome here if it's what you want. Most people sign up for the course by phone or online. But if you'd like to talk to Trudy while you're here . . ."

"Yeah. Since I'm here. Unless she doesn't have the time right now. It's not like she knew I was coming."

I realized, listening to myself speak, that I was sounding unsure. As if I could just as happily walk out the door and forget the whole idea. Which is probably the last thing they look for in a volunteer.

She picked up the phone, punched a button, and said, presumably to Trudy, "A *young man* is here, and he'd like to talk to you about our volunteer training."

She seemed to put an odd emphasis on the words "young man."

Then she hung up the phone and said, to me, "It'll just be a couple of minutes."

I fidgeted in my chair for what could only have been a minute or two. For some reason I was flashing back to that hospital in Denver—to all that time I'd waited for a nurse to come around and hover over me and tell me I'd done it all wrong.

I looked up to see a woman who looked surprisingly like Pauline Fischer. Her hair was cropped less extremely, and she had a more solid build. And she was much more casually dressed. Still, it made me like her immediately. I wondered if she could tally how many states away from home a person had driven, without looking at a map. She gave the impression of being smart.

"Hello," she said.

And I said, "Hello."

"I'm Trudy."

"So I hear."

Then I realized, a bit late in the game, that she was giving me the opening to introduce myself.

"Oh, sorry," I added. "Lewis."

"Come on into my office, Lewis."

I followed her into her office, which was not what I had expected. Speaking frankly, it was a mess. Not a mess as in actually dirty. No old coffee cups or food containers. Just files. Boxes of files. Stacks of files. Stacks of boxes of files. Everywhere. At first I wondered why they weren't all in filing cabinets. Then I wondered if there were enough filing cabinets in town to do the trick.

She sat down behind her desk and I sat down in front of it.

"We don't get a lot of young men your age in here to volunteer. I'm not suggesting it's unheard of, but it's . . . unusual. Tell me a little bit about what made you want to come in."

"Okay. Sure. I just finished doing a job that involved taking care of a man who was dying. I didn't have any training or professional credentials. He just needed somebody to be with him, to help him, and he'd driven everybody else away. I'd just gotten laid off from my job, and I needed the money, so I had to be that one person who wouldn't let himself be driven away, and at first I didn't think I could do it. I figured I'd be just as thin skinned as everybody else who'd walked away from him. But I ended up getting a lot out of the work. I ended up figuring out that I could let his behavior toward me roll off my back, and I didn't need to take it personally. And that's . . . it's such a freedom. To mostly rise up above the idea of someone being able to pull your strings. It's freeing. I don't want to lose that. I want to keep that going. I don't want to sound too corny, and maybe I'm saying too much, talking too much, but I feel like I want to say it was a gift."

She was fiddling with a pen as I spoke.

"To you? Or to him?"

"Well, both, I guess. He needed someone to stay with him till the end, and I managed to do that. But I meant a gift to me, actually."

"Do you mind if I ask what you were doing before? Workwise, I mean. You said you'd just lost a job."

"I was a software developer."

"This is a long way from that."

"Yes, it is. I noticed that."

"Did you hope to continue being a software developer?"

"Now that's a good question. I guess I thought so. I guess I figured I was attached to that career, but now I look back and I think my only thoughts about career were tied in with money. I didn't know a career could be more than money."

"I see."

She jotted briefly on a pad, then looked right into my face.

"Most of the people we care for will be much easier than your last experience. We can certainly find you someone who's more of a pleasure to work with."

"No, I don't want that," I said. "I want the toughest, most disagreeable people you've got."

She shot me a glance that was, at very least, quizzical.

"Talk to me more about why you would want that."

"Because . . . I'm beginning to think it's my . . . would it be too dramatic to say it's my calling?"

She didn't offer an opinion on that, so I kept going.

"I mean, they say everybody has something they can bring into the world. What if this is my something? What if I end up being of some use to somebody else, and all because somehow I learned not to take it personally, and that puts me in a position to help? You know what I mean?"

"I think so," she said.

"I'm about to take a course to be certified as a home health-care worker." I was surprised to hear myself say it, because I hadn't realized I'd already decided. I seemed to be telling Trudy and myself the news at the same time. "The daughter of the man I was caring for wants to pay my way through it, because she says some other families are bound to need what I just did for hers."

"Because you don't take it personally."

She sounded like she was adding me up in her brain and still hadn't come to any sort of sum total.

"Right. I'm starting to think . . . how do I put this so it makes sense? I look at the world now, and I think . . . if people knew how much they were revealing about themselves when they tell you what they think of you, everybody would just shut up and never say anything to anybody again."

We sat in silence for a few beats. Then her expression changed. A tiny smile formed on her lips.

"Oh, if you make it through the training, you're going to be a very welcome addition around here," she said.

I felt myself relax, and I sat back in my chair. I breathed deeply.

"Thanks," I said.

"You still need to take the thirty hours of training and commit to at least four hours of volunteer work a week when possible."

"Understood. I'm between jobs, so the timing is good."

"This is great. I love this." Then, "Hey, Connie!" she called. Loudly enough to make me jump a little, though maybe only on the inside.

The woman from the front lobby appeared in the open doorway.

"Guess what? We found a new volunteer for Gladys."

Connie's face morphed into a frown.

"Are we sure we want to do that to him?"

"It's what he wants."

"Yeah, but . . . Gladys? Is he sure? How much does he know about her?"

"Difficult people are my calling," I said.

"But . . ."

"No buts," I said. "I just got done taking care of Chester Wheeler. There's nobody you could possibly throw at me who would be too hard."

By the end of the day, owing to some nearly superhuman feat of endurance, I had Chester's house emptied out.

The furniture was all out in the driveway, along with more than forty garbage bags full of trash to be hauled to the dump. My car trunk and back seat were stacked to overflowing with odd items to donate to a thrift store.

I had even pulled up all that horrible shag carpeting, rolled it up, and left it in the driveway for pickup. And underneath it I'd found . . . this is going to be hard to believe, I think. I know it was for me. Hardwood. A beautiful old hardwood floor, albeit in need of some renovation. Now, I ask you: Who puts shag carpeting over a hardwood floor? Well, sure. Right. The answer to that question is obvious. But who *else*?

I stood in the empty living room for a moment, wrestling with a slight unease that I couldn't quite pin down.

The windows were still open, and the air was cold and fresh. And it smelled fine. Perfectly neutral. It contained no remnant of its old owner at all. And maybe that was the source of my unease right there.

I had erased him more successfully than I would have thought possible.

I shook the thought away again.

I locked up Chester's house and went home, where I showered for a seriously long time. Then I made myself a sandwich.

I had eaten about half of it when a knock came at my door.

I opened it to see a woman in her fifties in a smart skirt suit. A total stranger.

"Mr. Madigan?"

"Yes."

"Ellie Frankel says you'll have the key to next door."

"And you are?"

"The listing agent."

"Oh. Right. Okay. That was quick."

"Is the place not anywhere near ready to show?"

"Oh, it's ready. I just apologize for that nightmare in the driveway."

"What nightmare in the driveway?"

"You didn't see?"

"See what?"

I stepped outside in my bare feet, and walked along the sidewalk until I drew level with Chester's driveway. It was empty. Utterly empty. Perfectly clean.

"Huh," I said in the general direction of the real estate agent, who I could feel standing behind me. "I know Ellie was going to hire somebody to come get everything and haul it to the dump. But I didn't even hear anything. They must've come while I was in the shower."

"May I see the inside of the house?"

"Oh, right. Sorry. Let me just run home and get the key."

I ran home in my bare feet and grabbed the key off my hall table. Ran back.

I opened the door to Chester's house for her, and we both stepped inside.

I felt a swell of pride for my work. The place was perfect. I mean, if perfectly empty is what you're after, it was perfect.

"Oh," she said, and she sounded quite surprised. "This is great. I was told it would still be a bit of a disaster. Well. I shouldn't say disaster, even though *she* did. A work in progress."

"I managed to get it done today."

"Good. Thank you. This is just the way we like it. As though the former owner had never existed."

It was a decidedly odd thing for a real estate agent to say, and it hit like an arrow into my discomfort, running me through and pinning me to the wall of Chester's very clean house.

I'd made the place look as though Chester had never existed.

She seemed to sense my discomfort, because she backpedaled violently.

"Oh, I'm so sorry," she said. "I was thinking out loud, and I should never do that. I know when a person goes into a care home there's always this uncomfortable sense of them having been erased from the world, and it was very careless of me to feed into that. Please forgive me."

"He didn't go into a care home," I said. "He's dead."

"Oh dear." Her face flushed red. "I've really stuck my foot in it now, haven't I? I'll just take the key and go."

She reached one well-manicured hand in my direction, palm up, and I dropped the key into it.

We walked out together, and she locked up behind us.

I half expected another apology, but she was apparently more humiliated than sorry, and she got to her car and drove away as efficiently as possible.

I sat down on Chester's front stoop and tried to decide how best to atone for having erased him.

It was dusk by then, and quite cold. I wasn't wearing a jacket, and my feet were still bare. But I just sat there for many minutes, wearing the cold like some kind of hair shirt, wondering what part of Chester I could still salvage.

I had all that stuff for the thrift store in my car. I could keep some little piece of it for posterity. Something that fairly screamed Chester Wheeler by manner of its very existence.

There was that horrible cuckoo clock that no longer told time, and no longer sent its cuckoo out into the world on the hour. But it was so awful to look at. I couldn't imagine keeping it around my house.

Maybe something very small, but Chester-reminiscent, like that souvenir spoon from Niagara Falls, or the bottle opener made of carved wood, polished and lacquered.

Even a very small thing would be something. Just a reminder that he had walked the earth in this neighborhood for years. Decades.

Then I opened my eyes, figuratively speaking. They had been open the whole time, but without really seeing. I had been too caught up in the landscape inside my own brain. I focused outside myself for a moment, and there it was. Filling my line of sight. The unwieldy behemoth of Chester's Winnebago.

Nothing screamed Chester Wheeler as loudly as that Winnebago screamed it.

I got up and walked back to my own house. Picked up my phone and called Ellie.

"Oh, Lewis," she said. "I arranged for a hauler to clear the driveway. And a real estate agent is going to come for your key."

"They've both been here," I said.

"Oh, good. Did my checks come?"

"You know . . . in all honesty, I've been forgetting to bring the mail in. I'll do that as soon as I get off the phone."

"You can just tear up that other check if you don't want it."

"No. I'm not going to tear it up. I'm going to take the course and get certified."

"Oh, that's wonderful, Lewis. I'm really glad to hear you say that."

"So, listen. A question. Did you really mean what you said about Chester's Winnebago? You really don't care what happens to it?" I walked to the window as I spoke. Pulled back the curtain and stared at the monster. Briefly questioned my own sanity. "You don't even want any money for it?"

I heard her sigh on the other end of the line.

"I *should* want the money, I suppose. It's probably worth a few thousand dollars. But I'm just so tired, Lewis. I'm so tired of the whole thing with my dad. I just want to be done with it already. And the idea of trying to sell that huge beast when I don't even live in Buffalo . . . if you wanted to sell it, we could split the proceeds."

"Oh," I said.

"You sound disappointed."

"No, it's fine."

"What were you thinking?"

"I was thinking maybe I'd keep it. Maybe some other client will decide there's something they always wanted to see before they die."

"Lewis," she said, her voice firm again, "it's all yours."

"Thank you. That's very generous of you. So much so that I hate to even push my luck by bringing this up, but I never did find the title."

"I'll have my attorney write up something you can take to the DMV."

"Thanks," I said. "I'd better go check my mail."

"Let me know who comes to look at the house, okay?"

"Will do."

And we ended the call.

I emptied the mail from the box at the curb, and holy cow. It was full. The mail was actually wedged in, it was so full. I had to keep changing the angle of the stack, and bending, and pulling.

When I'd brought it into the house and weeded out the junk mail, what was left was mostly bills. But Ellie's checks were there. And the check Ellie had sent for my services was very large. Very generous. More than we had agreed on by quite a bit. So at least I didn't have to dread the bills. I'd have a fair chance of paying them, at least.

I put myself to bed and slept for a very long time.

———

I woke in the morning to voices outside.

I got up and crossed to the window in just pajama bottoms, and pulled the curtain aside.

A family was looking at Chester's house.

There were three medium-sized children running loose on the mostly dead lawn. Two boys and a girl. The husband and wife were standing on the front stoop, talking to that real estate lady with the bad habit of thinking out loud.

It seemed ironic. Young couple in love. Two boys and a girl. I wondered if any of the kids saw monsters under their bed at night. I wondered if the adults told each other everything, or if they had secrets.

I wanted to say, "Be kind to each other, and don't let anybody come between you. And if someone else does come in and break up the marriage, and there's no way around that, at least find a way to equitably share the raising of the children."

Needless to say, I didn't know these people, and they didn't want my advice, so I knew I would say nothing to them at all. That was just what the situation made me *want* to say.

My phone was on the bedside table, and it let out a tone announcing a text.

I walked back and picked it up.

The text was from Brian.

It said, What would you think about a real date, with dinner out, followed by a play or some kind of show? Maybe the steak house on the avenue near you and then the comedy club? What would you say to that?

I typed back, I would say yes to that.

He returned a little heart. But, again, not an actual emoji. Just the kind of sideways heart you make with that . . . I'm not sure what you call it. Maybe it's called a less-than sign? Like a caret, but lying on its side. And the number three.

<3

Brian was a little different. And I don't mean that in a bad way at all.

———

He showed up two nights later at seven.

He was wearing jeans with a crisp white shirt and a sport coat. His hair was neatly combed, which seemed too bad to me. I had liked it tousled.

We stepped out into the evening together.

"We could take my car if you want," he said. "But the restaurant is just a few blocks from here."

"It's such a nice night," I said. "Let's walk."

We made our way down my front path to the sidewalk together.

I had moved the Winnebago several feet forward so that it was parked in front of my house, not Chester's. The real estate agent had requested it. But I would have done it anyway, because it was mine now.

I stopped on the sidewalk in front of it, and he stopped, too, though it was clear he didn't know why.

"So here's a very important question for you," I said. "What do you think of my new Winnebago?"

Probably not very fair of me, I know. But I wanted to see how he would handle that one.

"It's . . . big."

"Oh, it's all of big."

"I'm not sure 'new' is the perfect description."

"Right. No. Of course not. New to me, I meant to say. I realize it's not the most attractive thing in the world. But you can go places and do things in it. You can go to the places you've always wanted to go, before it's too late."

"Are you planning on leaving the world soon?"

"No. But I expect to be meeting some more people who are."

I started walking again, and he did, too.

"It used to belong to Chester Wheeler," I said. "His daughter let me keep it."

This time he was the one who stopped.

We were just beyond the rear bumper of the great beast, and he stood there a moment, staring at it. Considering . . . I didn't know yet. Something.

"This was Chester's?"

"Yeah, this is the one we drove across the country."

"That seems surprising," he said.

"How so? It seems very Chester Wheeler to me."

"Based on the way you described him . . . I can't picture him having those bumper stickers."

"Oh, the bumper stickers," I said, barely suppressing a smile. "There's definitely a story behind the bumper stickers. Walk with me, and I'll tell you all about it."

Epilogue:

One Year Later

I spent a few minutes loading Estelle's belongings into the Winnebago. And then, finally, I loaded up Estelle.

I use the word "loaded" mostly jokingly. Estelle was, in fact, fairly mobile. She was wobbly, and a distinct fall risk, so I tended to walk at her elbow. But she got places more or less on her own power. The tricky part, for me, was keeping her steady with one hand and wheeling her oxygen tank with the other. Especially up the steps into the RV.

Once inside, she stopped. Looked around. She did a fair amount of looking up, as though she had expected a century-old theater with an ornate domed ceiling. Her hair was gray-white and about as close to nonexistent as a person's hair can get without literally falling out entirely. It was so thin that every inch of her scalp was visible to me as she surveyed the indoor scenery. She had a hooked nose that tended to look pinched where the nasal cannula of her oxygen system entered her nostrils.

Meanwhile I could see Brian standing on the sidewalk outside our house, waiting to see us off. He reminded me of a faithful beau in a 1930s movie who stands on the dock for no other reason than to wave goodbye to his sweetie as the ship sets sail.

Okay, okay. So I romanticize. Sue me.

Estelle finally offered her proclamation.

"Not exactly the Ritz-Carlton," she said, "is it now?"

She had a scratchy, nasally voice that had always struck me as the human equivalent of fingernails on a blackboard. If she had been more of a constant talker, it might almost have been a deal breaker.

"What did we talk about, Estelle?"

I figured there was maybe a ten percent chance she would remember.

"No idea. We talk about all manner of things."

"We agreed that if all you had to say was some form of criticism, you'd just keep your thoughts to yourself."

"You must be thinking of one of your other dying patients." This was her idea of a running joke. I had no other patients, dying or otherwise. Estelle was a full-time job and then some. "I'd never make an agreement like that. Being critical is all I've got left."

I walked her up to the passenger seat and guided and supported her as she sat.

I reached across her for her seat belt but she slapped my hand hard.

"I can do it!" she barked.

"You. Do. Not. Hit!" I said, my voice low and strong. "That's two strikes, Estelle. Next time you hit me I resign from this job and you can damn well get somebody else."

"But I can do it myself."

"Then you *tell* me that! With your *words*. How would you feel if I hit *you*?"

"You'd better not. That's elder abuse."

"My point is that anybody hitting anybody is abuse. I will work for you and I'll care for you, but under no circumstances will I accept your abuse. Are we clear?"

"Fine, fine," she said, buckling the belt herself.

But the trouble was that, in a minute or an hour, she'd forget we'd ever had the conversation.

"You sit right here," I said. "I have to go kiss Brian goodbye."

Her face morphed into an overdone mask of shock, like something from a silent-movie melodrama.

"On the *street*?"

"Yes, on the street. Where he's standing. Do *not* go anywhere."

I trotted down the steps and joined Brian in front of our house.

"I have such a sense of dread," I said. "Are you sure this is a good idea?"

"It was your idea."

"It was pretty much Estelle's idea. But yes, I agreed to it. And the question still stands."

"I'll tell you what you always tell me, Lewis. If you made it through Chester Wheeler, you can make it through anything."

He kissed me briefly on the lips, then seemed to focus on something over my shoulder.

"She's frowning at me," he said.

I looked around.

She was looking down at us from the Winnebago's high seat, looking like a judge on a bench. Again, overplaying her role.

"You're going to tell her," Brian said. "Right?"

"Yes. I'm going to tell her. But maybe on the way back, so I don't completely ruin her family reunion." I kissed *him* this time, also briefly. "Wish me luck. I'll need it."

"You'll do fine. Got your phone?"

"Yes. Got it. I'll call you every night."

I ran around the beast and jumped into the driver's seat. Started it up. I waved at Brian and he waved back. Estelle scowled. Then we were moving.

"We're on our way," I said.

"I find that so disturbing."

"What? That we're on our way?"

"No. The kissing. On *the street.* Men didn't do that in my day. Oh, there were men who were . . . you know . . . like that. And some women even, or so they say, though I never met any. So I can't say for a fact."

"There were women," I said. "And you met some."

"I just told you I never did."

"And I'm telling you yes you did, but you just didn't know it."

"Well, I don't know about that. But anyway, my point is that it all took place in private."

"Which underscores the point I just made."

"So much of the time when you talk, I have no idea what you're saying."

I gave up and fell silent.

I was navigating some fairly narrow streets on our way to the expressway, and I had forgotten how stressful city driving was in that boat.

Estelle would not let it drop.

"What I'm saying is, it's disturbing to me. It makes me a little nauseous. It would never have happened in my day. That's what I'm saying."

Already I could feel myself sinking under the strain of this endeavor. And we were only a few minutes in.

"I'm not saying this to be mean, Estelle, but this is not your day. I'm sorry. You have to let go and let things change. If you don't, you're only setting yourself up to be unhappy."

"I don't like it when things change."

So there it is, I thought. *My reminder that none of this is personal.*

"I know you don't," I said, and I could hear the sudden difference in my own voice. I could hear myself soften. "I know change scares you and makes you feel like everything is spinning out of your control."

I knew I had hit the bull's-eye, because she clammed up and looked out the window in silence.

"I'm not going to change myself to make you feel less disturbed," I added. Because I felt it needed to be said. "It's not what people do. It's above and beyond what we owe each other. What if I told you I wanted you to change into somebody who accepts me, because I get upset when you don't? Would you change?"

"Of course not. I am who I am and I've got a perfect right to be."

I waited for her to get it. Nothing happened.

"I'm waiting for you to get it," I said.

"Get what?"

I sighed.

Nothing more was said for several miles.

When I got out onto the highway, I set up in the right lane and breathed a sigh of relief.

"You can't just stay in the right lane all the way to South Dakota," she said a few miles later.

It briefly flitted through my mind that she might be channeling Chester Wheeler.

"Sure I can. Why can't I?"

"It'll add too much time to the trip. I'll be late to my reunion."

"No you won't. We're getting in tomorrow evening. Your family reunion doesn't start until Saturday morning."

"Tomorrow *is* Saturday."

"No, tomorrow is Friday."

"That would make this Thursday."

"Yes it would. And it is. It's Thursday."

I held my phone out to her with the screen turned in her direction.

"What am I looking at?" she asked.

"The little icon that looks like a calendar page."

"I don't see . . ."

"Top row."

"Oh," she said. Then, "What do you know? It's Thursday."

She didn't bring up timing again. And she never gave me any more trouble about driving in the right-hand lane.

—

Near the state line with Pennsylvania, Estelle opened up again and told me the story of Mount Rushmore. She was talking a lot, for Estelle, which meant the big trip had her more nervous than she was letting on. It also meant my nerves were in for a beating.

"Thirty-seven years I lived with that man in Spearfish, South Dakota. Maybe seventy miles from Mount Rushmore. It was new back then. Hadn't been finished all that long, and it was a big deal. Everybody either loved it or hated it, but it was a big deal. Controversial."

"It's still controversial."

She ignored me.

"But did I ever get to see it? No I did not. He was afraid the car would break down, he said. Maybe we'd get a flat tire, he said. Granted, it was a lot of nothing out there all those years ago, but seventy miles away is not the dark side of the moon, you know. I mean, show a little courage, am I right? Then he moves us to Buffalo but he says, 'Don't worry. When I retire, I'll take you there on a plane. *Business class.*' Listen to the big spender for once in his life. Business class! Seventeen years go by, he retires, and three months later he drops dead of a heart attack. Did I ever get to see Mount Rushmore?"

"No you did not," I said.

"No I did not," she repeated.

I hadn't literally counted, but if I'd had to guess, I'd say she'd told me that same story somewhere between fifteen and twenty times. A word or two might have changed here or there, but I could nearly have recited it right along with her by then. I didn't, so as not to offend her. It wasn't her fault that she couldn't remember what she'd already said.

My response to the story was the same as it always was. I figured if she didn't remember telling me the story before, she wouldn't remember my response.

"I just worry that it'll be a disappointment to you. I mean . . . after building it up in your imagination all those years. It's bound to be a little anticlimactic."

"It couldn't possibly be," she said. "Those are famous American presidents. It's an American tradition."

All things she had said before.

Then she added something new.

"Patriotism meant something in my day."

Then she paused. I glanced over to see her face fall. Her sturdiness seemed to dissolve.

"Then again," she added, "as you so rudely pointed out, this is not my day."

"I didn't mean to hurt your feelings with that," I said.

"No, no. It's fine. You are who you are, and you've got a perfect right to be."

I drove with my mouth open for a minute or so.

"Estelle," I said when I'd gotten my words together. "Your mind is very sharp today. I'm impressed."

"What are you so impressed about?"

"What you just said."

"What did I just say?"

"Never mind," I said. And I tried to keep my sigh as quiet as possible. "It's a long trip and we don't want to tire you out too early in the game. Maybe just put your head back and close your eyes."

She did as I'd suggested, and I was able to drive most of the day in perfect, healing silence.

———

We stopped for the night at an RV park somewhere in Wisconsin. I didn't note where, exactly, but we were on the 90 and had made it through Chicago and out the other side, and the 90 had turned decidedly north. We were between that northern turn and the place where it turned west again for a straight shot into South Dakota.

I'd been driving for over ten hours, and I was exhausted.

Unfortunately, Estelle had been sleeping sitting up in the passenger seat for most of that time, and she could not have been more wide awake.

She needed to use the toilet, but she didn't want to use the one in the Winnebago, though she could articulate no clear reasons why not. I walked her and her oxygen tank to the women's restroom provided by the RV park. I wanted to walk her in and help her sit down, which is legal for a caretaker, but she insisted on going in alone.

I hovered outside, wincing, waiting to hear a crash, and wondering if I'd made a dreadful mistake.

A minute later I heard the toilet flush, and she came teetering out, towing her own oxygen tank behind her.

"I didn't wash my hands," she said, "because I'm just about to take a shower anyway."

She pointed to a cinder block building behind me, and I turned around to look. It was a building that housed two individual showers, requiring several dollars in quarters to get inside.

I could have told her we didn't have quarters, but it would've been a lie, and I didn't like to lie to her.

"I'd be more comfortable if you'd shower in the Winnebago."

"I need more room."

"I think room is just what you don't need. You could take a fall."

"You'll be right outside the door. I won't lock it. I'll let you guard it instead. If I take a fall, I'll call out to you. You can be there in two seconds."

"But by then you would already have taken a fall."

Over her head I could see the sun setting through the trees, sending shafts of dusty-looking light out between their branches. It was beautiful, and I think I was reaching for beautiful. Because this situation was making me nervous.

"I could fall in the Winnebago's shower, too."

"No, you couldn't. And that's what I like about it. It's too small to fall down in."

"And that's what I *don't* like about it. It's not even big enough to fall down in. I get claustrophobia, you know."

I thought, *Now you tell me.* I didn't say it.

"Wait right here," I said. "Lean one hand on the side of that building and don't move a muscle. I'll be right back."

I ran back to the Winnebago and got soap, shampoo, a towel and washcloth, one of her nightgowns, and a folding camp chair.

I hauled all that back to where Estelle stood leaning, one arm on the building, as instructed.

"What's the chair for?" she asked.

"I want you to shower sitting down."

"The chair'll get all wet. It's a fabric chair. Who showers in a fabric chair?"

"So? Let it get wet. Who cares? We'll leave it outside to dry overnight. Small price to pay for keeping you safe."

I pumped quarters into the lock on the door, and opened it.

I set her up inside with her oxygen tank, nightgown, and towel over in the corner where they would stay dry. I put the soap, shampoo, and washcloth on the floor near her chair, which I set up right under the showerhead.

I did not instruct her on keeping her oxygen equipment dry, because she'd been doing it for years.

"Okay," she said when I led her over to the chair. "Now go away and leave me alone."

"I'll be right outside the door."

"You'd better be."

I stepped out and leaned my back against the door, and waited until I heard the water turn on. The sun was no longer shooting rays through the trees, but I could see a strong orange glow of it back there, behind their massive trunks.

I knew this was the most crucial time, while she was getting undressed and seated.

I briefly rehearsed what I would say to her family, whom I had never met or spoken to, if it turned out I'd made an unwise bet.

When I heard the water come on, I breathed out a boatload of tension.

I pulled my phone out of my pocket and called Brian.

"Hey," he said when he picked up the call.

"Hey."

I felt more grounded just hearing his voice. So much less lost. Not so far from home.

"How's it going?"

"Estelle is absolutely maddening, as always."

"If you made it through Chester Wheeler . . ."

"Right, but at least Chester knew what he couldn't do. She's constantly asking to do things by herself that I know are questionable, and it's really hard to know where to draw the line. I mean, I understand the need for independence. But I'm responsible for her."

"I know. You just need to do your best walking that line. It's all you can do."

We allowed a brief silence.

I looked back at the trees, and saw that their glow was less orangey. The sun was going down fast. Maybe it had been a mistake not to bring Estelle a coat to wear over her nightgown for the walk back. But it was too late. I needed to stay right by the door.

"Where are you?" he asked.

"Past Chicago. Somewhere in Wisconsin."

"You made miles."

"We did."

Another silence.

Then he said one of the many things he tended to say that under-scored why I loved him so much.

"Look, Lewis. It's hard. I know it's hard. You knew it would be hard. It's one of the reasons you got certified. So you could do the jobs that were too hard for most."

I didn't even bother to affirm that he was right, because we both knew it.

"I love you," I said.

"I love you, too, Lewis."

Just then the water turned off. Estelle's showers ran very short. It was another thing that made me feel she might be channeling Chester Wheeler.

And wouldn't it be just like that man to come back and haunt me?

"Gotta go," I said. "I'll call you tomorrow."

—

Chester and I had made a habit of sleeping directly on the ugly orange plaid upholstery. In that regard, Estelle was no Chester.

I'd been warned in advance that I had to make up her bed with real sheets—that there was no way she was bedding down for the night without proper linens.

She went to bed at 9:00 and fell asleep right away, despite having slept all day.

I, on the other hand, was not nearly so fortunate.

Estelle slept exclusively on her back, which I couldn't blame her for. She did it so she wouldn't have to worry about tangles in the oxygen line as she rolled back and forth. But the problem—for me—was that her mouth fell open, and holy cow could that woman snore! The sound made Chester Wheeler's snoring seem dainty. It had a rattle to it. Not a congestion rattle. More like some kind of loose skin flapping. I didn't know the details. I didn't have any kind of medical degree—yet. I only knew that sleep was going to come hard if it came at all.

I miraculously managed to fall asleep for an hour or so, but I woke up because I needed to pee. I got up, headed for the bathroom . . . and dislocated my toe on Estelle's oxygen tank.

I howled in pain, and jumped backward to sit on my own bed. I turned on the overhead light to see my second toe literally pointing in the wrong direction. I had to bite the bullet and pop it back into place, which was not fun to say the least.

Through it all Estelle only snored.

———

In the morning I woke to see her hovering over me, her face just inches from my own. A glow through the Winnebago's curtains told me that the sky had grown light.

"Lewis," she barked. "What's with you, anyway? You gonna sleep the day away?"

I rubbed my eyes and then held my hands up over my face, palms toward her, to indicate that I needed her to move back and give me some space.

"I doubt I got two hours," I said.

"Well, don't blame me. You should've slept when you had the chance. We've got to get miles behind us."

We really didn't. We had all day, and the family reunion wasn't until morning. But I was already awake, so I got up, made coffee, and got back in the driver's seat.

"Why are you limping?" she asked as she buckled herself in.

Yes, I let her buckle her own seat belt. I wasn't about to make *that* mistake twice.

"Because I kicked your oxygen tank in the dark."

"Well, that wasn't very bright."

"Maybe the miles will go better today with less talking," I said.

And, for a few miles at least, that seemed to work.

———

Around the time we neared the South Dakota state line, Estelle's misgivings began to surface.

"I'm not so sure this is a great idea," she said.

"But it was your idea."

"I know. But that doesn't mean it was a good one. Don't you ever have a bad idea?"

"Often," I said. "But if my ideas involve somebody else's help, by the time they go to a certain amount of trouble for me, I think I'd tend to follow through anyway."

Estelle wrinkled her pinched nose.

"There you go talking in riddles again."

"I said I'm not turning around now."

"Oh. Well, at least that I can understand. I don't like it, but at least I can figure out what you're saying."

"Are you afraid to see your family?"

"Of course I'm afraid to see them. I haven't seen them in seventeen years. And not by any coincidence, either. I mean, sure, Mel and I moved away, but there are planes and trains, you know. There must be reasons why they didn't want to see me."

"Well, they're going to see you now. Like it or not."

"What if they're cold to me?"

"Start out being warm to them. That tends to help."

"This might go badly."

"Yes. It might. But it might be your last chance to do it. And I really don't think any outcome could be as bad as knowing you chickened out and missed your last chance. And then you'll never know how it could have gone."

She sighed. She looked out the window for a few beats, as if the scenery were breathtaking out there. Note: it was not.

"Well, it pains me to admit it," she said, "but I think you might be right."

"And also, consider the possibility that it might go well."

"I wish I had your optimism."

"It's not something you have or don't have," I said. "It's like a muscle. You have to give it a little workout now and then."

"A bit late for me, don't you think?"

"Yes," I said. "A bit late. But not too late. Because you're not dead yet."

And yes. I did know I had said all that before.

—

We pulled into the site of the family reunion at a little after 6:30 p.m. Someone in the family had rented a farm, or a ranch—I honestly wasn't sure what to call it—in a very flat middle of nowhere, a fair distance west of the Missouri River.

It didn't seem to have a house, or any kind of living quarters. In fact, it appeared to be a gigantic rectangle of nothing, save for a massive and very high-ceilinged barn that could have doubled as an airplane hangar.

Estelle had said her daughter rented the place because it was more or less equidistant for all of the travelers—except, of course, us. I would have been hard pressed to find a single other feature to recommend it.

The good news was that we could camp right there in front of the barn. The bad news is that there was no hookup to water or electricity. There *was* water and electricity, but it would turn out to be inside the barn and not nearly close enough to anyplace we could park.

When I shut down the engine and killed the headlights, I was surprised by how dark it had gotten.

There was one other RV on the place already.

"Somebody else is here early," I said to Estelle. "You want to go say hello?"

"No, I do not want to go say hello. I want to go to bed."

"At six thirty in the afternoon?"

"I'm tired from all the worrying. Are you going to argue if I say I need the sleep?"

"You sure you don't want to say a quick hello first?"

"That's my grandnephew, and he's a horse's ass. So no."

I tucked Estelle into bed, which I had left made up from the night before. I placed her oxygen tank where I kept it while driving—wedged behind one of the seats, so it couldn't go flying in the event of a sudden stop. I had dislocated quite enough toes to suit myself.

"I'm going to limp out and look around the place," I said.

"I want a kiss good night."

It was a first, and an odd request, so I just stood there for a moment saying nothing.

"Just on the forehead," she said. "I'm not being weird with you."

But it was a little weird.

Still, I obliged her. I briefly kissed the crepey, papery skin of her forehead and then stepped out into nearly unbelievable cold.

Estelle's grandnephew was leaning against the outside of his RV, which was a much newer model built on a truck chassis. He was smoking a cigarette in the gathering darkness, and doing a poor job of hiding his curiosity over who had arrived.

I approached him, trying to walk as though I hadn't dislocated my toe, hugging my own arms against the chill.

"Who the hell are you?" he said. "You're not family."

He was probably forty, with close-cropped hair, but it was hard to see more in the dark.

"I'm here with Estelle Garnier," I said. "I'm her home health aide."

"Estelle did not come," he said.

Which seemed like a weird thing to say.

"Estelle did come."

"How was she even invited?"

"I guess the whole family was invited."

"But not Estelle."

"Well, she knew where it was. So I'm thinking you're wrong."

I realized we were off to a very bad start. Of course I hoped there was only this one horse's ass in the family, and that overall reactions to her attendance would be more positive. But it did set off some negative anticipation.

"Why does she need a home health aide?"

"Because she's dying."

"Of what?"

"A surprising number of things, actually. But let's not violate HIPAA too badly."

"I'll bet she's not. That old bat is too ornery to die."

"I'm going to take a look around," I said. "I'll see you."

But it was freezing, and nearly dark, and my toe hurt when I walked, and there wasn't much to see. And besides, the horse's ass seemed to be watching my every move.

I stepped back into the RV, closed myself into the back bedroom, and called Brian.

"Hey," he said.

I skipped the usual "Hey" and asked, "What's the treatment for a dislocated toe?"

"Well, you have to bite the bullet and pop it back into place."

"Did that already."

"Just take some medical adhesive tape and tape it to the toe next door. That will immobilize it some so it can heal. Other than that, there's not much you can do except . . . you know . . . ice. Elevation. Stay off it as much as possible. How did she dislocate her toe?"

"No, not Estelle. Me. I kicked her oxygen tank on the way to the bathroom in the dark."

"Ouch. You should have wedged it behind the seat like you do when you're driving."

"Great. Where were you last night?"

"Are you at the reunion?"

"Yeah, we're here. But I'm not quite sure where 'here' is. Being here feels a little bit like being nowhere at all."

Already I could hear the furnace cycling noisily on, trying to keep the inside of the cabin warm. Fortunately it could run without the generator. You just needed a full enough tank of propane and some battery, both of which we had.

I told him quite a bit about the drive, and the place, and the horse's ass of a grandnephew. Really quite a bit more than he needed to know, in fact. I wondered if he knew I was talking so much because I felt isolated and lost and totally alone.

Brian has never been a stupid man, so I guessed the answer to that question was a definite yes.

———

When we woke in the morning, the place was hopping. We could hear it over the roar of the furnace.

It was 6:45, and we already knew the festivities began with a pancake breakfast at 7:30.

I began to pull up the curtain on the barn side to see what was what.

"Put that down again!" Estelle shouted.

She was still in bed in her nightgown, sitting up. Before I did as she'd asked, I was able to see that an actual caterer had come in, with a logo truck, and generators, and outdoor tables with freestanding gas heaters.

"Why don't you want me to raise the curtain?"

"I want to see them before they see me."

She came over and sat on the bed on my side, and I scooted out of her way. She raised the curtain an inch or so. Just enough to get a view with one peering eye.

Channeling Chester again.

"Caterer. Caterer. Hell, there are more caterers here than there are family. There's my horse's ass grandnephew again. Caterer. Oh! There's my daughter."

"That's good. Right?"

"No. Not really. She's a horse's ass, too. Oh, and her husband. My son-in-law."

"Don't tell me. Let me guess. A horse's ass."

"He's not a horse's ass." I breathed a sigh of relief before she added, "He's pure evil."

Just for a split second I wondered why she had wanted to do this. But I supposed it made sense seen through the frame of end-of-life wishes. And maybe not in any other frame.

She seemed to read my mind.

"Why did I want to come here again?"

"Because you know it's probably your last chance. And because these people are your flesh and blood. You want to see if there's any way to repair those relationships, and if there isn't, you at least want to know you tried."

"Oh!" she said, and I could tell she was barely listening. "There's my granddaughter. Now *her* I like."

"Okay, then. We're getting somewhere. Let's get you dressed and get you out there to see her."

I limped with her, and her oxygen, to the table where her granddaugh-ter, a woman of nearly fifty, sat drinking light coffee. As I did, I tried to ignore cold stares from other family members.

Then I went back into the Winnebago to shower and get myself properly dressed.

I picked up my phone to see if Brian had called or texted, and as I did I noticed the date. It was one year to the day since Chester Wheeler's death.

While I showered, I tried to think of some fitting words. But all I could come up with was *You got me into all of this, you son of a bitch.* I know. It doesn't sound like much of a tribute for the departed. And yet, somehow, knowing Chester as I had, I figured he would laugh. And probably understand.

Face it, it was his kind of tribute.

———

When I went outside again, I brought Estelle's beret, so she wouldn't get a sunburned scalp.

Breakfast was in full swing. There were plain pancakes and blue-berry pancakes, and stacks of chocolate chip pancakes dripping with fresh strawberry sauce. There were scrambled eggs and sausages. There was coffee and there was toast.

The only thing missing was Estelle.

I limped around until I found her behind the barn with her mid-dle-aged granddaughter. They were leaning on the old dry wood siding together. They were each smoking a cigarette.

"What the hell?" I shouted.

Estelle dropped her cigarette and ground it under her shoe, leaving her foot there to obscure my view of it. She peered at the ground as though she'd lost something important there—as though the angle of her gaze was about something more noble and urgent than avoiding my eyes.

I waited, knowing she had to exhale eventually.

"It's too late, Estelle," I said when I'd gotten tired of waiting. "I already saw it."

She exhaled a great, guilty puff of smoke.

"What the hell do you think you're doing? You're dying of emphysema."

"Yes, *dying*," she said, switching into a defiant mode. "The operative word being *dying*. So what difference does it make?"

"Did you want to die in a fiery conflagration? Because your grand-daughter here might not know it's dangerous to smoke around medical oxygen. But *you* do."

The granddaughter took several steps back from Estelle and dropped her own half-smoked cigarette, crushing it into the dirt with the toe of one red cowboy boot.

"But we're outdoors," Estelle whined. "And I switched the tank off."

"But your hair and clothes and skin are still saturated with pure oxygen from your time inside. And you *know* all this, as you proved by turning off the tank even though it's uncomfortable to breathe without it."

"I'm sorry," the other woman said. "I didn't know about that fire stuff. I know it's not really good for her. But she said she felt like there might be a seizure coming on, and a cigarette would relax her, and maybe help."

I turned my ire back onto my patient, who averted her eyes in shame.

"Oh, so now you're manipulating people into letting you smoke."

She didn't answer.

For an awkward length of time, nobody breathed a word. Then I decided that after-the-fact anger was unhelpful, and we should move the morning along.

"Have you eaten, Estelle?"

"Not yet."

"Come on. Let's go get some of that breakfast."

281

———

We finished breakfast, sat back against our chairs in a synchronized manner, and a parade of relatives came by to greet Estelle. Not really enough of them, though. Maybe ten. And it's not like the others were waiting, thinking she'd come mingle with them. The oxygen tank and her obvious frailty made it clear that she was mingling from a sitting position.

For the most part, the older people who came by and greeted her wore tight looks on their faces. One even looked away the whole time.

As they left, she briefed me as to the relationship.

"Cousin."

"Cousin."

"Cousin."

"Cousin."

Finally, when the line thinned out, I asked, "How many cousins do you *have*?"

"Twenty-seven. I come from a big family. My mom was from a family of eight kids and my dad eleven. And I have six brothers and three sisters myself."

"Any of them here?"

"All dead. I'm the last one."

At that moment, Estelle's daughter came to the table and plunked down next to Estelle and across from me. She had long hair dyed a fiery red, and seemed to dress and style herself like a twenty-year-old when she was clearly pushing seventy.

"So," she said. "Health aide person. Do you really think it's your role to tell my mother she can't smoke?"

"She's on medical oxygen," I said. "So, yes. It's absolutely my job to make sure your mother doesn't set herself on fire. It's what she pays me for."

"Don't get me started on what she pays you," she said. "Why does she need a full-time . . . person, anyway? She's always been very independent."

Estelle spoke up, presumably in my defense.

"Because I'm dying, Einstein."

"Of *what*?" her daughter barked back, turning that acid gaze onto her mother.

Estelle looked down at the napkin in her lap.

"I don't remember," she said.

The acid gaze returned to me.

"Of. What?"

"I can't discuss details of her medical condition without her permission."

"Go ahead and tell her," Estelle said. "She needs to hear it. I just can't think straight when she looks at me like that."

"Non-Alzheimer's age-related dementia. Advanced emphysema. A seizure disorder that remains undiagnosed because she won't consent to an MRI, because no matter what it found she wouldn't undergo brain surgery at her age anyway. Which nobody's really arguing with her about. But it's most likely some type of brain tumor, because she's been tested for everything else. And congestive heart failure, which is why we came in a Winnebago instead of flying."

The daughter seemed a bit chastened, yet still determined to hold my feet to the fire.

"You can't fly with congestive heart failure?"

"Her doctor would have needed to sign off on it. And he advised against it."

"Maybe she just needs to be with her family. Maybe she needs to come live with us."

I looked over at Estelle to see if she cared to respond, but she only sat there in stony silence. She was looking at nothing, apparently. Maybe at the side of the barn.

It wasn't until I saw her eyelids twitching violently that I realized she was having the beginnings of a stress-induced seizure.

I jumped to my feet just in time. She stiffened, pitched to the right, and fell out of her chair. But I caught her, and lowered her to the ground. I rolled her over until she was mostly facedown, so she couldn't swallow her tongue or aspirate vomit. I got down on the ground with her and held her head gently but firmly against my chest, so she couldn't injure herself banging it on the ground.

Then I waited for the crisis to subside.

She lurched and jerked, and my gut reacted to each violent spasm, but I knew my job was simply to ride it out. So that's what I did. My emotions regarding the situation were beside the point.

It was only two or three minutes, but during that time I was fully focused on Estelle, and paying no attention to my surroundings. When I finally looked up, every single attendee, even the caterers, stood gathered in a tight circle around us, staring.

She struggled to rise, so I helped her into a sitting position, still holding her firmly.

All was silent as she gradually came back around. Nobody said a word. Also, unfortunately, nobody stopped staring, or moved their day along.

"Phew," she said after a time.

At that moment, conveniently, knowing the crisis was over, her daughter tried to step in and physically push me out of the way.

"She needs family," she shouted in my ear. "She needs her daughter."

Estelle shouted right back, panicky and loud and sudden.

"Get away from me! No! I don't need you! I don't want you! I need Lewis! Only Lewis!"

My heart fell to hear it. Because I knew I had to tell her soon that I was leaving.

The daughter jumped back and stood upright. I could see from her face that she was mortified over that dressing-down. And in front of the entire family, too.

"After she has a seizure," I said, "there could possibly be a period of dysphoria."

The daughter nodded glumly.

Then she wandered away, and every other family member and caterer took it as their cue to wander away as well. It was just me and Estelle, sitting on the ground together, giving her a little time to feel like herself again.

"Dysphoria my ass," she said near my ear. "I meant every word of it."

"I was giving her a chance to save face."

"You're kind," she said. "Too kind, in her case. So, listen. Lewis. Let's get out of here."

"You want to go back to the RV?"

"I want to go to Mount Rushmore. I've had enough of these people. I got what I came for."

"You sure?"

"Positive. Never been more sure of anything in my life."

"Care to share?"

"It's a long drive. We'll have plenty of time to talk on the way."

I picked up her fallen beret and plunked it onto her head at a rakish angle, and she smiled at me. And I smiled back. I couldn't help it.

"It's a good thing you scraped off those bumper stickers," she said as I lifted her to her feet, "because they'd get you an ass whipping where we're going."

———

Estelle's granddaughter came to the driver's side window as I was waiting for Estelle to buckle her own seat belt. I fired up the engine and powered the window down.

"I'm sorry about my mom," she said.

"Yeah, what was going on with that?"

"She didn't know Grandma had a full-time aide. She was hoping to inherit some money, and she just now got it that the money's being spent while Grandma's alive."

"Well," I said. And then I realized I didn't know quite what to say. I went with gut honesty. "That's just about the least magnanimous thing I've ever heard in my life."

She smiled wryly and shrugged her shoulders.

"What can I say? That's my family. And I'm sorry about the smoking thing. And also I'm sorry I told my mom about it. I had no idea she'd use it against you. But mostly I'm just sorry it ever happened in the first place."

"I know Estelle can make you do things against your better judgment."

"Hey," Estelle said. "You think I can't hear you?"

"No, I know you can."

Estelle's granddaughter stood up on the toes of her red cowboy boots, her fingers braced in the RV's window pocket.

"It was nice to see you again, Grandma."

"Likewise, dear," Estelle said.

I thought they would make some kind of arrangement for keeping in touch, but the granddaughter only wandered away.

I sat a minute with the engine running, watching her go.

"Hey," Estelle said. "Don't just sit there, Bozo. We've got a patriotic monument to see."

———

We drove a good third of the distance in silence. I couldn't help hoping that Estelle's reasons for leaving were nothing she would later regret. I was curious, but I didn't want to push.

"You know it's going to be much more crowded on the weekend," I said. "Right?"

"More crowded than what?"

"Than if we'd stayed at the reunion all weekend and gone on Monday."

"Oh. Right. Well . . . it's *up*, right? The monument. It's high. You look up to see it, right?"

"I can't argue with that," I said.

"So who cares what's on the ground?"

We fell silent again, but not for long. I had popped the cork on Estelle, and she started bubbling over.

"I feel very free," she said. "And do you know why?"

"I wouldn't venture a guess."

"Because I remembered why I haven't seen my family for so long. It's because they're a royal pain in the ass. Somehow I spent all this time wondering why *they* didn't want to see *me*. Like what was so terrible about me? And then this morning it hit me that I didn't want to see them, either. And it's very freeing. Oh, I'm sure they'd say it's me. But at least I know it's not *just* me. They think I'm too hard to get along with, but they're every bit as bad."

She looked out the window in silence for a few beats.

Then she asked, "Do you think I'm too hard to get along with, Lewis?"

"I think you're hard *enough*," I said.

It probably sounds like a harsh thing to say, but I was trusting her to hear it in the spirit in which it had been intended.

She chewed on that for a second or two, then brayed with laughter. Honestly, she laughed like a donkey. It was kind of fun. It was contagious.

"See, that's what I love about you, Lewis. Now hurry up and let's go see some dead presidents."

On the way, she told me at length about how she'd lived with her husband, Mel, in Spearfish, South Dakota, for thirty-seven years, not seventy miles from Mount Rushmore. But did she ever get to go see it?

Spoiler alert: no she did not.

———

I limped with her down the Avenue of Flags, very slowly, guiding her by the elbow and towing the oxygen behind. The monument itself was clearly visible above and beyond the rows of state flags. Under the presidents lay a sort of cone-shaped slope of loose rocks, with a few evergreen trees poking up.

On the ground, the place was packed. A sea of humans.

"Who knew all these people would be here?" Estelle asked.

"We . . . talked about it, actually."

"Did we? What did I say?"

"That the monument is *up*, so we'd be looking up. So it didn't matter what was on the ground."

"Right. I guess that's easy to say when you're not right in the middle of this crush of humanity."

She stopped, so I stopped, too. I could feel an unusual amount of her weight on me, as if I was holding her up more than normal. It had been a long day for Estelle.

"Look," I said. "You can see the damn thing from literally everywhere. Why don't we just go back to the RV, and I'll make us some lunch, and we can look at it out the window?"

"Eh," she said. "We can head for home. Once you've seen it, you've seen it. And now I've seen it."

We just stood for a moment, arm in arm, letting the crush of humanity spill around us like a river. Grown-ups jostled us with their shoulders and a kid stepped on my foot. The good one, fortunately.

"You know," I said, "I really didn't expect to say this, but . . . despite my many misgivings . . . just in its sheer size and scope, it's pretty impressive."

"Eh," she said again. "I think it's overrated. A little anticlimactic after all this time."

—

"So, listen," I said on our way back east through South Dakota.

Estelle said, "Uh-oh."

Then we just drove in silence for a moment.

"You're leaving me," she said.

"I just need to explain—"

"It's because I'm too hard to get along with."

"No. It's nothing like that."

"What's it like, then?"

"I want to move forward. In my professional life, I mean. I love working with people, but I want to take a step up. I want to start nursing school."

"You're going to be an RN?"

"LVN."

"I forget what that stands for."

"Licensed vocational nurse."

"Is that not as good?"

"It's more attainable. It requires less education."

"So not as good."

We drove in silence for a time. Her face was set like stone, so I pulled over, because I was afraid she'd have a seizure while I was driving. We sat there on the shoulder of the highway, on a stretch that I'm pretty sure was emergency stopping only.

"When I die," she said, "you'll do that."

"Actually, the semester starts soon."

"If it starts soon, it also starts a year from soon. It'll wait for you."

I opened my mouth to speak, but she cut me off.

"Look, Lewis. I don't know if you know how hard it is for someone like me to open up and trust someone like you. Think about a year from soon. Please. I'm down on my knees, figuratively speaking, begging you. Just think about it."

"Okay," I said. "I'll think about it."

But part of me already knew. In fact, part of me had known since she shouted at her own daughter that "Only Lewis" was allowed near her postseizure.

Now I just had to break it to Brian.

I pulled carefully back into the traffic lane.

"I've been meaning to ask you this for a long time," she said.

"Okay. Go."

"Why is there a paper bucket full of quarters in the map pocket? I can see if they were over in the console, where you could reach them. For parking meters or tolls. But they're not much use to you over here."

"They're not for parking meters or tolls," I said. "They're not for spending at all."

"I'll bite. What are they for?"

"They're . . . a type of monument. In their own way."

"Well, they're no Mount Rushmore," she said.

———

We pulled over for the night in a highway rest stop. Nothing better was available.

I fixed us a little dinner. Pulled all the curtains. Made up Estelle's bed with fresh sheets.

"What were you going to talk to me about?" she asked while we were eating.

"What do you mean?"

"After we left the monument you said you had something to talk to me about. But then we never did." She paused. Looked ceilingward, as if trying to find something in the air. "Did we?"

"We did, actually."

"What did we say?"

"Never mind. It's really not important."

I finished my food and got up to take my phone into the back bedroom. I wanted to call Brian and get the tough talk behind me.

"You're leaving?" she asked.

"I have to make a phone call."

"You won't leave me, right, Lewis?"

Which made it clear to me that she did remember our talk. Maybe not consciously. But it was in there somewhere.

"No. I won't."

"Good. Because I don't know if I could get somebody else. They all leave. They think I'm too hard to get along with. Bunch of lightweights. Do you think I'm too hard to get along with?"

"I think you're hard *enough*," I said.

And she brayed with laughter.

Even the darkest circumstances come with some sort of upside. When you're working with dementia patients, life is hard for both of you, but at least you don't have to keep coming up with new repartee. And I really don't say that to make light of the situation. I say it to *find* light *in* the situation, which I honestly think is a favor to all involved.

I closed myself into the bedroom in the back of the Winnie and called Brian.

"Hey," he said.

I jumped right in.

"I don't think I can start nursing school this year."

"Yeah," Brian said. "I knew that."

"You did? Then why did you push me to tell her?"

"It was worth at least hearing her reaction. Maybe she would have been okay with it. And, if not, she'll know to appreciate you more."

"You're amazing," I said. But it might have been hard for him to understand me, because I was laughing. "Are you disappointed in me?"

"For putting your patient first? Never. Nursing school will wait for you. It isn't going anywhere."

Then we talked about nonweighty topics for a long time. It was a big relief after my weighty few days.

———

I wouldn't be entirely honest if I didn't report that I was sure Estelle would die on the way home.

The human subconscious is a funny thing. If it never happened before, it tells you it never will, which is why I was so shocked when Chester died. If it happened once, it tells you it will happen that way every time.

I woke the following morning, and the morning after that, in a state of utter dread.

But Estelle did not die on the way home. In fact, she soldiered on for another sixteen months, letting me hone the skills of my calling every day, and forcing me to wait "two years from soon" to further my education.

But nursing school didn't go anywhere. It waited for me, just as Brian and Estelle had promised me it would.

And guess what? It turned out to be my calling.

BOOK CLUB QUESTIONS

1. From the very first line of the book and continuing through the story, there is significant friction between Chester and Lewis. What deep-seated feelings and beliefs are being triggered in both characters that contribute to this outcome?

2. When Lewis meets with his friend Anna, she says about Chester, "Look, I get it. . . . He upset you . . . It usually takes me about three days to let a thing like that move all the way through my system and move on. But while you're waiting, try not to feed it." Do you agree with Anna that an upset of this level takes about three days to move through you? What does she mean by advising not to feed it?

3. There is a famous quote often attributed to Joseph Campbell that says something like "We must be willing to let go of the life we planned so as to have the life that is waiting for us." How does this quote apply when Lewis decides to take the job of being Chester Wheeler's caretaker?

4. One of the themes running through this novel is whether amends or apologies are appropriate. When Chester finally meets up for the last time with his ex-wife, Sue,

she tells him, "I couldn't help falling in love with somebody else, so I'm not really apologizing for it, but there's a right and a wrong way to handle a thing like that." What do you think of her statement, and do you agree?

5. After Chester's visit with Sue, she kisses him on the forehead and tells him to pack in as much life as he can in the short time left. In her own way, perhaps, she was trying to make amends. Do you believe in the power of forgiveness, or do you think some things can never be reconciled?

6. After Chester's death, Lewis ruminates about his experience with the man he'd been in conflict with for so long. "He wasn't a great person," Lewis says, "but he was a person." What does this statement mean to you?

7. While caring for both Chester and Estelle, Lewis comes to know himself better. What do you see as some of his biggest areas of growth and most significant shifts in his beliefs about himself and others?

8. Something Lewis realizes toward the end of the book is "All the way down to my gut I *got* something I'd never gotten before. I got that when a person is rude and abusive to me, it's not about me at all." Do you agree with this statement and all that it implies?

9. By the end of the book, each main character has irrevocably altered the other's life. Have you had a similar situation in which someone irrevocably altered your life?

10. Ultimately, Lewis decides to choose a career that might not be as profitable as his previous one, but will provide him more fulfillment, and honor the gift he can share with others. Do you believe that everybody has something special that they can bring to the world?

ABOUT THE AUTHOR

Photo © 2019 Douglas Sonders

Catherine Ryan Hyde is the #1 Amazon Charts and *New York Times* bestselling author of over forty published and forthcoming books. An avid traveler, equestrian, and amateur photographer, she shares her astrophotography with readers on her website.

Her novel *Pay It Forward* was adapted into a major motion picture, chosen by the American Library Association (ALA) for its Best Books for Young Adults list, and translated into more than twenty-three languages for distribution in over thirty countries. Both *Becoming Chloe* and *Jumpstart the World* were included on the ALA's Rainbow list, and *Jumpstart the World* was a finalist for two Lambda Literary Awards. *Where We Belong* won two Rainbow Awards in 2013, and *The Language of Hoofbeats* won a Rainbow Award in 2015.

More than fifty of her short stories have been published in the *Antioch Review*, *Michigan Quarterly Review*, *Virginia Quarterly Review*, *Ploughshares*, *Glimmer Train*, and many other journals; in the anthologies *Santa Barbara Stories* and *California Shorts*; and in the bestselling anthology *Dog Is My Co-Pilot*. Her stories have been honored by the Raymond Carver Short Story Contest and the Tobias Wolff Award and have been nominated for Best American Short Stories, the O. Henry

Award, and the Pushcart Prize. Three have been cited in the annual *Best American Short Stories* anthology.

She is founder and former president (2000–2009) of the Pay It Forward Foundation and served for more than twenty years on its board of directors. As a professional public speaker, she has addressed the National Conference on Education, twice spoken at Cornell University, met with AmeriCorps members at the White House, and shared a dais with Bill Clinton.